ULTERIOR
MOTIVES

BOOKS BY MARK ANDREW OLSEN

Hadassah: One Night With the King[1]

The Hadassah Covenant: A Queen's Legacy[1]

Rescued[2]

The Road Home[1]

The Watchers

The Warriors

Ulterior Motives

[1]with Tommy Tenney   [2]with John Bevere

ULTERIOR
MOTIVES

MARK ANDREW OLSEN

BETHANYHOUSE
MINNEAPOLIS, MINNESOTA

Ulterior Motives
Copyright © 2009
Mark Andrew Olsen

Cover design by Lookout Design, Inc.

Published by Bethany House Publishers
11400 Hampshire Avenue South
Bloomington, Minnesota 55438

Bethany House Publishers is a division of
Baker Publishing Group, Grand Rapids, Michigan.

Printed in the United States of America

Library of Congress Cataloging-in-Publication Data

Olsen, Mark Andrew.
    Ulterior motives / Mark Andrew Olsen.
        p.   cm.
    ISBN 978-0-7642-0275-9 (pbk.)
    1. Terrorists—Fiction. 2. Prisoners—Fiction. 3. Clergy—Fiction. 4. Undercover
operations—Fiction. 5. Terrorism—Prevention—Fiction. I. Title.

PS3615.L73U67   2009
813'.6—dc22

                                                                      2008051035

To Bret,
who helped birth this novel's
"high concept" premise, and so many
more creative babies through the years.

Admittedly, this proposal has the potential to be incredibly controversial. It will strike some as being contrary to every fiber of America's body politic, not to mention the spirit of our Constitution. Nevertheless, Tabula Rasa remains squarely centered on our latest understanding of modern global conflicts.

This is because military strategists wishing to prevail on the field of battle can no longer treat hatred, genocide, and international terrorism as divorced from ideology and religion.

To put it simply, religion forms the basis of our enemies' compulsion to destroy us. And if we do not address it clearly and directly, religion will fuel the inferno of their eventual victory.

Excerpt from the prologue of the "Tabula Rasa Protocol," classified Defense Department policy proposal, drafted by Captain Delia Kilgore, United States Army.

Current status: reviewed without comment, archived with prejudice—no action taken.

CHAPTER 1

Palmdale, California

The boy's outline danced, ecstatic and elusive, across the razor-thin crosshairs of a spotting scope. Trying to follow its exuberant path caused the hidden watcher to grit his teeth in frustration. Even the finest military-grade optics could not keep his lens focused on the youngster's manic figure. The child would not quit leaping out of view, veering away, seized by sudden peals of laughter.

The excitement was understandable, though. It was, after all, Robby Cahill's sixth birthday party.

At last, the boy paused to catch his breath. Just as quickly the intruder took advantage of the interval to reacquire the young body in his sights and bore in on his tousled head. He lingered over those eyes, glowing in the sunlight. Cheeks as ruddy as an apple. Sandy hair swaying in the breeze.

Good, thought the watcher. *Almost within range. Not one foot too close, not an inch too far.*

The intruder's stealth grew more pronounced with

every passing second. The closer he crawled beneath layers of concealing leaves and shrubbery, the more he worried about early detection—an inadvertent reflection from the scope, a stray glint of light that could instantly give him away.

The man wouldn't let that happen. He was too good for that. Too experienced.

And today the stakes were too high.

Neither Robby nor his mother, Donna, could see the man, but they each suspected, in their own silent ways, that he might be near. Only brief, sidelong glances betrayed their suspicions. And yet they had no idea he'd already made it so close to their location, inching toward them through the underbrush.

The very potential of his presence had brought the police cruiser there, idling conspicuously beside the curb in the shade of Armstrong Park's vast hundred-year-old magnolia tree. It was the reason for the drawn, tight mouth of the boy's mother. And for the unusually terse nature of her comments to the other boys' mothers. Donna Cahill was taking no chances.

At that moment, the intruder was in fact less than 120 yards away from the birthday party, slithering slowly through a cluster of pungent rosemary bushes under an improvised mat of native twigs and leaves. He wore camouflage perfectly suited to the ground cover, selected on several reconnoitering trips the week before. His face and lips were covered in carefully applied swirls of camo paint. Even his army boots were smeared with dark polish to prevent any shine and to blend into the terrain.

The man was so well concealed that the boy might have stepped on his back without ever seeing him, without even a second's awareness that anyone was underfoot.

The factors capable of betraying his presence ticked through his mind in a cascade of crucial data. *Time, brightness, temperature, wind, sun position*—each contributed to the play of light upon him. He had chosen the shadow of these bushes for the angle and blending of illumination they would provide at this time of day. His mind continually monitored the exact position of both key persons—Robby and Donna—to make sure he did not move while they were facing his way. Fortunately, there were no dogs about; one of the worst threats to a well-hidden asset. He had nothing left but unobstructed brush to traverse before reaching the perfect position.

He kept the mother firmly planted in his peripheral vision. She ranked first on his list of vigilant, even paranoid, observers of whom to beware. He knew she would be looking for him. He also knew that she remembered what kinds of areas to watch. Indeed, the woman knew more than most folks did about sniper stealth tactics. Fortunately for him, she had been eyeballing the trees all morning rather than the ground, distracted by her knowledge that most people rarely looked upward, and that as a result leafy canopies made the ideal approach route.

Now she seemed engrossed in chatting with the other mothers over by the picnic tables. Better still, her glances around the park had grown more and more sporadic. He hoped she was, at last, entertaining the prospect that he might not be there after all. And yet, he could tell, she was also wrestling with a vague, emerging awareness of his presence.

He wriggled one more foot closer, taking almost a full minute to do so. The boy would be in range soon. He reached into a side pocket and extricated the tool he had chosen for the mission.

Great day.

"Donna, you seem tense," said the mother of Robby's best friend. "Is everything okay?"

"Nothing unusual," replied the party's hostess with a quick world-weary grin. "Just a little tired."

"I was wondering about the police car," the mother persisted. "Are you sure there isn't anything we should be worrying about?"

"No!" she responded, a bit too emphatically. "There's nothing for you to worry about. It's, uh, just a new regulation . . . something about private parties on city property. Gotta pay for police protection."

"I didn't know that," said her friend. "It's just that you seem really on edge today."

Donna Cahill looked down at the ungarnished hot-dog bun in her hands and sighed. "Nothing new. You know how parties are. No matter how well you think you've prepared, there's always something that goes wrong at the last minute."

"Don't I know it," the woman laughed. "Just a fact of life."

Donna shook her head. "Good thing the kids are clueless about what we go through," she said softly, "or no one would have any fun at all."

Twenty yards away, little Robby Cahill was also looking around for signs. He had seen none, but then he'd been playing hard with his friends. Star Wars Jedi combat, laser tag, and even Transformers, stomping around the yard and growling as pretend robots.

But his gaze kept drifting back to the sidelines, scanning for a glimpse.

Suddenly the event he'd waited all morning for happened. His eyelashes flickered against a blinding assault, and he winced. A small flare of light glittered in his retinas, washing out his world. Robby knew right away what it was, and that it was too strong and steady to be an accidental reflection from a passing car. Robby squinted and shielded his eyes with an uplifted hand.

Then he jumped high in the air and squealed.

He started running toward the light. He giggled loudly, pumping his arms and stocky legs like a superhero.

Donna screamed and lunged for the boy. Her fingers grazed his waist but failed to capture him.

"Stop him!" she shouted in the direction of the police car. "It's *him*! It's *him*!"

The police car's engine switched off. The door flew open. A young officer jumped out and sprinted across the grass, fingers fumbling with his gun holster.

Seventy yards away, the ground erupted in a flurry of upward motion. The bushes flung debris up and around a figure that rose from their midst. Leaves and branches flew about the standing man, who was clad in shades of green.

Running to catch up, Donna fell to her knees, transfixed at the bizarre sight. Her breathing stopped and her heart seemed to flutter to a halt in her chest. For a moment, the sight struck her as an apparition disgorged by the earth itself, like some gnarled creature of soil and root.

The man stood and extended his arms, hands empty to the sky.

Robby Cahill kept on running, his face contorted with emotion. His mouth opened and a shout ripped forth from his heaving lungs.

"Daddy! Daddy!"

Robby had made it halfway across the park green when the police officer caught up with him and swept him up off his feet in a single motion. The boy screamed and began writhing furiously.

Greg Cahill took in the sight of his boy's agony and felt a physical sensation of something shredding inside him. Everything in him longed to throw itself at the man and free his son.

But Greg knew that would be the worst thing he could do. He could not move another inch forward now.

Instead, grimacing in anguish, he pointed at the officer with a level stare. "You keep your hands off my boy!" he shouted. "You so much as scratch him, and I swear—"

"Daddy!" Robby screamed, weeping now.

Greg Cahill waved at his boy. "Stay right there, son. You know we can't come any closer."

"But, Dad!"

"I love you, son," he called out, his voice cracking. "Happy birthday!"

The words seemed to loosen the officer's hold on the boy so that Robby slipped from his grasp. His sneakered feet neared the ground and began churning again, as though the mere proximity to grass had switched on some internal motor. Still, the officer held him fast.

The sight of it caused the ache in his father's chest to double its throbbing. He wondered if he could bear it a moment longer.

"Can't you just let me hold him for a second?" he called out.

"Are you armed?" the officer asked sharply.

"Nothing but a scope. Please. Look." He raised his arms, holding his camo jacket so that it flapped open, revealing the emptiness of its interior pockets.

The officer squinted. Greg could feel the man's gaze take in the camo paint on his face, smeared by the descent of tears. The officer's clenched features relaxed.

"I'm sorry, but the order prohibits you from having unscheduled contact with your son. You're not to come within one hundred feet of the boy. You know that."

"I haven't moved one step beyond that distance. My son approached *me*."

"I know. That's the only reason you're not under arrest. But I can't let him come any closer."

Donna's voice rang out behind them, sharp and angry. "Greg, what's the meaning of this stunt?"

"I just wanted to get close enough to tell my son happy birthday. The only way I could."

His eyes bore fiercely into the youngster's weeping face, and for a moment he felt like the worst, most thoughtless father who had ever lived.

"Son, please don't cry. I didn't want to ruin your birthday. I just wanted you to know that I was here. Just don't you ever forget how much your daddy loves you, okay? Don't forget that I was here. That I came."

Robby nodded, still held back by the officer, his face streaked with tears.

Greg made the hand signal for *I love you*, then slowly he turned and ran away. His camouflaged figure swiftly melted into the surrounding brush.

Shaking her head, Donna knelt down and hugged her son's limp, dispirited form. The birthday party had been upstaged. But she had to admit: the restraining order had been obeyed, the proper distance observed.

Greg would have made sure of that.

CHAPTER 2

Animal shelter, Pasadena, California

The cocker spaniel puppy gazed pleadingly up at the man watching through the glass and blinked twice. But it simply refused to die.

True, its furry, stubby legs twitched and wobbled. Its fuzzy sides bumped briefly against the glass, shakily regaining balance. Instead of closing, its large brown eyes seemed to merely cloud over. The puppy jerked its snout forward several times, as if wracked by a silent cough. Somehow the spaniel remained upright.

The young man standing on the other side of the glass spat a curse at the animal's infuriatingly endearing face, although he was not exactly surprised by its survival. This was the first shot of the poison, less than a thousandth of an ounce.

He was still perfecting the dose.

Nevertheless, the man was filled with tension, his every muscle a coiled band of anxiety. The dumb little beast seemed the closest target on which to vent his frustration.

He switched on the contraption he'd rigged to suck out the lethal air. It was an improvised design the average American would never manage, he thought with an inner twinge of pride, but only ten minutes' work for someone like him—a gifted graduate student in physics at the California Institute of Technology, or Caltech.

Not only a purer soul, he reminded himself, but a superior mind as well.

The disemboweled hair-dryer motor whined and sucked invisible fumes out through a hose to the outside, where a customized air filter awaited it. He smiled grimly at the small machine's efficiency. *The things you can do when people leave you alone for a while . . .*

When a minute had passed, he turned it off, opened a small window and pulled the animal out. He tossed it into a small pen. The animal would live and, due to its young age, possibly even outgrow the neurological damage inflicted on it. He opened another cage where a second puppy panted, one nearly the same size. This one, not yet logged in, had been brought to the shelter less than a half hour before by a returning driver.

With this second puppy he would double the dose, and still the droplet would be barely large enough to see.

He tossed the puppy, a Labrador retriever, into the sealed cage and locked it inside. Then he picked up the pipette and retrieved a tiny amount of liquid from a bottle.

He felt beads of sweat forming on his forehead. A quiver crept into his fingers. He tried to banish from his mind the knowledge that this dose was easily enough to kill him. If he so much as dropped the pipette or squeezed out a stray drop onto his shoe, he had a terrifyingly clear notion what would take place.

His mind raced back over the well-traveled images. First, a sudden dryness and a smell akin to burnt almonds would sweep through his nasal passages. Next, his airway and his lungs would sear with a burning like that of battery acid. Seconds later his limbs would fail and he would fall to the concrete as quickly and unceremoniously as a puppet whose strings had been snipped. His lungs might heave spasmodically and his brain fire for a minute longer, grasping desperately across paralyzed synapses for his gaping eyes and drooling mouth. And his heart would be slowing to rest after a lifetime of labor.

Soon his short time on earth would be over.

Yes, he was quite familiar with the gas's deadly pathways, for he had carefully chosen every one of them himself. The men who would soon taste his wrath had even paid him to develop them, *the idiots*. He laughed every time he considered the irony of America's government paying him to craft its own doom.

Classified research, my foot, he thought. *Just because I'm not an Arab, just because I have a surfer's blond hair and blue eyes, they overlook me. They think I'm safe. What racists. As if brown skin, dark eyes, and an Arabic name were the sum total of what it meant to be a faithful servant of jihad.*

He breathed out his wrath in a single trembling breath. With any luck, each one of his concoction's torments would soon afflict thousands, perhaps millions of the moronic infidels who surrounded him. The evil ones who had sent his father away to die in the deserts of Kuwait would pay for shattering a toddler's heart and destroying his family whole.

Someday in the near future, he just knew, some sharp-dressed pretty boy from a network documentary show would stand right here, after visiting all the haunts of his childhood years, having already interviewed his clueless mother and his contemptible classmates, and recount for a breathless America how the greatest killer in American history had spent his formative years *on this very spot*.

The young terrorist chuckled, then refocused on the task at hand, for he had no wish to become his own first victim. Rather, he was soon to become a great hero, right up there with Osama bin Laden. That is, if his mixture was as potent as he'd hoped.

The chain-saw rasp of the door's buzzer assaulted his ears. He turned with an exasperated wince at whoever was seeking entry. "It's five minutes after closing time," he muttered. "Go away." The interruption caused his hands to shake even more fearfully. He exhaled with a fierce hiss. He had carefully chosen the day and the time for maximum privacy, but of course life's randomness had seen fit to shatter his plan.

He willed his hand to stop moving. Taking a few deep breaths, he threaded the pipette through a tiny perforation in the rubber gasket, concentrating harder than ever. His fingers shook only slightly.

Now a knocking thundered from the door—his unwanted guest had switched tactics. He gritted his teeth, doing his best to ignore the sound. Ten more minutes at the most was all he needed.

But the latecomer had grown insistent. The knocking not only failed to quit, but grew louder, more emphatic. He found himself picturing his hands around the person's neck, choking the dim-witted life out of whoever it was.

And then matters grew worse. He heard familiar steps approach the door from inside the building. The stooped figure of Hal, the old night janitor, tottered into view. The young man groaned audibly. Hal was not supposed to start his shift for another hour. Compounding the disaster, Hal leaned into the door, peered out, and after a moment's listening to a female voice, opened it wider for the offender to come inside. He saw the worst: a clean-cut brunette woman in her thirties, hand in hand with a weeping little blond-haired girl.

He thought of the loaded revolver lying inside the backpack at his feet. He realized, for the first time, that he had both the equipment and the will to take human life with his own hand. Just a few more seconds and he would have the weapon out, tight in his grip, and be pumping bullets into all of them.

A rush of adrenaline coursed through his veins. He felt lean and powerful, filled with purpose. The light around him seemed to shift into a shade of gray, and a ringing sound began at the periphery of his hearing.

He swallowed hard. This whole endeavor was all about killing as many Americans as possible, but until now it was something to be done from a distance. He'd helped rationalize his complicity by imagining that even though they would use a weapon he had developed, it would be al-Qaeda's lead attack cell actually doing the killing, not him.

Now he could almost feel the weight of the gun in his hand, the trigger's resistance, hear the recoil of the blasts, see the bodies falling limp to the floor.

"I'm sorry!" he yelled down the hallway at them. "Come back tomorrow!"

But the woman turned to him, her face earnest and open. "Sir, if we could just have a moment of your time. We called about fifteen minutes ago. We think you may have my daughter Brooke's cocker spaniel. She just got it for her birthday and he ran away this morning. Someone on the phone told us a driver might have brought him in. Could you just check, real quick, and see if he's here?"

He winced into his pipette. Of course. The puppy was right in front of him. He was about to dispatch it to doggy heaven.

"Sorry, ma'am. You'll have to come back in the morning."

Ignoring her, he gently squeezed the bulb and released the predetermined dose. The droplet vaporized even before hitting the ground, as it was supposed to. He narrowed his eyelids and focused all of his energy on pulling out the pipette without breaking it. Slowly, agonizingly, the narrow tube came free with a faint popping sound.

He glanced into the cage. The puppy had its wet nose pressed against the glass, staring amiably at him. Then it leaned away and began to sway sideways. A second later it fell hard onto the floor, its tongue protruding from its mouth.

The mother was walking toward him. "Please?" she insisted, her voice rising. "Couldn't you make an exception? It's a two-month-old cocker spaniel. Brown spot across its back the shape of Italy. Brooke loves it more than life itself."

He hurriedly stashed the pipette into the backpack and grabbed the revolver lying inside. "There's no such puppy here," he said, feeling the ringing in his ears grow more intense. "Maybe you talked to a different shelter."

But Mom and little girl had turned down the hall and were coming his way. He groaned. They wanted to approach and plead their case. They were almost upon him. He glanced in the cage's direction. The puppy's eyes were still open, but its eyelids were twitching. The dose was working!

Despite the stress of the moment, a surge of triumph raged through him. He had achieved a great victory for Allah. As a new convert, and one of al-Qaeda's few non-Arab members, he'd just perfected the most lethal chemical agent in history. The New Year's Day attack cell would receive their batch right on schedule. Less than a month from now, thousands of unsuspecting Americans would pay with their lives for what their nation had done to him and his family—dying just as this puppy had, only live on national television before untold millions of their countrymen.

Flush with the thrill of it all, he hid the gun behind his back and raised his free hand abruptly against the intruders.

"This is a restricted area. You cannot come back here."

"But they let us in when we adopted Buddy."

"They shouldn't have. Do not approach. I warn you."

The woman stopped, apparently alarmed by the tone of his voice.

He eased off the revolver's safety, then moved his finger to the trigger. One jerk of his arm and their fate would be sealed, his choice made.

The woman narrowed her eyes, and a twitching around her eyebrows betrayed that she had made a decision. She walked forward.

The young man took one final glance inside the cage. Then he clicked the safety back on and tucked the weapon away.

As they stepped beside him, the woman's eyes followed his to the cage. Her hand flew to her face. The little girl beside her screamed.

Their puppy lay in the cage, its eyes open and lifeless, tongue clenched between its teeth.

"I tried to keep you away," he said. "The puppy was struck by a car and there was nothing we could do."

The woman nodded, holding her little girl tight. As they turned to leave, she whispered, "Thank you for trying. I should have listened."

"You can have the body if you'd like to bury it," he offered.

She smiled. "Okay. And I'm sorry. I know you were only trying to protect us."

He smiled back at her for the first time.

CHAPTER 3

Reseda, California—26 days remaining before the attack

The young student resembled every other cyber-café patron
out late that night, clad in ragged jeans and a Caltech T-shirt.
He peered through the steam swirling up from his latte toward
the screen of the rented computer. Perhaps the only difference
was that he couldn't help but beam with a glee that not only
lit up his features but seemed to invigorate each of his jangly
limbs.

He gave his fellow customers a glance laced with contempt
and began typing with such enthusiasm that he almost pounded
the keys to the edge of breaking them. A pair of his neighbors
turned and glared at him.

Fortunately, none of them could make sense of the bizarre
mishmash of characters filling his screen, let alone the message
they concealed. . . .

*Dar al-Harb to Dar al-Salam base: The weapon is tested and ready,
the perfect time and place chosen with great care and cunning.*

Hundreds of thousands of infidel souls will flood into hell, their New Year's stillborn. Praise be to Allah!

                 —*Azzam the Younger*

Palmdale, California

It was midnight. Outside, the air was laden with a cool breeze and the hum of dwindling auto traffic.

Inside Greg Cahill's small apartment, however, the bed lay empty and neatly made. The kitchen table stood spotless, the sink barren.

It did not mean nobody was home.

Just outside the front door, within a darkened gap above the entry causeway and perfectly positioned to watch for any hostile approach, drifted the tiniest blur of motion. No one could detect it without a handheld spotlight, but a man sat crouched there, still wearing the camouflage outfit he'd sported for almost an entire day.

It was a tactical sentry point, perfectly positioned for maximum visibility and minimum exposure, including even a backdoor escape route through a narrow crawl space. Greg Cahill had used this place often to keep watch over his home, at times of high anxiety.

But right now he was crouched tightly against the night, hugging his knees.

And weeping.

After running an evasive four-mile route home from Armstrong Park, he had found it simply impossible to reenter his empty apartment, its every inch drenched with the cruel absence of his family, its every bare surface a screaming reminder that he now lived alone.

He could not endure the thought—Greg Cahill, onetime loving father, earnest husband, fiercely dedicated public servant, now eking out the hours of his life in the company of a thirteen-inch television and a mechanical alarm clock. As if he were just another child-support dodging, marriage-vow betraying, indifferent head of household, crashed in a dingy party pad like some perpetual teenager.

As if he didn't crave with every breath in his lungs to return to his wife and child, to restore what had once been the cradle of his affections, ground zero of his boy's whole world.

Inside his cubbyhole, Greg leaned his head back and tapped it lightly against the dirty stucco wall, wishing he could just bash on through and somehow end the pain.

He shut his eyes, then opened them again, for the image of a boy moving through crosshairs would not relinquish its hold upon his tortured mind. However, this sight was not today's memory, that of his Robby playing Transformers.

No, this was a different boy. The tormentor of his dreams.

The ruiner of his life.

This boy's head only appeared in a split second, as a mere silhouette through a shadow-flattened screen door. The fleeting sight of it, seven years earlier, had instinctively caused Greg's index finger to tighten around the trigger of his FBI-issue Winchester .308 sniper rifle and squeeze gently to cancel out its remaining pound and a half of pull.

Even now, thinking about it, he opened his mouth in a silent scream of protest, of agonized revulsion at the enormity of his mistake.

He had thought the head belonged to the boy's father, a crazed madman. Instead, he heard his earphones fill with the screams of his colleagues: "Nooooo! That was the boy! The boy . . . !"

The last syllable echoed through the caverns of Greg's imagination like a primal scream resounding through the halls of his own guilt-ridden, private hell.

A growing voice inside him called him out of the perch, to go and drink away the pain in the semi-comforting gloom of a nearby bar. He could almost feel the rising stupor that alcohol would grant him, the relief of feeling his pain dim into the soothing throb of inebriation.

But no. He could not do that. He forced himself to remember that along that route lay only more agony. In fact, that same route had brought him to this place, had caused Greg's final measure of self-destruction.

"Please, God," he whispered. "Don't let me fall. Don't let me give in to that lie."

Searching for any alternative to the distraction, he tried to replace the scene with today's similar but monumentally different sight. The image of his own son, playing, exultant, completely out of danger. But the other silhouette, falling under a pink mist through the distant doorway, would not go away.

He groaned under the strain of trying to control his thoughts. Finally, little Robby's face flickered into Greg's mind and this time remained.

Yet, without his bidding, that imaginary trigger finger pulled again.

In his perverse nightmare, it was now Robby's turn to jerk back against the speeding bullet and fall.

And then Greg's turn, for the millionth time, to let out a silent scream as the other father had, from his tense crouch against the wall.

Robby . . . Oh, Robby . . .

Palmdale, 3 miles away, Cahill residence—that moment

Donna Cahill held her son in a gloom, broken only by a pirate night-light in a poster-strewn child's bedroom. It was incredibly late for such a young boy to remain sleepless, but hardly the first time.

"Try to think about something else," she urged, "and let yourself get some rest, would you please, honey?"

"But I can't stop thinking about him. He was crying, Mommy. Crying for me. I thought grown-ups didn't cry."

"You've seen Mommy cry plenty of times lately."

"I guess I meant grown-up daddies."

"Daddies cry too. Most of the time, they cry inside so no one can see their soft side."

"Mommy, why can't you just forgive him and let him come home?"

"Honey, it's not that simple. We've talked about this before, remember? Yes, Daddy loves you—"

"And you too."

"Yes, maybe he loves me too. But the problem is he's sick, and he's not safe. I mean, the sickness makes him not safe to be around. Think of the accident. Remember all the fright and the pain. I know you've tried hard to forget and that's a good thing. But sometimes, when it's tempting to let down your guard, you have to remember too."

"I think he's gotten better. The accident was a long time ago. He's been sober . . ."

"Robby, you have no idea how long Daddy's been sober."

"Yes I do. He told me on the phone, just last week. It's been—"

"Yes," she interrupted, "and he told me that too, a hundred times. The sickness made him lie to me, and makes him lie to you. Please understand. He doesn't want to lie to you. He wants it to be true. He wants to be a safe daddy again. But he can't help himself."

"But, Mommy, just suppose one day he did get better again.

What would he have to do to make us believe it was true? Are we not going to believe him forever and ever?"

Donna Cahill paused, allowing the poignancy and piercing truth of the question to wash through her. At last, she spoke again.

"God will tell us, sweetie. He'll let both of us know, so it won't be so painful. Okay?"

SBC Communications Building, San Francisco, CA

A great river snaked up from the bowels of San Francisco's underground utility grid, through the surface pavement and into the walls of the former AT&T building on San Francisco's Folsom Street.

Yet this great current was not composed of water. Instead, it whisked along billions of light pulses in a prodigious flow of data—optical flashes comprising a primary backbone of the Internet, shooting through a bundle of fiber optic wires no wider than a desk-side garbage can.

In the old days of analog telephone transmission and inefficient copper lines, a cable of that size would have barely managed the traffic coming from a large neighborhood. Today, however, it represented the primary node in the whole West Coast's Internet traffic. Combined with data merely passing through from across the globe, this river of light flowed at a speed of several dozen gigabytes per second—more than the entire Library of Congress—every fifteen minutes.

This precious tributary harbored a concealed detour.

Unknown to most of the technicians who occupied AT&T's three floors of the SBC Communications Building, the overlooked, innocent-looking cabinet along a seventh-story hallway was actually crammed with beam splitters—customized devices that duplicated every incoming flash of light and routed it into a parallel network all its own. The original optics left the room with only a faint signal loss to betray that they had ever been compromised.

From there, the pirated impulses flowed to the sixth floor and the secret room behind a plain orange door whose sign was innocuously labeled *641-A*. Behind this nondescript entrance lay a windowless room, 24 by 48 feet, filled with racks of computer monitors, cabinets, cable bundles, and other highly specialized electronic gear.

In the most secretive backwaters of the country's intelligence community, this room was a celebrated, nearly hallowed space, known by the nickname "Mae West"—rivaled in importance only by its counterpart on the Atlantic seaboard, aptly named "Mae East." Company records labeled the chamber *Study Group 3 Secure Room,* but the title's bureaucratic banality obscured a far more cunning function.

It was here, before even leaving its enclosure, that the newly diverted tsunami of data was covertly analyzed, on behalf of the nation's intelligence community, according to a complex series of alert criteria.

One of those warning factors was the detection of unknown encryption algorithms—the elaborate codes devised to scramble and protect important data from prying eyes. The nation's spy community watched for these for two key reasons. First, the intelligence world routinely fought to keep itself abreast of the ever-multiplying and sophisticated schemes developed by the nation's hackers. Uncle Sam employed scores of young computer geeks, some of them students themselves on West Coast campuses, to crack those codes and remain constantly ahead of the game.

Most of the codes proved benign in nature, written to cloak adolescent rantings against the adult establishment and notices of things like illegal raves, skateboarding trespasses, and off-limits bonfires. Illegal perhaps, but hardly within the scope of these prying eyes.

However, a frighteningly large slice of the encryption codes were written for vastly more sinister purposes.

For that reason, the second motive for monitoring encryption codes was more straightforward. The nation's Internet traffic was constantly monitored to detect one of the most eager markets for their use—terrorist cells, communicating covert plans of mayhem across the oceans to their foreign handlers.

On this night, the email message originating from a Reseda Internet café blinked on to the room's third computer monitor, plucked from the web's backbone because of its greatly original encryption structure.

Within a millisecond its meaningless jumble of digits, letters, and random characters was whisked across the country to Fort Meade, Maryland, headquarters of the National Security Agency. There, a team of three software analysts went to work breaking the message's devious cipher scheme.

Before long they discovered that rather than being wholly homegrown, the code was in fact an augmented version of an old algorithm favored by al-Qaeda operatives. The discovery vaulted this action item to the top of a very long list, and spurred the analysts to double their efforts.

At dawn, just before their shift's end, the team broke the code and lofted a shout that nearly echoed across their floor—quite a feat considering their surroundings' considerable padding and soundproofing.

The two men and one woman stared at the screen for a long moment, then at each other. They had reason to cheer. A readable message blinked menacingly at them from their screens. But they also had reason to stare ominously at its contents.

Within seconds of the text's identification, the message had triggered no less than four of the Agency's content thresholds. The trio would be late leaving for home.

The first triggers were Arabic nicknames chosen by their writer to label the message's origin and destination—Dar al-Harb and Dar al-Salam—terms referring to the Place of War and the Place of Peace in Koranic lore.

Both were well-known jihadist terms of battle.

Second was the adamant tone of its threats. *The weapon is tested and ready. . . . Hundreds of thousands of infidel souls will flood into hell. . . .*

Third was its closing salutation: *Azzam the Younger*.

That name had immediately triggered a flash warning from TIDE—the Terrorist Information Datamart Environment—one of the world's largest databases of suspect names and identities housed at the National Counterterrorism Center.

It turned out the original Azzam was notorious as the father of the global jihadist movement, personal mentor of Osama bin Laden, and author of the movement's guiding slogan—"Jihad and the rifle alone: no negotiations, no conferences, and no dialogues."

Azzam was al-Qaeda's very own patron saint.

In the history of jihadist terrorism, no one had ever been brash enough, or genocidal enough, to assign himself the moniker of Azzam the Younger. This kind of reckless yet informed vocabulary raised the message beyond the level of most faux-terrorist and wannabe communiqués. Instead, the designation hinted at the possible emergence of a dangerous new arrival on the global terrorism scene.

As quickly as it had arrived, the email disappeared again,

now whisked up into increasingly secretive pathways, toward America's highest corridors of power.

During the minutes that followed, the message bounced between the networks of various agencies assigned to national security—from Fort Meade to the CIA in Langley, Virginia, the FBI in nearby Quantico, Homeland Security in Washington's Nebraska Avenue Complex, on to the Pentagon, and still onward to an alphabet soup of more obscure groups like the Defense Intelligence Agency, the DOD Counterintelligence Field Activity, the U.S. Strategic Command, the Special Operations Command, the Joint Forces Command, and the Joint Warfare Analysis Center.

And still on it continued, racing on to its ultimate destination—the cavernous operations room of the National Counterterrorism Center, housed in a nondescript building at the intersection of two major highways in McLean, Virginia. The secretive federal agency now served as the new and expanded post–9/11 clearinghouse for centralized collection and analysis of intelligence on the subject.

There, the message's text and several paragraphs of accompanying commentary were spat from a printer, snatched up, and swiftly read by a midlevel watch officer attached to the Domestic Terror Unit of a larger team called the al-Qaeda and Sunni Affiliates Group.

Minutes later, the information was carefully inserted into a thick folder bearing the heading *Read Book Number One*, along with several lines of secrecy codes across its black cover, then dropped onto the desk of Vice Admiral Howard Gansky, the Center's director.

The following morning at precisely seven o'clock, Gansky, an African-American Navy veteran in his midfifties, read the account now labeled *Item One* three times. He leaned back in his chair, looked up at the ceiling, and took a single, exceedingly long breath.

A half hour later he stood holding that same sheet of paper at the head of a conference table lined with dark-suited functionaries and heavily decorated soldiers.

"Item One and its accompanying Item Two are some of the most promising and frightening enigmas we've seen in quite a while, folks," he began. "I'll start with the promising part. NSA decoded the message's destination. And it's a site in western Pakistan we've been curious about for a long time. A *Madrass* in Quetta. We'll have satellite and drone imagery within the hour, and confidence is high that it may lead us straight to Nirubi himself."

Eyebrows shot up around the table. Osama bin Laden's successor, his associate Omar Nirubi, had emerged as al-Qaeda's new leader and, accordingly, America's new global Enemy Number One. Capturing him would represent the War on Terror's most spectacular coup ever. While it was true that Nirubi had proven every bit as elusive as his predecessors, he also presented his pursuers with a new challenge. Though born in a refugee camp in West Beirut, he was Oxford-educated, a fluent English speaker, and a keen student of Western culture, along with its most subtle weaknesses. This made him the most prized catch in the history of American intelligence.

"The bad news," Gansky continued, "is that if it's truly Nirubi, that means the message is authentic. And that means—"

The general closest to Gansky turned and met his eye. "It means we've got twenty-six days to find the sender," he interrupted, glancing down at his BlackBerry. "Whatever holiday plans you folks have made, better plan on canceling them. You can tell your kids you're keeping someone else's family from being murdered."

CHAPTER 4

The White House, family dining room—25 days before the attack

The grandfather clock struck nine. The folders, their crisp spines perfectly aligned like a pair of breakfast menus, sat on gleaming mahogany alongside a cup of Ethiopian coffee and a hand-rolled croissant perched on bone china.

The doors flew open and the telltale murmur of power swept into the room, then into the leather chair. The manicured left hand framed by crisp double cuffs grasped the top folder first, long before the coffee cup handle or the napkin with its neatly embroidered *W* and *H*.

The top folder contained the Threat Matrix—a secretly ranked list of the day's top ten developments in the War on Terror. The ranking had long ago evolved into the most compelling part of the President's Daily Brief.

The email message from Reseda ranked both number one and two.

"First on the list this morning, Mr. President," began

Vice Admiral Gansky, "is your approval on a snatch-and-grab mission in Pakistan. We believe it may yield Omar Nirubi himself."

"Wow," said the president. "Which part of Pakistan?"

"Western. The lawless provinces."

"Great. It's where we suspected him all along. Which one?"

"Baluchistan. Quetta, specifically."

"Why is this even on the Threat Matrix?" he asked with an air of mild exasperation. "The chance of catching Nirubi isn't exactly a threat—it's an opportunity."

"You're right, Mr. President," Gansky replied. "But Item Two explains that the opportunity is also closely linked to a major threat, and that's what makes it so troubling. See, if we find Nirubi, that also validates the message. And the message promises the mass murder of hundreds of thousands of Americans on New Year's Day."

The president turned, stared hard at his adviser. "Where's this terror cell located?"

"That's the problem, sir. We don't know. The email's point of origin wasn't successfully decrypted."

"Great. And is this mass murder set to go off no matter what? Regardless of the response this emailer gets back?"

"It appears so. He's not asking for approval, just gloating to his superiors. The mass murder plan appears to be under way, independent of any central authority. You know how these cells are organized."

"Right. Compartmentalization." The president exaggerated each of the word's syllables, like a schoolboy being forced to enunciate. "Well, at least let's get Nirubi. But instead of telling the world, let's take him dark right away. Then turn him over to the right people. Aggressively interrogate him. Do everything we can to get the cell's location out of him. And I do mean *everything*."

Gansky slowly nodded his assent. Each listener knew what *everything* meant. In this context, it brought up words like *rendition, black site, waterboarding.*

In other words, torture.

"Mr. President," Gansky said at last in a low tone, "I must bring up the obvious. As you well know, you campaigned quite vocally on the promise of ending the practices usually associated with extreme interrogation."

The president exhaled forcefully through his nostrils, clearly exasperated at being confronted with this truth.

"I know, I know. But in this case, we have a very clear instance of a specific threat and a clock ticking down on our chances of stopping it. Legally, isn't that supposed to make all the difference?"

"Some difference. But it doesn't erase the very categorical promises you made on the campaign trail. If it came out that you authorized old-style tactics, it would be political suicide. Neither your political opponents nor the press would focus for a moment on the altered legalities of the situation."

"Even if it was to prevent a mass killing on American soil?"

"Sir, the old tortures themselves were carried out to prevent mass killings on American soil. And they worked too. Nothing more happened. But the problem is, nobody is ever impressed by successful prevention. You can't cheer for the neutralization of a threat you never knew about in the first place. It's like proving a negative. The urgency of the cause didn't impress the critics then, and it won't now. The only thing with enough traction would be a failure. Another 9/11. Thousands of American fatalities."

The president leaned over and gave Gansky a look that said he was growing irritated.

"All right, since you people are so stinking familiar with all of my past pronouncements, then draw up an interrogation plan that's as aggressive as possible, given my paper trail, and follow it. If it doesn't work, if it becomes necessary to consider other options, then we talk again. In the meantime, I'm tired of all this mealymouthed talk. We need to move."

"Do you want to see the aerial shots of the place?" asked the general after an awkward pause.

The president shrugged, clearly in no mood for preliminaries. "What's your confidence level on the target package?"

"The highest, sir."

"Well then," said the leader of the free world, "let's not waste another minute. Let's go get this guy."

Quetta, Baluchistan Province, Pakistan—3 hours later

The *muezzin*'s call to worship rang out from a narrow minaret six stories above the bleached-gray streets of Quetta, piercing the morning mist with a thin, almost sirenlike wail.

Thousands of eyes darted skyward at the sound, for it signaled the moment to offer the *Fajr salat*, every Muslim's predawn prayers. Citizens of Quetta—everyone from the wealthy Pashtoon merchants on Jinnah Road to Afghan refugees in outlying tent colonies—had reason to welcome the *adhan*, because adherence to the five daily prayers was one of the few unifying aspects of daily life in the city.

The Baluchistan Province, which called Quetta its capital, was one of the most lawless and chaotic regions on earth, a free-fire patchwork of tribal chiefdoms even Islam's power could not unify. In the fractious and bloodthirsty wastelands between Quetta and the Afghan border, the Pakistani government maintained only the thinnest pretense of control, and medieval traditions held the rule of law. Here, Sunnis and Shiites killed each other even more freely than they did infidels. As a result, the ritual of the five prayers was one of the few observances that both of Islam's major factions could practice in common.

Even in the radical Madrass schools, where pupils as young as three learned the ways of jihad and global terrorism for eighteen hours a day, the song signaled an immediate pause for prayer.

On the rooftop of the most notorious such Madrass, a large school run by Taliban sympathizers in the city's Pashtunibad district, a cordon of Kalashnikov-toting guards put down their machine guns with wary expressions, then knelt on their rugs to face Mecca.

It was a rare concession of security, for the man kneeling at the group's center happened to be the most wanted man in the world.

It would be the only touch of direct sunlight in which he'd dare to indulge himself all day.

Al-Qaeda protocol called for Omar Nirubi to be spirited from the building in an hour's time, and from the entire region by midday. The man rarely spent more than three hours in a single place. Only the most important of conferences—a briefing of al-Qaeda leaders about an upcoming slaughter inside the Great Satan, America—had compelled him to enter the city limits proper. And within that reluctant visit, even these brief minutes of exposure had been contested among them.

But their leader would not be swayed. He simply loved the sight of the rising sun at prayers.

Hardly audible above the sound of their voices, a dull *whoosh* like a burst of wind blew across the rooftop, followed by four soft overlapping thumps.

All four of the bodyguards had just begun the *sujood*, the prostrate posture where foreheads touch the ground. The thumps had been the sound of silenced sniper rounds hitting their targets. Their bodies rolled limply onto their sides, each of their prayer rugs bearing a fresh stain that glistened red in the dawning light.

It took the unharmed man between them a dazed moment to understand what had happened. He broke from his prayers with a scowl. Cocking his head, he stared at the bodies around him. Turning from one to the other, his eyes widened with realization.

Americans!

He ran to the side, where he snatched up the nearest AK-47. He swiftly raised it to his forehead.

But he was too late.

In the half second it took him to raise the barrel to his temple, five Delta Force commandos had swarmed over the lip of the roof and converged on him like linebackers blitzing a helpless quarterback.

A single shot rang out, lofted wildly into thin air as the soldiers wrestled the weapon from his hands. There would be no merciful death by suicide.

The sound of the gun was swallowed up by a roar of thunder. A Black Hawk helicopter floated into view, its front canopy lined up even with the roofline, rotor wash blowing the prayer rugs clean off the roof.

While one soldier threw the prisoner into the Black Hawk's open side door, the other three crept to the roof's edge with weapons brandished and fired warning bursts to the sidewalk below, the source of several hostile shouts.

With a head-spinning suddenness the rooftop exploded with incoming gun blasts. The outermost commando reared back and fell, blood spraying from his neck. The Americans turned to each other and bellowed warnings through the crossfire, faces contorted with rage and determination. All around them windowsills and rooftops erupted with muzzle flashes, pouring bullets onto their position.

The tactic was now clear. Rather than being lightly defended, the Madrass had recruited its surrounding neighborhood to serve as its very own defensive sniper's nest.

The Black Hawk jolted sideways, its flanks peppered with steaming bullet holes. Its canopy rumpled under the impact of ricocheted bullets.

The distant sniper and the chopper's gunner now added their fire, ratcheting the scene above the school into an inferno of dust, careening bullets, and flying shards of debris. The surrounding buildings were hardly visible now, their mud walls shattering into gray clouds that swirled about with each passing round.

Another shout rang out from the chopper door, barely audible above the roar. The surviving commandos backed toward the craft, guns still trained on their surroundings. Finally, when their backs were against the Black Hawk, they turned and jumped inside. Their fallen comrade was pulled in with them.

The chopper banked upward violently, its side gun still belching out cover fire.

Two minutes later, it was skirting the hilltops east of the city, flying to safety.

From the time of the first sniper shot, the raid had lasted fifty-three seconds.

CHAPTER 5

CIA headquarters, Langley, Virginia—24 days before the attack

In the middle of the evening, lights flicked on inside the most secure conference room of the sprawling CIA complex. Three men entered the densely carpeted expanse and sat down with the briskness and energy of former military officers. Together they comprised the rubber-meets-the-road contingent of the National Security Council.

They were the officials responsible for executing the majority of the Council's decisions regarding the War on Terror.

Two of them were officially employed by the president's own staff. Thomas Little, a rangy fifty-year-old with a coif of unruly gray hair, held the title of deputy assistant secretary for Homeland Security. Joseph King, a stocky man with piercing blue eyes, outranked him as deputy assistant to the president for national security.

Their host and fellow member of the Council was Matthew Snipes, director of the CIA National Clandestine

Service. Snipes was not only the country's most formidable espionage chief but possessed one of the most shielded identities within the CIA. To his colleagues at Langley, he was referred to simply as José.

"José," began King, "you know we always enjoy your company. So I'm sure there's a perfectly good reason why you called us away from our nice, warm living rooms to drive all the way here for a meeting."

"You know about the operation," José said.

"Of course we do," King replied testily. "The CIA isn't the only agency with real-time intel feeds."

"True," said José. "I was only introducing the case. Anyway, it's going to present the White House with some very delicate, very dangerous dilemmas. And I think you guys are the kind of clearheaded types who can start thinking about a solution while there's still time."

Their faces relaxed somewhat, and they slowly offered the flat smiles of men who knew they were being flattered and yet accepted it.

"I know where you're headed," Little said with a nod.

"The president wants us to interrogate Nirubi," continued José, "in case there's any chance the lowlife has any info about the New Year's Day bomb plot. That's understandable. Nirubi could save millions of American lives by talking. But what happens after that?"

"After what?" King asked. "Failure or success?"

José's voice dropped to a conspiratorial growl. "Either one."

King contemplated his freshly manicured nails. "I see. Look, we all know we can speak freely here. And we all know what the preferred outcome of the capture would have been, had the prisoner's intel not been so crucial."

"Exactly," said José. "It's still operational policy for a terrorist of this importance to . . . *not* survive apprehension."

King sighed. Everybody in their circles knew this. Death during capture was the cleanest, most expeditious way of handling the delicacies of holding such a revered prisoner. No drawn out, unpredictable, publicity-producing trial. No hero worship or galvanizing of militant Islamists around the world. No chance of escape. No hassles about extradition or citizenship. Just a flat press release implying that the dirtbag had taken a round or two in the head in the heat of crossfire.

"This is especially true for the head of al-Qaeda," added José. "He's nearly as much trouble in our custody and alive as he is on the loose. Even under normal circumstances, we wouldn't let him live. And our usual need to make him disappear would double after an aggressive interrogation that made a mockery of international law. There's no way he could ever be allowed to surface and tell the world we've gone back to extraordinary renditions and black sites just months after the president signed a law saying America had changed its tactics. So here's problem one."

"Not to mention," said King, "that with a fish this big, and a plot this dangerous, and with so many agencies involved, we'll probably risk a leak at some point."

"I'd say it's almost guaranteed," said Little.

"If we have any hope of preserving the president's deniability," José continued, "he can't be told anything more about what happens to Nirubi after today. Period. No matter if Nirubi talks or not. And no matter what happens to him subsequent to that. If he talks, and the attack is stopped, the president can stand up in the East Room and tell the world that his intelligence services thwarted the plot. As an aside, he can add, 'Oh, and Nirubi was killed during a raid to apprehend him this morning.' End of story. Nothing needs to be any more specific than that."

"What if Nirubi breaks down and offers us full cooperation?" asked Little.

"Yeah, right," José said with a smirk. "And what are the odds of that?"

"I'm just wondering if there's any scenario that allows us to let Nirubi live."

"Why would you want something like *that* to happen?"

"It just puts the president at a slightly lower risk, that's all. You do realize that we've never terminated a suspect this long after his apprehension before. In the past, they always just got caught in the crossfire. Now we're going to have to terminate him months after his arrest. Maybe even after he cooperated with us. Are you really up for that?"

King's and Little's gazes met, then quickly looked past each other. Little sighed and stared absently down at his BlackBerry sitting on the conference table. "In the interests of national security, you betcha."

King nodded. "To save thousands of American lives, I'd put a bullet through that monster's head myself."

The White House—minutes later

There would be no fanfare, for the capture of Omar Nirubi had to be, for the moment anyway, kept completely secret. Given the nature of the stakes, a person leaking this story could potentially be prosecuted for treason, and everyone involved knew it. Any leaker could even face the death penalty. Which didn't make a leak impossible, only a bit more dangerous.

A solitary phone call came to the Situation Room, announcing to the National Security director that Operation Quetta Capture had been successful, with the notable exception of one service fatality.

The president was informed by a whisper in his ear as he sat in the Rose Garden listening to a federal judge candidate express her gratitude for being appointed. The only signs of his inner exultation were the sudden brightening of his countenance and the slow clenching and unclenching of his fists.

The confirmation ceremony was discreetly cut short, and the president whisked away to the Situation Room.

The "Salt Lick" Detention Complex, Bagram Air Base, Afghanistan

Light had vanished from Omar Nirubi's world. Blackness reigned, his eyes no more than impotent holes in his head. For longer than he could remember, a blindfold had gripped his face so tightly that he could not even blink.

Outside sound was also a distant memory. His ears were wrapped in sound-dampening muffs. He could barely make out the faint murmur of his own heart, a slight cough, a swallow. Or a muffled scream.

But nothing more.

His mouth was gagged. He sucked anemic puffs of air into his nostrils, fought to keep panic from sparking his lungs into a claustrophobic frenzy.

He could not move an inch. His naked limbs were bound with a vengeful snugness to a stretcher using duct tape. Not a single muscle responded to him. He could not even twitch his pinkie finger.

In fact, Omar Nirubi was so cut off from the rhythms and impulses of being alive that he was unsure if he'd survived the firefight in Quetta or had actually died in the crossfire.

One thing he knew: if this was death, it was certainly far from what he'd expected. No fanfare. No blasts of light or trumpets. No meeting Allah. In fact, this death of utter blackness and blankness most resembled the oblivion promised by atheists.

But he refused to give up faith. So for an eternity that in reality lasted only two hours and forty-five minutes—long enough for him to be flown across the Afghan border and over to Bagram Air Base—Omar Nirubi prayed incessantly. He screwed his thoughts down tight upon the single urge to supplicate Allah for forgiveness, and this he continued with hardly a pause.

A hard tug, then light.

A searing, blinding glare, like ice picks stabbing the eyes.

A face, wrapped in a halo of light.

Faces. Eyes.

Cold.

CHAPTER 6

"Omar Nirubi. You are in the custody of the United States Army."

The voice was that of a woman, although no woman Nirubi had ever heard speak before. Her speech was low and clipped. Almost masculine—although some tension in her cadence told him the manly aspects were forced, not her natural tone.

He forced himself to focus on her face and meet her gaze.

What he saw seared his spirit as an abomination. There, within an arm's length, stood an uncovered young woman, her attractive face and hair exposed, her bosom's rise under a plain blue shirt obvious to the eye. An offense to the holy way of things.

The sight of her made his every muscle seize with rage, and his body, despite its confinement, surge to rise up and destroy. He lifted, but the alien hands about him tightened and forced him back down into the chair. Had he possessed the strength to resist, he would have gladly struggled until death.

The woman was barely out of her twenties, his mind registered almost despite himself, with pale blue eyes and shoulder-length blond hair that curled about her face in a way that inflamed him. He had not seen a woman wearing anything other than an *abeya* in several weeks. Not since his last visit with his wife in a tiny Pakistani hideout. And none who looked like this in a very long time.

"I know you speak English," the woman said. "Mr. Nirubi, I am Captain Delia Kilgore of the U.S. Army. You are my prisoner. Life as you once knew it has ended forever. And your fate is completely in my hands."

Pelican Bay State Prison, Crescent City, California

In another location, under different circumstances, the man might have been just another six-foot-four, baby-faced, chubby-cheeked man wearing a disarmingly childlike grin and a bright orange jumpsuit.

Here, in a bare room at the center of California's highest security prison, the picture also featured handcuffs around the man's wrists and chains about his ankles. Not to mention the loathsome identity of Alex McCarry—one of America's most notorious serial killers, blissfully awaiting the arrival of his best friend.

A much shorter, fitter man in a simple black suit entered the room, followed by a burly prison guard. The man in the suit stepped forward, smiled even wider.

"Greg," the prisoner said with all the carefree whimsy of a frat brother greeting an old pal. "I knew you'd come."

"I wouldn't miss it," said Greg Cahill in a far more somber tone.

The prisoner lunged forward and engulfed Greg in his arms. Standing only two feet behind them, the guard stiffened and reflexively reached for his nightstick. After a brief moment of shock, a wide-eyed Greg held out his hand behind him. All was well. And indeed it was—for over Greg's shoulder, the mass murderer was grinning like a toddler. The embrace was no threat, but a bear hug of affectionate gratitude.

"I wanna thank you," McCarry said, pulling back with tears in his eyes. "Thanks for looking past all my junk and bringing me to Christ."

Cahill smiled. "What are you talking about? It was He who brought you to me. It's what He's called me to do, and it's been one of the biggest privileges of my life."

Nodding, the prisoner grabbed a metal folding chair and swept it under his ample behind. "Hey, did ya see what I told that CBS lady?" he exulted. Without waiting for Greg's reply, he continued, "I told her that Greg Cahill, the bravest, most pure guy I've ever known, came here to the pit of hell to share Christ with me when nobody else would even look my way. And thanks to Jesus, I can sit here knowing that no matter how many bars and fences I've got around me, I'm actually a free man. I'm forgiven. I don't have any of the killing urges anymore. And soon I'll be going home to see my heavenly Daddy. Did you see it? I told her all that without even blinking an eye. They put it on TV too. I saw it."

Greg shook his head in disbelief, still smiling. "So did I, Alex. I am so proud of you."

McCarry leaned back and laughed. "None of the guys understand what I'm feeling right now," he said. "They're all bummed out for me, like I lost the big fight or something. I try to tell them I'm about to win the race, but none of 'em get it. They're not in the Word."

"Don't worry, Alex. After that, you'll have left behind the most powerful testimony anyone could ever imagine. And I'll be right back here to talk with every one of them and make sure they understand what gave you the strength to face it like this."

McCarry leaned forward and his eyes suddenly narrowed.

"You know what I'm gonna do when I get to heaven? I'm gonna find every one of those people whose lives I stole. If they'll talk to me, I'll kneel in front of them, take their hand, and beg 'em for their forgiveness."

Cahill stared at him, unable to respond to the outpouring.

"You know something, Greg? I know which ones were believers too, those that I'm gonna find up there. I don't like to talk about this much . . ."

He paused, inhaled a trembling breath.

". . . but people's last moments tell everything about 'em. Some of those folks cursed me and spit at me with every last breath inside 'em. And of course, they had every right to do that. But some of them got this light in their eyes, and started talking to Jesus. One even forgave me, can you believe that? Knowing full well what I was about to do. She smiled at me. So much kindness and understanding just sort of flooded out of those eyes."

Cahill reached out and took the convict's hand, causing the chains to rustle loudly across the room's barren surfaces.

"I got a letter off to the very last relative yesterday."

"That's wonderful. Congratulations, Alex."

McCarry had been on a relentless letter-writing campaign ever since his conversion, sending out letters to the families of the people he'd killed, expressing his remorse in the strongest possible words. Following Greg's advice, he had only discussed their forgiveness in the most offhand of terms, leaving the decision to forgive entirely up to their discretion. Many of the letters had gone unanswered. Other people had written back letters filled with bitterness and hostility. Greg had helped Alex to see that these came from people still suffering the aftermath of his crimes. He needed to have compassion for them and let their plight deepen his understanding of what he'd done. They were, in a real sense, his most wounded victims.

"It's an honor to know you, my brother," Greg said hoarsely. "And I want you to know something. I'm going to miss you. You're a changed man from what all those cable TV shows used to say about you."

"Yeah, and I saw on TV what they're saying about *you* now," said McCarrry. "Being my friend and all. They haven't been very nice."

Cahill shrugged. "It's easier for them to hate you for what you did than to look inside their own hearts and see the blackness there."

"But what I don't understand is the people who say they're Christians, then go on to say all these awful things about you just because you're my friend and shared the gospel with me. That's not right."

Greg winced, but said nothing.

"Look, whatever price I've paid for befriending you," he said at last, "I would pay again in a heartbeat. It's been an honor. And a healing for me too, don't forget. Remember, I'm a killer too. Jesus forgave me of something unforgivable. It's just a fluke of circumstance that it's you in that jumpsuit and not me."

"Time!" shouted the guard.

The two men looked into each other's eyes, as if unable to verbalize their feelings at that moment. Finally, Cahill rose. McCarry followed suit, accidentally kicking over his chair with a clatter. Now it was Greg's turn to extend the bear hug. He reached around the murderer's torso as best he could and squeezed his hardest.

"I'll be there," Greg said.

"I know you will."

"You stay in the Word between now and then, you hear?" Cahill whispered.

"You can count on it."

Greg wiped his eyes and walked slowly toward the door.

CHAPTER 7

Skies over northern Poland—12 days before the attack

A pair of Rolls Royce engines throttled higher and, nudged by the wave of an upraised aileron, lowered one elegantly fluted wing tip into a graceful dip across the frigid air currents of a clear blue winter sky.

With only some different clothes and maybe a pair of skis in her luggage, thought Captain Delia Kilgore, she might have been a movie star jetting in to Gstaad or Aspen.

After all, here she was in a Gulfstream V, the preferred private jet of the glitterati, and tilting just outside her oval window was a crystalline landscape of pine-clad slopes and blinding white snowfields.

Granted, it was by Air Force terms officially a C-37, and hardly configured for comfort and luxury. Yet the plainness of her military trappings could not belie the reality of her surroundings.

They had flown at low altitude for some time now. Watching the unfolding beauty had proven a welcome

distraction from the shrink-wrapped lump of detestable humanity lying on the fuselage floor beside her.

The pilot had been making the most of his aircraft's power and
maneuverability, even if his flight plan had clearly ordered him to
fly this way. He'd descended to somewhere around five thousand
feet, she reckoned, then used the engines' heft to power through
every dip and ridgeline of the vast forestland below them. From
her seat just aft of the wing, the ride had been exhilarating.

She glanced outside again. They were preparing to land, the
engines feathering back to a low hum with the nose rising as part
of its final flare. A scattering of tall wooden lodges and hotels for
tourists now punctuated the treetops.

The remote airport revealed itself just ahead as merely a half-
dozen small buildings, built to service hunting parties and winter
getaways.

The field had been designed for the use of a tiny few aircraft
at once. Today she saw, as the jarring thump of tires announced
their landing, six aircraft parked just beyond the runway. Three
were clearly identifiable as U.S. military. The other three, like the
one that held her, bore very few identifiable markings at all.

She looked away, back to the comfort of trees. Truly, it caused
her an odd sort of cognitive dissonance to remember that this airfield secretly carried one of the world's most dreaded and loathed
labels. A pair of words that could hardly have been more at odds
with such surroundings of tranquility and wild beauty.

Black site.

Stare Kiejkuty Military Base, Poland—11 days before the attack

"You are a traitor to Allah! A betrayer of Islam!"
Bound to a bare steel-boned chair in a dimly lit concrete

basement, the near-naked Nirubi spat out his words, then spat for real. Only the tiniest drops of saliva reached the shoulder of the black-robed Islamic cleric facing him. The al-Qaeda leader had not been given water for many hours.

These were the first words he had spoken in hours.

An *imam* deeply opposed to violence in the name of his faith, the object of Nirubi's wrath closed his eyes for a long pause. Unceremoniously, the man scraped two flecks of saliva from his robe and shook his head in futility, cutting his eyes toward the room's darkened perimeter.

He had been flown to central Europe by the CIA the day before, for the express purpose of trying to soften Nirubi's unwavering resolve. It was now manifestly clear to the shadowy row of glowering officials that his journey had been in vain.

"I have done nothing but quote the Koran to you, my brother," the cleric said in the voice of someone nearing the end of his patience. "Which words of Mohammed do you throw away in your lust for blood? Indeed, it is you who discredit the name of Islam. I implore you to consider all of the prophet's words, not only those which tickle your ears."

From her vantage point amidst the torture chamber's deepest darkness, Captain Kilgore crossed her arms and stared through the shadows. Shaking her head with a frown, the head interrogator turned and crossed a gloomy corridor to a steel door. She pulled the metal slab open with a wince of effort and entered a large room lit mainly by the glow of several dozen video monitors.

Standing at the room's center was the familiar cordon of somber-eyed men she'd wrangled for days—two CIA case officers in rumpled suits, a very large African-American with ties to the Department of Homeland Security, and an Army colonel who just happened to be her superior officer.

She knew of many more, perhaps even hundreds more American intel types of every rank and variety crowding the upper floors of the heavily guarded Polish base above her. The vast chain of command, however, appeared to have siphoned its power down to these men. Their stares revealed a keen awareness that significant reservoirs of authority had distilled themselves into their elite group.

Delia swallowed a vague sense of intimidation at the sight of their glum faces turning toward her and the claps of their cell phones shutting, one by one. As she stepped into their tight circle, she faced each one eye to eye, reminding herself to swallow her feelings of inferiority and take charge of her case.

Clearly, this was the most important assignment she would ever handle, the proverbial opportunity of a lifetime. *Own it!* she told herself with an invisible clench of her teeth. It was *her* case, after all. It didn't matter how many slights the men had tossed her way—disregarding her, conferring in her absence, dropping demeaning comments or patronizing glances. It didn't matter how many times they had pointedly reminded her of the high-powered cloud of scrutiny surrounding her every move. Despite all those things, no one could argue that circumstances had placed her there as lead interrogator.

She had the authority.

At least on paper.

Besides, their treatment of her could easily be explained as merely helpful warnings to remain respectful of her rank, to not forget the amazing good fortune directed her way.

Delia found it impossible to gauge, and not worth trying to decide, how it had happened. Perhaps she'd earned the assignment through demonstrated skill in her last posting. Or maybe the powers that be had simply opted to rattle Nirubi by making him subservient to an attractive woman.

What she did know was that the assignment would never have come her way had she stunk at her job. Besides, the posting came loaded with countless intricacies and chances to screw up. And she hadn't done that yet.

Thankfully, the assignment gave her just as many chances to shine brightly.

Delia had chosen to grit her teeth and resolved to do her best despite the minefields. Which was why, seeing the lidded gazes of the men follow her entrance into the command center, she merely straightened her spine and tightened her face into a mask of determination.

"Good morning, gentlemen," she said flatly.

The greeting earned her two barely perceptible nods.

"Seems the good imam has done his best," she said, making sure her voice contained only steely assessment without a hint of questioning. They would second-guess her conclusions quickly enough, without her appearing to ask for it.

"Looks like this tactic has run its course," she continued. "It may have even backfired. The subject seems to despise the man. Amazing how little respect these zealots show even their own clerics."

She exhaled commandingly.

"I'm for ending this phase and sending the imam home at once."

"That call's already been made," said the Homeland Security official dismissively.

"What do you mean, already made?" she asked with a cold stare. "I hadn't heard anything about that. I've neither signed off on a shift in tactics nor received word from command authority."

"I didn't mean 'call' in that sense," the officer relented, subtly rolling his eyes. "I just meant that there seems to be a consensus, a shared assessment, that none of the tactics we've used so far have done any good."

"We don't have time for this," began the senior CIA man. "We're now under two weeks before the attack date. We've been here a day, and all we've gotten is a smattering of operational intel out of the man. Nothing about New Year's."

New Year's. Delia nodded at the term, trying her hardest to conceal her bemusement at how swiftly the men had assigned the threatened attack its own cute little operational nickname. New Year's—it sounded more like a holiday vacation itinerary than a possible massacre of fellow Americans.

The coining of inside phrases had always struck Delia as yet another collegial way of demonstrating how deeply intelligence workers were "in the know." Her work seemed to be full of such people, those types who seemed to find under every rock another way to remind the people around them how high they ranked on the classification ladder. How much inside knowledge to which they were privy.

She brushed away her reaction and rejoined the conversation. Truth was, falling in line and repeating their nickname was easier than spouting any of the other half-dozen monikers intelligence bureaucracies had attached to the impending attack.

"Speaking of which," broke in his CIA colleague, "we just got another communiqué from Langley. Our human sources in the Mideast are sending back nothing but confirmations on the validity of the New Year's threat. Gaza, Damascus, Tehran, everywhere—the whole jihadist world is buzzing about how America's going to be brought to its knees."

"Great. As if there's not enough pressure."

That last sympathetic rejoinder had come from her commanding officer.

Since their arrival in Poland, the colonel had declined to speak with her directly about the political intricacies of her assignment. Yet it had not escaped her attention that most of his public arguments had tended to support Delia and point out the difficulties of her position.

"Well, you haven't seen pressure if we don't start providing results," insisted the lead CIA man. "And I mean soon."

"Five years ago, the next step would have been simple," the other CIA man continued. "We would have just turned the screw a lot tighter. Ratchet up the interrogation. Bring in a foreign national who knew how to make people talk, give him some power tools and plenty of towels, then walk out for a three-hour cup of coffee while he did his job. Maybe bring in a waterboard. But now, after all the media whining, they hardly need us. They need political analysts. Publicists. Consultants."

"They always said torture didn't actually work," said Delia's superior, staring at the pitted concrete floor. "But all the softer techniques have failed, I have to admit." He turned to her. "Captain Kilgore, what's the basic list of tactics we've run through thus far?"

"Well, if you start with the transport, we have his being hooded and duct-taped to a stretcher. A long flight. No bathroom. No sleep. Since he got here, when he hasn't been strapped to the interrogation chair, he's been in the hole."

They nodded, each of them wincing at the thought of occupying such a space. The so-called hole was actually an aperture in the concrete a little larger than a coffin, offering very little maneuvering space on either side of Nirubi's body. The man could not even turn around. If he was even remotely claustrophobic, then he'd spent hours in psychological agony.

"He still hasn't had any sleep. No food or water. He's been interrogated for a total of twenty-six hours. We've played Devo over the speakers during breaks at around 140 decibels. That was, of course, until the imam showed up."

"Man, in the old days that would have been called a walk in the park."

"It's definitely a classic non-torture approach, that's for sure," Delia conceded. "But that's contemporary rules of engagement. And it's definitely had an impact on him. I certainly wouldn't call it a walk in the park. He may not be cooperating, and he may be retreating constantly into his religion, but he's hardly the firebrand who came in here. We've succeeded in burning the rage and bombast out of him. The treatment has definitely taken the edge off of his fanaticism."

"What do you mean?" asked the colonel. "He just bawled out one of his own clerics for not being jihadist enough. I don't see him being less fanatic."

"True, he's relying more and more on his faith as a basis for resisting. On a belief level, he's as fanatical as ever. I'm simply talking about his psychological resiliency, on the basis of pure emotional strength. He's got less fire in him."

"Well, this whole situation may be about to change," said the Homeland Security official. "I just got a heads-up on the latest idea that's about to be run up the flagpole by my superiors. Remember, there's huge propaganda value in having captured Nirubi. Only we can't cash in any of it so long as we keep him a secret while we search for answers. So my bosses are proposing that we announce the capture like it happened today, then have a quick show trial and execute him before he becomes a pariah."

"But then all his intel dies with him!" Delia exclaimed.

"Who cares? At that point, they would just say that the intel community had its shot and failed. The assumption would be that nothing actionable was forthcoming anyway. I'm telling you guys, if we don't come up with something soon, this is all going south, and our careers with it."

"I'm going to recommend a throttles-up on the old-fashioned tactics," said one of the CIA men. "They were never fully out of the question, you all know that. Given the severity of the threat, they were always on the table as a last resort. Washington just wanted to try the soft stuff first. Obviously, it hasn't worked. We reached last resort—yesterday."

Delia glared at the man and said, "I believe that would be a mistake, sir. The guy's mentally already checked out. He's already counting the virgins, if you know what I mean. He seems to retreat further into his set-in-stone version of Islam with every new twist I throw his way. You've heard him—the only words out of his mouth are about Allah and Mohammed. His faith seems to be giving him more strength by the hour. And I'm convinced if you start using brute force on him, he'll become even more entrenched. If we take it one step further down the road to torture, and start confirming all his worst opinions of the West, we'll lose any chance we ever had."

"I agree with the captain," interjected her superior. Delia kept her gaze aimed straight ahead in an attempt to mask her surprise. He had never backed her this openly before.

"I do too," broke in the Homeland Security man.

"Fine," sneered the CIA officer. "What kind of change do you all suggest?"

"We need something completely different," said her last champion. "Something fresh. A change in direction." He looked around at the group, notably excepting Delia. "Any ideas?"

Nobody spoke. The moment elapsed in a miserable silence.

"No? Then let's reconvene here at thirteen hundred," said the CIA officer. "And be ready for some changes."

CHAPTER 8

The colonel grabbed Delia by the elbow on her way out of the room, motioning toward a stairway. Together they climbed the stairs and found themselves in an abandoned hallway that reeked of cigarettes and sweat.

"I want to give you a warning," he said, looking around nervously. "If this whole thing goes down, you'll go before anyone else. Those guys would gladly jettison you in order to salvage the situation."

"I understand, sir. I kind of got that feeling already."

"Personally, I think you've done a terrific job against some pretty big obstacles, and I would have supported you more, but that would only have hurt you with the other men. They're scrutinizing the situation for any signs that you're just a prop. You've managed to avoid that, but it's always a danger. But sheer persistence isn't going to save you anymore. I'm afraid that, barring a massive last-second sea change, you'd better steel yourself for a quick plane ride back home."

Locking eyes with the colonel, Delia said, "Look, if I had a rabbit to yank out of my hat, I'd have done it along time ago."

. "I'm sure you would have, Captain. I would have expected nothing less. Just sit tight and be prepared."

"Yes, sir," she said with a salute, then turned and started walking away.

"Just figure out how to surgically remove the religion from the man's head," he called after her, "and we're home free."

She nodded and continued walking, staring at the floor. At that precise moment, it came to her. She stopped as though frozen in place and remained there for a full thirty seconds before moving again. When she took her next step, it was with renewed vigor and purpose.

Delia emerged from the building and stepped into a scene straight out of Currier and Ives: a grove of pine trees weighed down with clumps of snow. A bucolic winterscape, provided she banish from her mind the presence of armed sentries guarding its every square foot from various vantage points. She glanced around and took in a deep breath of cold, bracingly clean air.

Once again it struck her as supremely ironic to drink in this serenity, the thick forest framed by a clear winter sky, yet here the place was a key destination in America's notorious rendition program.

That was the reality. *Her* reality. Whether she liked it or not, she now stood quite vulnerably poised between the opposing knife points of one of international law's sharpest controversies. In fact, she thought with an incredulous chuckle, at the moment she probably embodied everything that many Americans found dark and repressive about the War on Terror.

And given the moral ambiguities of the situation, it seemed fitting that she be standing right here, of all places. Fragments of the briefing she'd received on the flight over came floating back to her.

The complex behind her was a venerable haven of intelligence training dating all the way back to the days of Nazi occupation. During WWII, it had served as headquarters for the German SD, the intelligence arm of the SS. The airstrip on which she'd landed had launched Luftwaffe raids during the Warsaw Uprising. After the war, Soviet agents had used it as the launching pad for reprisals during the Prague Spring of 1968.

Looking out at her billowing breath, she was reminded that normally she would have used the interlude to grab a quick cigarette. Today she was not only trying to quit but entirely too preoccupied to entertain her own personal cravings. She threw her head back, trying to find courage in the pale blue of the sky above, and pulled out the satellite phone she'd been assigned upon her arrival.

She held out the bulky shape like an unpinned hand grenade, feeling dread overwhelm her. This wasn't going to be easy. Closing her eyes to remember the numbers, she pressed the buttons using her thumb and then lifted the unit to her ear.

"Dale?" she said finally. "It's me. Delia."

"What?" growled a male voice on the other end. "What are you doing calling me this early? I told you to never contact me again."

She sighed. This could prove even harder than she'd anticipated. The man on the other end of the line had very little reason to want to speak with her, let alone help her overcome one of her life's greatest challenges.

"Please don't hang up," she said with as much intensity as she could muster. "This isn't about . . . *us*. Okay?"

"Then what in the world could it possibly be about?"

"I have a very strange, very interesting reason for calling you. Unfortunately, I can only tell you about a tenth of it right now, but you'll understand."

Yeah, he'll understand, she reminded herself. After all, she'd first set eyes on his tanned, handsome face from her seat as a student in the Interrogation School at Fort Huachuca eight years ago. Dale had ranked as the school's most feared yet most admired instructor, a veteran of the Cold War's most pivotal and precarious interrogations. He'd entered Delia's life as a relentless tormentor, an instructor who recognized her latent gift for the job, then seemed to punish her for the talent from that point onward.

Only later, much later, had their relationship turned into something more. He'd been too conscientious to let something like a fraternization charge ruin a long and storied career.

She wondered what it meant now for him to have a bitter divorce on his record. Not an offense, but hardly a bright spot.

"I'm in Poland, Dale. Calling you on a CIA sat phone. Get the picture?" She tried to mark her words. Despite the unit's alleged security, given the intensity of her situation, one could never be too paranoid. "Look, I would be really grateful if you could help me with something. Not only that, but your country would be grateful. I'm in the middle of something very important, very sensitive, and very dangerous. Dale, do you remember that weird protocol you mentioned near the end of that first semester? You called it 'highly unorthodox,' one of your puns, since it had to do with religion. It dealt with a subject whose religion formed the foundation for an unusually stiff resistance to questioning?"

"Yeah, I remember that wild-haired, cockamamie excuse for a protocol. I only mentioned it as a joke. An off-base anecdote. I'm surprised one of you young hotheads didn't report me for it."

She grinned and nodded her head. "Good. I wasn't sure you would remember. Of course, you *are* the one with the steel-trap memory."

She'd said it while wincing at the thought. They both knew

he had used those same fail-safe memory banks to barrage her with unending accounts of her failures as a wife.

"Is there any way we can dredge that up? I know it's buried deep, from what you said. Somewhere in one of those defense think tanks, maybe?"

"Oh, man. I first heard about it over beers somewhere in Georgetown, from that wacky psy-ops guy who was always floating around some D.C. intel think tank or another. What was his name?"

"Please, Dale. I really need you to remember."

She grew perfectly still, waiting.

"He had a name that reminded me of one of those old nature painters. Ruskin. No . . . Ruffkin. I think I know how to find him, even though I haven't talked to him in years. This is really something important? 'Cause I'm not all that interested in giving you a career nudge. Not that you need it, from the sound of it."

"This isn't about me, Dale," she said. "I'll email you some contact info. And someday I'll be able to tell you what you helped me pull off. If we're all lucky, you won't be hearing about it on the evening news."

CHAPTER 9

The Pentagon, B ring, Arlington, Virginia—10 days before the attack

It wound up taking Lieutenant Colonel Dale Scheer more than ten phone calls, and nearly as many hours, to track down the author of the strange protocol Delia had inquired about. By that time, thankfully, the quest had blossomed for Dale into another test of his manly powers, compelling him to obsessively persist in flushing out his quarry.

In the end, it turned out the quarry was dead. Felled by a massive heart attack at age fifty, in some back corner of New Hampshire where he'd hidden away to telecommute.

The bizarre protocol he'd authored had slipped into the digital half-life of defense papers deemed too odd to implement, yet too well-reasoned to destroy.

Which was why within hours a phone rang in a large computer center at the Pentagon's second most sensitive concentric building, the so-called B ring. The request, even though it came from outside the New Year's team *per se,* was immediately tagged with a red-light priority rating and fed into the Defense Department's elaborate document retrieval system.

In this case, the task was far from simple. Following the document's negative evaluation, it had been filed deep within the Pentagon's tactical database for psychological operations, or psy-ops, there to remain available for any number of properly cleared interrogation and intelligence usages.

This particular retrieval had been complicated by yet another factor. In order to save space, Pentagon computers continuously ranked and arranged documents in order of their usage frequency. Documents found to be rarely used were moved further back into the database's filing structure. It was survival of the most frequently read. Data-entry Darwinism.

Furthermore, this paper had been labeled with a redundant checkout notification, which raised a covert alarm by notifying a short list of intelligence staffers of just who had requested it. The clerk noted this status with an arched eyebrow, for that kind of classification was rare these days, especially with older files.

Apparently someone wanted to keep close tabs on anybody foolish enough to even consider the protocol in question.

Stare Kiejkuty Military Base, northern Poland

Four hours later, Delia convened with the other officers in one of the building's rudimentary excuses for a conference room. She strode in briskly, holding a blue folder in both hands, positioning herself at the head of a bare table lined with peeling wooden chairs.

Nirubi was back in the hole, with the imam already winging his way back to Saudi Arabia. All was on hold, she knew, pending the conversation now facing her. Her cheeks were flushed, her eyes bright with the gleam of someone who believed she'd successfully pulled victory from the jaws of defeat.

"Thank you for meeting with me so quickly," she said with a confident smile. "As you know, there's not a second to waste, so I wanted you to be the first to hear. I've located something which I believe fits the parameters of what we're all looking for to turn this interrogation around."

She picked up the blue folder and held it out before her, as if it were a cardboard barrier against the resistance to come.

"Remember now that you asked for something fresh, something new and outside the box. Something equal to the danger our country faces. What I've dug up fills that bill and more. In fact, the person who first showed it to me called it highly unorthodox, which was always a bit of a pun. So remember your admonitions, because this is definitely out there."

"Duly noted," said her boss, his eyes watching her intently.

"I doubt whether any of you, despite your considerable experience, have ever heard of this. The officer who briefed me on it only knew of its existence by a fluke. Turned out a brilliant and eccentric friend of his, who at the time worked for the Defense Threat Reduction Agency, or Deetra for short, dreamed up this protocol. It was passed around a few covert agencies yet never went anywhere. Just too extreme. But again, remember that we're up against extreme threats. At least that's what you gentlemen keep telling me."

She grinned at that last dig, not wanting to appear bitter. She was enjoying this moment of vindication. No need to cheapen it with petty reprisals, she chided herself.

She opened the folder, pulled out four stapled sheaths of paper, and slid one to each man across the pitted tabletop.

"It's code-named *Tabula Rasa*. As in Clean Slate. It's designed for one highly specific scenario—one precisely like the situation before us. The case of a subject resistant to interrogation, for one and one reason only." She paused and glanced at each man in turn. "His religion."

The White House basement, National Security Council— that same day

The Tabula Rasa Protocol blasted through America's intelligence community with all the speed and devastation of a neutron bomb shock wave. It crossed the Atlantic in a mere split second, then spent approximately fifteen minutes in the grasp of several dozen officials across the greater D.C. beltway.

National Security councillors Little and King nearly collided in the darkened hallways of the White House basement, both of them grasping their respective copies. Both were headed to the other's office. Shaking their heads in bemusement at the coincidence, they settled on King's.

The two immediately placed a secure conference call to Matthew Snipes, aka José, director of the National Clandestine Service.

"Matt," King said into the speakerphone, flagrantly ignoring the CIA's alias directives, "have you had a chance to read it yet?"

"Yes, and I can't believe they're even wasting our time with this madness. It's one of the worst notions I've ever heard."

"Come on, Matt," said Little. "You know everybody's hunting for a bold new idea. It's out there, but you've got to admit that it speaks to the problem at hand."

"You mean you guys actually *like* this thing?" Snipes's voice rose to a plaintive whine. "I can't believe what I'm hearing!"

"We're all holding our noses right now," King broke in, "but again, remember that we're in last-ditch territory here. We know some of your rivals in the administration are suggesting we take Nirubi public. That's pure PR. No operational value whatsoever— and a total failure from an intel point of view. We'd get nothing out of him. So this idea may be our last chance."

"I can't believe this is even a government protocol!" Snipes snarled. His voice sounded like it was about to jump out of the black console at the table's center, then reach out and grab the two men by their throats. "I mean, you're talking about mixing Uncle Sam up with religion at the deepest level. We're not sup- posed to denigrate a prisoner's religion, but this . . . this is far worse. Far more serious. You think assassinating Nirubi would be a damaging leak? Try this operation on for size. It'd be the biggest PR disaster for the American government since Watergate!"

"I think you're overreacting, Matt," interrupted King. "We're not talking about flushing a Koran down the toilet, or saying nasty things about somebody's prophet or anything. We're just talking about the removal of something that's been identified as the prime obstacle in a subject's cooperation."

"In the past, we've been willing to kill a man to soften his resistance," added Little. "To break his health. To shatter his mind. Get him hooked on drugs. If all those things are within bounds, then isn't breaking his faith the next logical step?"

"Sure, the next step into insanity! Listen to yourselves!" Snipes was now shouting. "Doesn't some part of you recoil at the whole idea of mixing up our intelligence community in airy- fairy stuff like this? Even assuming it could work, which I highly doubt."

"Think of this, Matt. If it doesn't work, you've lost time, which is, yes, very important. But little else. You haven't waterboarded the man. You haven't left physical evidence of torture. You can still do whatever else you want. It's clean."

"It does involve the president, though."

"That's true," Little conceded. "The president has to record a few dummy video recordings. All deniable. After that, he's out."

"That's not all the liabilities. This thing has to be conducted on American soil."

"Yeah, I'm not crazy about that part. Although the rationale does make sense. The subject will never believe anything we tell him unless he's on our territory. That's basic to the op."

"And then there's this so-called person of influence."

"Right. The outside party. I didn't say this thing was neat as a whistle. Nothing is. But this outside person doesn't even have to know anything about the protocol. He'll act without direct knowledge. He's just incidental."

"Incidental, my foot. That's a huge unknown variable. You're assuming everything is going to go right."

"It will if we choose the right person. Listen, you may not like this plan, but it is quite detailed and thought out. Have you read the whole thing? It's chock-full of hardcore research on the psychology of religious conversion. The outside party is clearly brought in through a series of overlapping cover stories. He never knows the whole truth. In theory, it could work quite effectively."

"What if we gave it three days?" asked Little. "Three days tops, after which the whole intel strategy has run its course. Remember, it's our last good chance."

José snorted, clearly not convinced. "It's not a good one. But it's a chance, I suppose. Tell you guys what. You take a shot at it, but know that if it blows up in your faces, don't expect any solidarity and brotherly love from me. I'll be your harshest critic."

"We understand," King said gruffly.

CHAPTER 10

The Oval Office—2 hours later

"Good news, I hope?" asked the U.S. commander in chief, standing up from the refuge of his usual roost behind the famous Resolute desk.

His national security adviser, the only other person in the room, replied, "Not really, sir. Nirubi's interrogation has hit an impasse. The only thing he seems willing to share is the name of Allah, chanted over and over again. So they either go off into hardcore torture tactics, with all the attendant risks and low-yield expectations the approach brings with it, or they try a completely new, admittedly bizarre interrogation protocol. It comes with a pretty extensive set of its own disclaimers, warnings, and worst-case scenarios."

"Let me hear it."

"Well, the team on the ground has become convinced that if they could only undermine Nirubi's religious conviction, they would have a serious chance of rendering him quite pliable and cooperative. And as you know, the military has on file protocols for addressing nearly every contingency the human mind can dream up, this one included. It's called Tabula Rasa, and it falls within the realm of psychological operations, because of all the mind games and subterfuge involved. But the net result is to completely remove a man's religious underpinnings."

"How in the world does it propose to do that?"

"Brace yourself, because it's fairly radical. It proposes to do so by leading the subject into a religious conversion to another faith altogether."

The president unleashed a pithy swearword, following it up with a question.

"You're telling me there's a *procedure* for this?" Disbelief dripped from his words.

"Not necessarily tried and true, but yes, one does exist, sir."

"Unbelievable. And scary. What kind of Geneva Convention or United Nations pronouncement or other does this thing violate? The mind reels at the thought."

"Mr. President, this whole area is so unprecedented that no one has even thought to address it. There are, of course, many international laws and treaties against the denigration of religion. But that refers to something quite different. Insults against religious figures. Desecration of icons and scriptures. Blasphemies. This is something else entirely. A person's ability to convert to another religion is actually protected by most international laws. And an important point—in this protocol, the so-called witnessing, or inducement into the conversion, is carried out by a completely innocent party who has no connection whatsoever with the United States government."

"I don't know," the president said, now staring out a south window toward the ellipse. "This sounds like trouble, like the kind of desperate, loopy idea that can sink a presidency forever."

"I understand the concern, sir. But if I may take you back

in time, let's remember that some of the greatest masterstrokes in history appeared wacky and dangerous when they were first presented. Think about how insane it must have sounded to cross the freezing Delaware River in rowboats on the coldest night of the winter. Or how crazy the notion of splitting the atom must have sounded to Harry Truman. Or think of how the moon-rocket idea must have first sounded to JFK."

"You put this on a par with those events?" the president asked.

"I'm just saying that while this solution sounds loopy, as you say, many great ideas initially strike a president in a similar way."

"That may be true, but I don't see that as an excuse to throw away your instincts, your common sense. I mean, we're talking about reaching in to try and rearrange the insides of a man's soul!"

"Sir, please remember that the contents of this man's soul presently consist of a homicidal mutation of religious faith. And most of all, that the souls of many more hang in the balance. Truly innocent souls. Let's think of them."

The president encircled his forehead with trembling thumbs. "All right then. I suppose it's not the first time religion came front and center in the midst of a national crisis. But, please, insulate me from this. I don't like it. I don't like it at all."

Stare Kiejkuty Military Base, northern Poland

Captain Kilgore saw the colonel approach in the base's ad hoc lunchroom with an unusually intent expression on his face, broken only by the faintest hint of a smile. Reaching her, he took her by the arm and led her back out into the winter air.

"You're on," he muttered at a low volume, looking past her at the deep blue horizon. "The president has signed off, but off the record, with extreme misgivings. You may think you've won this one, but if you think you were under pressure before, honey, you have no idea."

"So I can move ahead?" she asked, feeling a bit sheepish at her need to reconfirm.

"Roger that. Proceed immediately to Phase One. Find your agent of influence. And I warn you, this person has to be perfect. If you can't find someone who's exactly what the protocol calls for, we simply must call it off. Understand?"

Delia nodded, then quickly said, "Sir, I think I've found him already. I read about him in the papers at the JFK waiting area, and later found him in our database. He hits every marker."

"But you say he's in the papers? That's hardly in our target profile."

"Yeah, but there's a wrinkle. The man's got a past. Some pretty major black spots on his record, both military and civilian. He's got some mighty strong reasons for playing along. He used to be in the FBI. A sniper."

"You're not telling me he's—"

"You got it. The very same man. Changed his name after the hearings and tried to start a new life, but it was all too much. He crashed and burned in a huge way."

"If he's the man I remember, how is he going to be religious enough for the objective?"

She smiled at that. "He's become an Evangelical. And a bona fide freelance minister. Did you ever know any of those people to shut their yaps about their faith?"

"Got a point there. I grew up Evangelical, and I can't go to a family reunion without having to account for my soul at least a dozen times an hour."

"Like I said, he's perfect."

CHAPTER 11

Palmdale, California—9 days before the attack

Donna Cahill sat alone, staring at the walls of what she'd once called "the family room." She glanced away from the lengthening shadows, back into the nightcap in her hand, trying to erase all the memories that seemed to project themselves like some phantom video stream onto those empty surfaces. The once-happy recollections of wrestling matches, cuddling times, long winter naps, even Robby's first steps, right there in the middle of this very same floor.

Daddy, Mommy, baby. Back before everything had gone wrong.

Little Robby, her last vestige of what had once been, was hardly a presence now. At that moment, he was up in his room, unwilling to spend time alone with her. He was probably up there playing on his game unit, more invested in Caribbean pirates than in her. His sullenness had lasted for days now. The boy was still bitter toward her, still blaming her for keeping Daddy away.

She thrust forward the TV remote as if it were a sword to cut through the darkness. Immediately the television came to life, sending shards of bright colors across the divide. But despite its manic vibrancy, it could not still the stubborn argument taking place inside her.

Should I give in? Or should I listen to the voice of reason and professional expertise?

She tried to picture Greg as he had once been, back when he'd asked her out that first time. It was her freshman year of college, and she admired his intensity, his habit of leaping up with some wild idea in his head and executing a wild-eyed stunt with perfect results. On their first date, he decided at the last second to leave the highway and swerve onto a hidden side road leading to his favorite cliff-top view. They had already been traveling at a healthy rate of speed, which made his unannounced skid turn even more traumatic and precarious. Grinning at her, he'd thrown them sideways in a wild screech of tires and rubber smoke, then gunned the Camaro's engine at just the right instant to catch the unpaved road. The trauma had culminated, as promised, with a view of city lights she had never witnessed before. Along with their first kiss, just as impulsively shared.

He had proposed to her by sneaking into the bank where she worked, then popping out of a corner of the vault when she walked in to return a safe-deposit box. She never told him, but she'd actually wet her pants in the scream that accompanied his sudden appearance. After receiving his apology, and his reassurance that the bank manager had agreed to the stunt, she tearfully accepted his proposal. Even as she kissed him, she glanced over his shoulder, scanning the room for a coat or sweater to borrow.

Thoughts like these always made her smile, and want to forget what always came next. His joining the marines. The long absences to Kuwait and Afghanistan. When she'd given him an ultimatum, the months of qualifying to join the FBI. Always long hours. Brooding silences. And explosions of anger that only seemed to grow stronger and easier to provoke.

What had happened to end his career, she could hardly blame him for. His explanations seemed both sincere and plausible—he'd been set up by incompetent superiors and made the scapegoat for a highly public failure.

But the drinking that ensued, and the slow descent into self-pity and self-destruction—those she had nobody else to pin onto.

Then that very night, the accident. The hospital. Almost losing Robby. The arrest. The separation. The injuries they had both inflicted on each other—verbal, emotional . . . and worse. Followed only by further disintegration. The divorce. The wild harassment.

It had only gotten weirder since those black days. She hardly knew how to interpret Greg's wild swerve into religion. Somehow she wanted to resent the conclusion that his sudden fervor meant she should forgive everything, forget all the damage they'd inflicted on each other, throw open her arms and her life and simply act like nothing bad had taken place.

And all because he'd figured out how to smile again, adding new words like *God* and *Jesus* and *saved* into his once-profane vocabulary. Perhaps he'd even learned to straighten out his act, for a while.

But a voice of warning deep within her would not stop whispering to her that Christianity was just another addictive swerve in his path, another reckless and random leap in an already cursed journey. Someday, the bubble would burst. God would not prove enough, just as adrenaline hadn't been, and combat hadn't been, and law enforcement hadn't been.

And fatherhood hadn't been . . .

And *she* hadn't been . . .

Maybe someday he'd truly get well again. The fatalistic tone of her childhood told her that no, it probably would never happen. But maybe it could.

She just needed to wait out the Jesus stuff. Wait for it to explode, for Greg to hit bottom, and maybe, just maybe, recover his hold on what was truly real.

Like her and their son.

She didn't want to think of any of this anymore. So she took the remote and switched the channel.

And found herself staring at the figure of her very own ex-husband, right there on the local news.

"As death penalty supporters and opponents alike began to gather on both sides of the walkway," intoned a young female voice, obviously in the midst of severe intimidation, "only a single person walked through to pay the accused killer a visit. He is local minister Greg Cahill, who says he has a 'ministry to the condemned.' "

Donna scowled and turned away. *Minister? Since when?*

". . . and he's braved the contempt of both sides to show what he calls 'love and support' to a serial killer he refers to as his 'brother in Christ.' "

Then came his voice. The very timbre of Greg's words made her stiffen on her sofa and stab ahead with the remote, desperate to lower the volume. Robby might hear and come down more confused than ever.

"I'm not saying Alex doesn't deserve what's happening to him today," said Greg. "That's not the point. The point is he's a child of God. And as much as I hate what he did, I love the man who's been forgiven of those awful things."

Great, she thought, switching off the TV and tossing the

remote to the floor. *That's all I need—Greg becoming famous. Some kind of celebrity bleeding heart, religious nut-job.*

Pelican Bay State Prison, Crescent City, California— 10 days before the attack

Greg Cahill sat inside a bare, gray holding room on a bent folding chair, holding a cup of scalding prison coffee he knew he would never drink. He forced himself to look away from the steaming Styrofoam lip, and across the room at a man only less than an hour away from his death.

He could hardly breathe, so crushing was the sense of dread and grief upon him. The feeling felt so powerful that Greg wasn't entirely sure, just then, whether he was not condemned as well.

All about him, loud clangs and echoed shouts seemed to fill the air with foreboding and menace, with a sense of unpredictability. The sounds of a powerful, invisible authority gathering its might. Preparing for its most solemn and sovereign task.

Greg forced himself to ignore those superficial distractions and focus instead on the sight that, for once, he'd rather be spared from at the moment.

The pale, puffy face of Alex McCarry.

The condemned man's features did not form a picture-perfect tableau of serenity and anticipation. Rather, peace alternated there, along with flashes of panic and terror. Greg could see the latter pierce the calm of Alex's eyes in a sudden clenching of cheek and jaw. He forced himself to remember that as fully transformed as Alex had been by his newfound faith, the man was still human. And only a superhuman being could endure an ordeal like this moment without also suffering a crushing weight of fear.

The mass murderer had come from a large family, yet none of his relations were here at this time. Too few had seen fit to visit their relative while he eked out his last months of life, and of that number none wanted to share in this present horror. In a way, the intimacy of this terrible wait struck Greg as a somber honor. It felt like a great privilege to be the only friend sharing a man's last moments on earth.

A clamor of voices drifted over from the outer walls, faint but certain. Their eyes met, and Alex's gaze fell.

Protesters. Hundreds of them, enraged at the senselessness and savagery of what those thick hands had done, those very fingers that now clenched and unclenched themselves before him.

Greg looked up. His eyes found the clock. Forty minutes left.

"I'm going to have to leave soon," he said in the lowest, most comforting voice he could produce. "You want to pray now?"

Alex looked at him with large round eyes, seeming to question whether prayer was even possible at such a moment. Still wild-eyed, he found Greg's smile and formed the faintest of grins.

"Sure," he muttered.

Greg gently grasped McCarry's hands, unshackled for once, and took the lead.

"Lord, here come two broken men who want to bring you praise," he began haltingly. "You said that where two or more of us are gathered, you'd be there too. Well, we desperately need your presence. Please come inhabit this terrible place. Please come and fill Alex with your . . ."

Greg paused and looked up. Something had changed in the room, something his senses could not quite register.

He found that Alex had already opened his eyes and was looking about him too. Their gazes met, and they both realized it was useless to comment in any other manner but a knowing smile.

The room felt aglow with some kind of radiance, but one beyond the visible spectrum. One indiscernible by the verdict of earthly eyes. An invisible warmth bathed Greg, yet it was far more than mere temperature. It seemed a mixture of physical warmth and pure joy. As though he were swimming inside a vast smile. He looked across and knew, with a certainty beyond the natural realm, that Alex felt it too.

Now, unbidden, came Alex's husky voice. "I can't wait to be with you, Jesus. Much as I hate what's coming, please redeem it. I give it to you. Anoint it. Make it, somehow, a time of healing for the people I hurt."

"Thirty minutes! Visitors gotta go!" The booming voice belonged to a tall muscular man nearly bursting from the freshly starched seams of his California Department of Corrections uniform.

The glow seemed to diminish in Greg's awareness, though he could not tell whether it was due to the intrusion or merely his diverted attention.

He stood, feeling the blood drain from his upper extremities. The importance of the moment felt like a hundred-pound weight across his shoulders. He struggled to lean forward and grip his friend's hands even more tightly.

"He'll be with you," he whispered, before feeling strong hands take him by the forearm and nudge him away. "I know He will."

Their fingers separated, and just at the second of their parting, Greg felt himself transported far away, months before. He experienced again the agony of feeling his son's hands ripped from his own by the iron grip of a social worker. It was a morning Greg fought hard to never, ever think of, vowed to leave behind him at all costs. He flinched, and fought to chase the thought from his mind once more.

A strangled cry echoed across the hallway's concrete surfaces.

"Thanks, bro . . ."

CHAPTER 12

What came next unfolded in a blur, carried out in a slow-motion state of foreboding and horror. One barren hallway gave way to another wall of bars. Another ten-second wait, then a buzzer, followed by more walking. Finally, just as Greg had lost all sense of where he stood in the prison complex, he realized he was approaching the windows of a small viewing gallery. Ushered inside, he sat down on a wooden chair, alone in the room.

The condemned's side. Somewhat obscured by the reflections of several glass panes between them, he could make out faces—family members of the victims. A sense of anguish seemed to drift from their eyes and seep into Greg's heart. He formed a silent prayer for their peace and looked away.

It felt strange, being here on Alex's side. Before meeting him and the other convicts he'd ministered to, Greg would have been the first one to stand outside a prison gate with his buddies. He would have gladly held up a hand-lettered sign calling for the needle or the chair. Violent crime enraged him like it did most Americans, and even more strongly members of law enforcement.

Once, he would have glowered in hate at the kind of human being who could sit on the side of the condemned and seemingly denigrate the slaughter of innocents with a show of support for the guilty. Just like the one he was giving now.

He wished for a moment that he could cross the execution chamber and explain himself, help them understand that he was no softer on crime than any of them. This wasn't about belief in the death penalty. But about life, and God, who had led him down an unexpected path. He now believed a man could be forgiven by God, his heart cleansed. He'd seen this in a long string of criminals, starting with himself. As a result, he believed that even as Alex received his punishment, he also deserved to be shown compassion.

His ponderings were jarred loose by the clang of the death-chamber door, followed by the backs of two uniformed men who seemed to be carrying Alex into the space. Greg took in Alex's appearance and gasped. The transformation of ten minutes' time was truly shocking, heartbreaking. His friend's face had now slackened into a mask of almost childlike stupor. Greg was certain he'd taken no calming drugs, even though the prison would have offered some. Terror alone had done this to the once-formidable visage of America's most hated serial killer.

The officers struggled to lower Alex onto the gurney, yet it seemed more like an effort to overcome physical clumsiness than actual resistance. Watching the straps being secured about Alex's wrists, Greg felt a swoon in his spirit.

A command rang across his consciousness. *On your knees.*

He glanced about him, despite knowing he was alone. The words seemed to ring through every cell in his body. For a moment, they seemed so powerful and tangible that he could have sworn they'd come from the mouth of a warden or prison guard.

Get on your knees, Greg.

Slowly, with a numbed woodenness he would have found pathetic at any other moment, he realized where the voice was coming from. It was a divine command. Coming to him from somewhere beyond the pathways of his own tympanic membrane. He was being spoken to directly, more directly than at any time since he had turned his life over to God.

Despite the realization, some ridiculous, stubborn pride within him refused to obey. Greg flat out did not want to leave his seat. An inner voice seemed to whisper to him that it was degrading enough, having to sit here and suffer the silent loathing of the victims' families. He shouldn't have to embarrass himself further by violating prison protocol, risking being thrown out for adopting some weird religious-nut posture. . . .

On your knees!

At last, something inside him moved. His muscles flexed and he found himself rising, leaning forward to the window, then bending his left knee toward the floor. Another strange compulsion animated his right arm, which straightened upward. His palm found the glass and flattened against its cool surface.

Greg closed his eyes now, feeling a smothering urge to pray without pausing. He started, then almost stopped at the sound of an intruding voice that began reading words in the kind of flat monotone guaranteed to set Greg's nerve on edge. The realization broke through.

It was the warden. *The death warrant.*

He forced himself not to listen, to keep on praying.

Then came the question: "Alex McCarry, do you have any last words?"

Greg felt a strong temptation to open his eyes and watch Alex speak, but he just as quickly realized there was little worth seeing. He was overcome by an odd insight—that this moment's ultimate importance was not being played out in the physical realm.

The words that now left Alex's mouth were quite familiar to Greg. He had heard Alex practice his memorization many times before this day. But the voice that filled his ears did not even sound like Alex. It met the air sounding more like the softness and eloquence of a child blessed with poise beyond his years.

"I am so very sorry for my horrible deeds," he began mournfully. "So sorry that I gladly pay with my life for the pain I caused you all. In fact, I wish I had twenty more lives to lay down for each precious life I stole from you all. I do not ask you for your forgiveness, not because I wouldn't love to have it, but because I do not want to ask you today for anything. I have taken enough from you. Anyway, God has forgiven me, and that matters the most. I only pray that He will bless you with the same peace and healing He has showered on me. I hope someday in heaven, we can all embrace and leave behind us the grief caused by those horrible acts committed by some twisted man who used to be Alex McCarry. I hope you will embrace me too, as a sign that you will be healed of all the grief and pain my sins inflicted on you. Because I cannot wait for that day to come, I am indeed the blessed one today. For you, I can only hope my death brings you some earthly relief."

Alex's statement ended, replaced only by a shocked silence. Greg resumed praying for Alex and those listening to his words.

After what felt like a half hour, he heard a loud beep, then a metallic *thunk*.

He winced, knowing it was the sound of the valve being opened. The fatal dose was being administered.

Greg felt an inner release, a sense that it was now all right to straighten up and look through the window.

The first thing he saw was the creased face of an elderly man. Someone's father, slack-jawed in amazement. Beside him, a middle-aged woman held a hand over her mouth, weeping. A gray-haired man beside her stared in obvious shock.

He knew that all of them had heard about McCarry's death-row conversion. Many had publicly expressed the usual derision at his inevitable "coming to Jesus." That was to be expected. Greg knew better than most how many jailhouse conversions were dubious and self-serving in nature.

But clearly, most of these people had expected Alex's serenity to melt away during the final moments. They had fully anticipated the last-second unveiling of a heart still darkened by denial and justification.

Instead, the group was now stunned to the core.

Greg focused closer on the sight he'd hoped to avoid having to take in. The gurney itself. He began to pray again, asking for strength not only for his friend but for himself.

He did not finish the prayer. His thoughts trailed off inside his mind, their request abandoned. In fact, he fought to keep his mouth from gaping stupidly.

A death chamber that had been oppressive only minutes before now burst with a white luminescence. The light was so intense that a part of Greg felt himself unworthy somehow, too dingy and stained to face it. On the precise spot where Alex's body lay on the gurney, the glow grew so blinding that he could not make out anything more than flimsy, transparent outlines.

Yet one thing was for sure. Most of who Alex had been, and what he had been, was not strapped down any longer. He was being released from the straps by visitors too wondrous to be described in words.

Once more, Greg found himself grateful that he was alone in the condemned's gallery, for he was now weeping openly. Gasps and a heaving chest had overtaken his breathing. He was powerless to stop them. Furthermore, he wasn't sure he cared to try.

His sense of awe and gratitude at this confirmation of his faith overpowered all other impulses. He could hardly believe what was unfolding before him.

Not more than five feet from him, a man's spiritual being was separating from its earthly shell, being escorted someplace else.

He risked a glance at the victims' relatives, but he could not tell whether they were seeing the same thing. The expressions he could make out were just as they'd been moments before. No more, no less.

He peered forward, for something else was now happening. Alex was being taken up, out of the death chamber. For a split second, Greg caught sight of his friend's face and saw it as he remembered it best—not the drooping caricature of a minute ago, but smiling, vibrant, focusing upward with strength and anticipation. Then, just as quickly, it was gone.

The death chamber, however, was still overflowing with light. What happened next amazed Greg even more. He saw an angel float downward with a grace and a deliberateness that sent chills down his spine, then cross the barrier into the victims' family gallery. It reached out a luminous hand and caressed first one, then another of the faces contorting with grief and anguish.

First came the wizened old man. Whether he saw or sensed the presence upon him was impossible to tell, but his expression softened and his eyes relaxed with a gleam of acceptance. Next, the young woman, who still wept. At the moment of the invisible fingers grazing her brow, her eyes flew open. She did not move a muscle, and it seemed as though she was keenly aware of someone, some unseen entity, at her side. One by one, the angel moved along the row, reaching out and touching hands, hearts, cheeks.

Greg smiled and thanked God inwardly, for he knew that

his friend's last request had been granted. If the execution itself had not given them solace, the intervention of spiritual hosts had been sent to provide healing.

Another long beep sounded. It was clear beyond any doubt that the sentence had been carried out. Alex was gone.

Greg stood slowly, inexplicably torn between an inability to leave this place, this sacred moment, and a human wish to run out of there as fast as his feet would take him.

CHAPTER 13

Greg heard a raucous cheer go up as he reached the prison yard. Stepping out into the cool night air, he fought back the urge to condemn the protesters. He understood their relief. Knowing that Alex McCarry had been put to death meant that, for the moment at least, their fear of violent crime, that ever-lingering awareness that they or their loved ones could be the next victims of random slaughter, had been laid to rest. The system had worked. Law enforcement had stopped the savagery, and the perpetrator would never hurt another innocent soul again.

And yet, fresh from the solemn and hallowed experience of a few minutes past, Greg recoiled. No matter how much of a relief the execution might have been to them, he wished they could have shown more respect for the taking of a life. The crowd before him resembled one at a rock concert or a wild frat party more than a group marking the ultimate penalty. It struck Greg as unseemly, as out of place.

He lowered his head, turned away from a shaft of television lights, and tried to make his way through the clamor of cheering voices and the shuffle of bodies.

"Hey you!" A fist struck him hard across the jaw, sending him reeling downward. "You that friend of McCarry's? You that killer lover?"

Greg tried to stumble away, but the crowd had already surrounded him. He felt more than pain inflame his jaw. He felt the old flare of rage, which would have once fused with his military training and transformed him into a blur of savage hands and feet. But he couldn't do that here. For a dozen good reasons, starting with his own safety and moving on to motives even more compelling. He took a deep breath just as a roar of jeers and hisses flowed over him.

"You call yourself a Christian?" This time the voice was female. He recognized her face from the victims' family gallery. "A minister? Well, how come you never saw fit to visit us in our pain? How come you valued the killer over the victims? What kind of sick, twisted excuse for a minister is that?"

A desperate wish to reply overcame him. He had so many answers for her. Replies that would take time, and calm. He shook his head sadly, anxious to impart as much empathy as he could.

A hocking sound shredded the air close to his ear. Spit struck his cheek.

That was enough. Greg squared his shoulders and thrust himself forward—anywhere but the center of this group. He felt shoulders glance off his and heard cries of protest. Just that quickly he broke from the knot of bodies and felt his feet running underneath him, dodging more people, more protesters. He saw a sign, fleetingly, in his peripheral vision: *Respect Life*.

Great, he thought. *Counter-protesters*.

He continued running, reaching his car a minute later. Then he looked down and a groan ripped from his mouth. The tires had been slashed.

Collapsing against the side of the car, he closed his eyes and prayed.

Please, God, what's this all about? You carry me through this horrible event on the wings of an incredible experience, seeing your angels carry my brother away. I feel all the horror melt out of me. I sense your presence and your power more strongly than ever before. A new flood of purpose flows into me. I get your reassurance that I'm on the right track, that I'm where you want me to be. My ministry matters. It's touching lives. And then this. Many of my so-called brothers and sisters hate my guts. What's the point, God? What am I supposed to get from this day? Can you give me an answer? I'm totally confused. . . .

He stopped, because he felt the distinct sensation of someone's presence behind him.

His lungs still heaving from running, he did not turn around at first. His heart sank, because the way this day was going, it was probably someone out to kill him.

But then he tensed his muscles, hoping to be mistaken, and whirled around.

It was an attractive blonde, standing there in an army uniform. She was staring at him intensely, with a gaze brimming with interest and sympathy.

"Greg Cahill?" Her voice sounded musical, feminine, yet strong at the same time.

"Yeah."

"I'm sorry about your car, sir. And about that mob. That's inexcusable. I know this isn't a good time, but I urgently need to speak with you."

He faced her squarely and looked her in the eye. Instinct told him that despite all the turmoil washing through him right now, this was not something to take lightly.

She extended a hand.

"Captain Delia Kilgore, United States Army. Mr. Cahill, I

would appreciate it very much if you'd allow me the chance to offer you a drive home. I'll have some associates of mine take care of your car, change the tires, and have it back at your house within the hour."

Greg cocked his head, processing. This officer knew where he lived. This was no random encounter.

He nodded numbly and followed her to a blue sedan with government plates.

"Mr. Cahill, I know you've had an eventful and draining couple of hours. But I've come from across the country just to speak with you, on national business of the highest priority. I promise that your day will improve dramatically if you hear me out."

A familiar fight-or-flight wariness constricted his shoulders. He hadn't heard words like this since the old days.

"Do you want to grab a cup of coffee? A sandwich? I'd offer you a stiff drink, but I know that wouldn't be a responsible thing."

Greg glanced at her questioningly. "You seem to know a bit about me."

She smiled. "You better believe it. Like I said, I'm here on very important business."

"Why don't we just drive, and I'll let you do the talking. I'm completely spent."

"Sounds perfect," she said.

A few minutes later, the two of them were in the car and heading onto a freeway on-ramp.

"Mr. Cahill, your newfound ministry has made some fans in high places. My superiors and I, as well as some government officials far higher than that, have taken note of your singular ability to befriend the unlovable. You've got an amazing gift for finding redeeming qualities in what many would consider the most despicable human beings on the planet."

"That's nice to hear, after what I just went through," he said with a sigh.

"I can assure you, Greg, that you're not alone. Another thing we have noted is your ability to reach in and make a profound difference in these convicts' demeanor and behavior."

"That," he countered, "I can't take credit for. That's the work of God, moving in and doing His redemptive work just as He did for me."

"Fair enough. I won't disagree with you one bit. I will insist, however, that you have a unique ability to trigger this blessing in others' lives."

"I just share Him because I'm compelled to, Captain. You know everything about me, so you probably know my record. You know I've hit bottom myself. I've spent some time behind bars. I can't keep myself from sharing how dramatically God turned my life around."

He said it with a touch of defiance, because as a government servant he expected her to resist the injection of religion into his biography. Separation of church and state and all that.

Instead, she turned to him with an even brighter smile. "Trust me, all that has been duly noted and is part and parcel of why I'm here. As I said, you have fans at the highest levels. And I do mean the highest levels."

He frowned at her questioningly, wondering. Did she mean the White House?

"So, besides conveying good wishes, Captain Kilgore, what's this really about? I mean, what is this urgent government business?"

She grinned at his impatience and then stared back at the road, just in time to swerve around a slow-moving station wagon.

"Mr. Cahill, what I'm about to divulge to you must remain confidential upon the strongest penalty of law. Do you understand me?"

He stuttered his agreement.

"All right then," she continued. "U.S. forces have recently apprehended one of the few men more universally hated and feared by the American people than your friend Alex McCarry."

"Who could *that* be?" he asked with a disbelieving look.

She paused, and her face darkened. "Omar Nirubi."

He let out a low whistle, but said nothing for several moments.

"You're right," he said at last. "You found maybe the one man more hated than Alex. But what does this have to do with me?"

"Mr. Nirubi's capture is being kept secret, as you might have inferred. The main reason is that we are about to make an experimental overture to him. Something that has never been tried before in the history of terrorism."

"An overture?" Greg asked, feeling lost.

"An offer with grave repercussions and earth-shattering consequences. An offer of clemency."

CHAPTER 14

Greg stared, unable to process her meaning. Finally, he repeated, "Clemency? You're going to offer to drop charges against the most hated terrorist on the planet?"

"That's right," said Captain Kilgore, "in exchange for a written vow of nonviolence. And a recorded repudiation of any hostile tactics, past and future."

Greg laughed. "Yeah, well, good luck with that."

"Oh, we're not relying on good luck. What we need is a personal connection. Someone who is gifted in the art of quickly forming trusting relationships."

"You mean *me*?"

She looked at him with a pained expression that seemed to indulge his incredulity. "The person who makes this connection cannot be linked to the government, cannot have a professional stake in whether or not Nirubi accepts the offer of clemency."

"So I just happen to mosey along somewhere near Guantánamo, stop to tie my shoelaces, and strike up a conversation?"

"Not exactly, no. You'll be introduced as a civilian host at the base where he'll be held."

"And I have no stake in it?" he asked. "I assume there's *something* in it for me."

She raised her eyebrows and smiled. "Well, the project is budgeted to take a week. All your expenses would be paid, of course, and at its successful completion you would be paid a cash, nontaxable consulting fee of $35,000."

"Not bad."

"In addition," she continued, "your record would be expunged upon completion. Both criminal and professional. That would start with the reason for your dismissal from the FBI. Your brushes with the law since then as well. Convictions, prosecutions, investigations—everything."

"What about my wife's protective order keeping me from my son?"

"Well, that would be more difficult."

"C'mon, Captain. If you've checked it out, then you know it's totally bogus and unjust. True, I might have needed to stay away from them a while, but I've been sober for eight months now. I've turned my life around, and I've made every effort to resume a positive relationship with my son."

"Yes, including a few grandstanding stunts," she said, "like making a sniper incursion into your son's birthday party."

"You heard about that too? Amazing. But it was the only way to get close enough to tell him happy birthday, to tell him that I love him."

Kilgore nodded, giving in. "All right. If the operation is successful, the restraining order will be rescinded without prejudice."

Greg blew out his breath loudly. "Now *that* is an offer," he said emphatically. "And what exactly am I going to do to earn this?"

"You're going to do your thing—befriend a prisoner who's

in a highly agitated and traumatized state. You're going to show him all the goodwill and personal charm that endeared you to the likes of Alex McCarry."

"Now wait," Greg said. "Anything I've accomplished in the lives of these men, I've already told you. It doesn't come from me. It's Jesus Christ. I couldn't shut up about Him any more than I could stop taking breaths."

"Nobody expects you to, Mr. Cahill. That's the beauty of it. We want you to be yourself, and to engage Mr. Nirubi in the most natural way you see fit. There are no restrictions on any personal or religious convictions you may bring to the table. Believe me, it'll be hard enough simply befriending a man filled with a compulsion to wipe all Americans from the face of the earth. If you can succeed at that, nobody is going to ask questions about your tactics."

"So I just spend these days trying to convince him to accept this clemency offer."

"Essentially, yes."

"Should I ask how much wiggle room you've given yourself in that word *essentially*?"

"No. You probably shouldn't."

Greg decided not to pursue the matter any further.

Cahill residence, Palmdale, California

Donna Cahill awoke with a cannonball pull of alarm churning deep in her stomach. She rose up in bed, panting into the near darkness, and tried to think back to a possible cause. She had eaten a light dinner of soup and a sandwich, so there was little chance of heartburn. She leaned over to the nightstand, opened its drawer, and pulled out the revolver. The gun had been there ever since Greg's long-ago transition to the FBI. Cocking it silently with a pounding heart, she remained still and listened hard, straining to pick up on any strange noise in the house. Nothing drifted to her ears.

That left only one probability: another recurrence of the horrible night traumas she had endured since the breakup of her marriage and her ex-husband's descent into addiction. Granted, it had been a month or more since the last one. But in the early days, they had been a nightly affliction.

Then she felt it—the faint, singular sense of a presence. Someone was in the house, someone besides Robby. She knew the feel of her son's nearness like the scent of her own skin, the weight of her own limbs.

She breathed deeply and willed herself to be brave for his sake. Gripping the handgun stiffly in front of her, she slipped out of bed and began inching toward her bedroom door.

If Greg had been there, she thought, he would have probably shot down her feminine, touchy-feely notions about intuition and instinct. Ever the tactical nerd, he would have told her something concrete and empirical like her alarm being the result of two or three sensations just below the threshold of her conscious awareness. Or perhaps that it was the vaguest hint of a strange air current in the house, a shadow or ceiling reflection out of place, the tiniest variant in all the background hum of machines regulating the home's physical environment.

Doesn't matter, Greg, she said to herself with a grit of her teeth and another internal reminder to stop arguing with him in her mind. *What matters is that I'm sure something's not right.*

With a shake of her head, she told herself that of all the unpleasant contingencies, this was one that made her wish Greg were still there with her. A terrifying walk through the house in the middle of the night, frightened by strange noises—that was the time to be grateful for a SWAT-trained, law-enforcement gun fanatic of a husband.

This is not a mommy job, she thought, hearkening back to the days when a stable husband-and-wife division of labor was a constant topic of banter between them.

She took a nerve-wracking step forward, hoping to hear the tiniest noise above the pounding of her heart. Frantically, she forced her mind into an analytical mode. "Tactical thinking," Greg would have called it.

She knew she'd spent enough time sitting silent in bed to rule out an intruder in her master suite. That left the greater threatening world beyond the doorframe at the room's far corner. She skirted the end of the bed slowly, trying to minimize her exposure to the hallway that led to Robby's bedroom. After a maddening minute, she reached the doorway and peeked out, the gun held at the ready.

The hallway was empty. A rush of doubt swept over her. Maybe she was just being paranoid. Conflicted, she tiptoed down the hall and looked into Robby's room.

All was well. A shadow-splashed lump on the bed told her that her boy was sleeping normally. And yet, somehow, that sense of an intrusion still lingered, more strongly than ever. She stepped forward.

There was something on the bed. A flat shape, reflecting moonlight from the window not far from Robby's face.

It was a folded piece of paper.

A note?

This is the moment, she warned herself, when the dumb woman in the movies lurches forward, not bothering to check the closet or behind the door, and gets whacked. So, postponing her urge to look at the paper, holding the gun in front of her, she checked the room's corners, behind the door, inside the closet, under the bed.

Satisfied that whoever had left the item was now gone, she moved to Robby's bed. She picked up the paper, noticed Greg's handwriting on the folded note's center.

To Robby, from Daddy.

She let out a breath of exasperation and snatched it up. Why didn't she think of it? Another showy stunt by an absent father, meant to enthrall her son with his dad's coolness and concealment skills.

She unfolded the paper and began reading.

> *Robby,*
>
> *I was here tonight. I gave you a kiss on the cheek, because I love you more than anything. I couldn't wake you up because I didn't want to cause a problem. But I have to tell you something. Daddy has to go away for a while. I don't know how long it will be. I know that tomorrow is Christmas and that we would have spent some time together. I would love that more than anything, but Daddy has to go do a secret project for the government that's really, really important. That's all I can tell you. Be good for Mommy. And don't be afraid, just say a prayer for me and I'll be back as soon as I can.*
>
> *Love, Daddy*

Donna felt a reeling sensation as half a dozen conflicting emotions roared through her. What sort of mad crisis had this man gotten himself into this time? No way was he working on some secret government project, of that she was certain. Greg's record was so sufficiently mangled as to rule that out.

She felt rage and resentment flail at her. How could he do this to her? After all the pathetic requests for reconciliation, the pledges of renewed responsibility and stability, now to disappear without even a decent explanation?

She inwardly kicked herself for having briefly harbored the

notion of believing him, of someday working, however gradually, toward healing their wounds and reconciling.

That was it. When he surfaced, whenever that was, she would tell him to forget about ever cobbling this pathetic excuse for a family back together again.

CHAPTER 15

Stare Kiejkuty Military Base, Poland—7 days before the attack

Omar Nirubi. Yes, that was his name. He struggled to remember, to force his brain to hang on to the words that framed the earthly parameters of his identity.

Somehow the question of who he was seemed fleeting at the moment, strangely inconsequential in light of the physical and emotional assault against him. Even the ancillary things, such as his nationality, his faith, his fame, jihad, and his mission—these felt like a wispy cloud of irrelevant facts and affectations.

All that truly mattered now was making it through the next five minutes.

And yet, paradoxically, another part of him knew that his identity could be the most vital, most important thing he might ever lay hold of. Something as wispy yet as precious as his own soul, beckoning to be recaptured and apprehended. He had to hang on to *something*. He no longer had his freedom, his dignity, control over his fate, his sensations, even his bodily functions. But perhaps he could hang on to who in the world he actually was, even if it was as elusive as a morning breeze.

There was a pause in the shouting, in the rain of fists upon his face and chest. He heard footsteps, but he was too wounded to open his eyes and register their direction. It seemed some transition was afoot, a change in tactics. He silently prayed that his darkest forebodings were not about to burst to life.

Once long ago, when he was a free man upon the earth, he had spied a peek at some descriptions of the torture he was certain lay ahead. He had taken in the facts, just in case. One of his Iranian liaisons had provided his leaders with a smuggled videotape of a victim in the clutches of the ISI, the Pakistani secret police.

What he had watched did not seem at first to have frightened him deeply. But he had dreamed about the waterboard that night, and the night that followed, and dozens more after that. He had felt himself stretched out on that wooden slat, his feet bound by iron rods, his hands held fast over his head. He had felt a vicious hand stuff a washcloth into his mouth, then pour cold water over it. He'd felt his throat clench in a relentless gag reflex.

More than that, he felt the fear, each and every time.

Death was upon him, the moment of his life's cessation. The one instant which ended all the others, all those predecessors that had formed his earthly existence.

The reality of that knowledge soured like a metallic taste in his mouth, cold and biting. He felt his entire neck and head throb with the drumbeat of a terror he had never before known possible.

Here in the present moment, he saw the board being carried toward him in the hands of the impassive Polish torturer, who had just replaced America's president as the leading character in his vilest dreams of retribution.

He heard his mouth unleash a long moan, and some part of his mind hated himself for the pathetic sound of it.

The Pole dropped the board to the ground with a clatter. Omar recoiled at the echo of it, as well as its inescapable meaning.

Inwardly he tried his hardest to die, to simply let go. He retreated emotionally into the deepest recesses of his being, clawing invisibly for some release, some inner lever which would allow him to relinquish his body's hold over his soul.

He found none.

He screamed out to Allah for help. To take him—snatch him up into the escape of his eternal destination.

Nothing came . . . until a second later, the room flooded with light. Whether someone had switched on an overhead lamp or some angelic presence had suddenly invaded, he was not sure, except that the space echoed with the voice of a man he had not heard before.

American. Loud. Angry.

"Stop this now!"

And it was no hallucination, for every face in the room turned swiftly in the direction of its source. He forced himself to open his own eyes, and caught a hazy glimpse of a pale-skinned man in blue jeans and a chambray shirt, striding resolutely across the interrogation room floor.

The man reached the waterboard and kicked it. The contraption became airborne and crashed into a nearby wall, splintering at its edges.

"What's going on here? What's the meaning of this?" the man shouted. "This is not what I was led to expect! It's against everything I was brought here for!"

The Pole seemed to owe the man some latitude, despite the

civilian attire, for he allowed the newcomer to snatch up the waterboard.

Nevertheless, the torturer then turned and glared at the newcomer with a scowl of pure defiance. "And who are you, exactly?" he asked, looking around at an ever thickening cordon of military men even as he spoke.

"That's none of your business," snapped the red-faced intruder, "except this one thing. I come on direct authority of the president of the United States. And every single person in this room is to follow my orders as if they came directly from the Oval Office, which they do. Now unbind this man."

The Pole stood motionless, panting hard and staring at the American. He seemed to be waiting for his breathing to calm down before obeying, but the civilian would not wait for him. The man turned toward Nirubi and knelt beside the chair, shaking his head.

"Mr. Nirubi, my name is Gregory Cahill. I am here to ensure that you are not treated in this manner one moment longer. I am not, repeat not, a member of the United States military or its intelligence services. I have nothing to do with the way you have been treated until this minute. Yet the president himself has sent me here to take you back to our sovereign soil and present you with an offer of clemency. Do you understand me?"

Nirubi nodded, more emphatically than one would have expected from a man so deep in agony.

Cahill reached forward gingerly and began pulling away the tape binding Nirubi's wrists to the wooden chair that had been his hell for so many hours.

From the haze of his disorientation, Nirubi tried to gain a sense of himself, to determine whether this man was real or some wild construct of a dying mind. Omar Nirubi had once been considered a prodigiously keen reader of human motives. The gift had helped him stay alive on many occasions, allowing him to spot infiltrators, spies, and assassins sent to kill him. It had eventually grown into a potent part of his legend.

Now, whichever of those once-vital instincts survived within him screamed that Cahill's voice, eyes, and body language were completely genuine. It seemed impossible, for he had not sensed an unconflicted person since his capture.

But this man, real or imagined, seemed to be the first exception.

A truly sincere heart.

Cahill pulled off the first length of tape from Nirubi's arm, and the prisoner knew at once that this was no hallucination.

The American slowly, almost tenderly, unbound his restraints. When Nirubi's bare chest and legs were exposed, for he wore nothing but tattered underwear, the American looked at the filth and the exposed wounds for a long time. He sighed mournfully.

"Makes you proud to be an American," he mumbled under his breath, with Nirubi probably the only other person close enough to hear it.

"Do we have any clothes for this man?" he asked loudly, sharply, without turning away.

No reply was offered.

Cahill began to pull off his own clothes. More than one hand flew up to cover their mouths, for the sight was jarring—an American stripping himself to his underwear and handing over his clothing to a grimy prisoner. Cahill laid first his shirt, then his jeans on the armrest of the prisoner's chair. He also gave up his shoes.

Nirubi lifted one arm almost an inch, but laid it down again with a grimace. He was too weak to get up and put on the clothes.

Shivering in the basement's chill air, Cahill noticed the

problem. He leaned forward and took Nirubi by the hand. The Arab looked up at the touch, for its benign softness felt alien to him. He hadn't been touched for any purpose but to inflict pain for longer than he could remember. The American paid no mind. He gently pulled him up, took the shirt, and helped him to put it on, slowly, one sleeve at a time.

A few minutes later, their roles had been reversed. The American was now in his underwear, and the man who'd been brought here and treated as a rabid animal was stepping away in fresh clothes.

CHAPTER 16

Captain Kilgore followed the two men out of the interrogation room, keeping her distance from them and ignoring the frowns of the former tormentors. It was no longer their game, she realized with a surge of pleasure. The baton had now been passed, thanks to her.

This was no accident; it had been carefully planned to spark an unrehearsed reaction in Cahill. Phase One of the protocol was labeled *Compressed Bonding*, which meant introducing the subject and his civilian host into a variety of situations designed to induce an accelerated sense of kinship. There was no time for the usual building of trust, an already gradual process that could have been dramatically slowed by the prisoner's ill treatment. Therefore, they'd needed a dramatic moment to speed up a very normal human response.

Only she knew for certain that Cahill was being completely genuine. Of course, anyone with his level of empathy and compassion—or any human being untainted by weeks of exposure to such tactics—would have been moved by the sight of a man facing the waterboard. The severity of Cahill's explosion had been a bonus.

This was only the first. Phase One had only begun.

The departed author of Tabula Rasa was now in charge of all their destinies.

Greg Cahill escorted Nirubi to a small officers' mess within the Polish complex, where the prisoner showered and was given another set of civilian clothes, picked out for him earlier.

By the time they emerged from the prison complex two hours later, both men were equally clean and clad in the casual attire of ordinary American civilians: blue jeans, T-shirts, and glaring white sneakers. They boarded a van on their way to the Stare Kiejkuty airfield, watched by a ring of military officers wearing sullen expressions.

The C-37 awaited them. As they approached, Nirubi recoiled and shot Cahill an apprehensive glance. Was this just another excruciating rendition to another black site? The American only smiled and extended a helping hand forward.

From the man's demeanor, something became clear to Nirubi. There would be no duct tape or gurneys on this flight.

Nirubi's bewilderment only deepened with every passing minute, for as he boarded the aircraft an American officer stepped forward and introduced himself as if some sort of subservient flight attendant, offering his services. Turning away from the proffered hand, he stared warily as he moved to a soft leather seat pointed out by Greg.

"It's going to be a long flight," Greg told him in a low voice, like any other seatmate on a commercial airliner.

Nirubi finally spoke up.

"We are going to . . . Guantánamo?"

Cahill drew back in surprise at the question, then smiled. "Oh no. When I said United States soil, I was being serious. I'm going to be truthful with you, Mr. Nirubi. We're headed to Arizona. A landscape you'll be quite familiar with."

Nirubi narrowed his eyes. Cahill had made the statement as though their destination had been picked out for the sole purpose of setting him at ease. But that couldn't be true. As much as he welcomed the change in treatment, and as much as he was utterly confused by the abrupt shift in tactic, he still refused to trust it.

It may be that Cahill was guileless, and that possibility certainly unsettled Nirubi, yet there was still an agenda at work here. There had to be. Nirubi had been told of vastly shifting modes of treatment designed to unsettle and destabilize prisoners even further. Perhaps this was one such tactic.

In either case, Arizona sounded far more welcoming than Guantánamo Bay.

They flew for ten hours straight, utilizing the full span of the Gulfstream's nautical flying range.

Nirubi sat unrestrained in his chair, a change that while exhilarating also felt odd to him. He had become perversely acclimated to physical bondage and privation.

Three army officers sat in the cabin with them, each of them sporting conspicuously worn side arms on their belts, but otherwise unthreatening.

During the first half hour of their flight, which began in silence, the officers brought Nirubi one bottle of mineral water after another. Each was sealed, Nirubi noticed with some measure of relief. He drank each one, four in total. They also brought him two large plates of eggs and toast, which he devoured without any pretense of table manners.

When Nirubi was through eating and drinking, Cahill nodded to one of the officers, who then produced a slim electronics case and offered it to Nirubi. The officer opened it slowly, displaying an empty screen, and set the contraption on the prisoner's lap.

"Please watch this," Cahill said.

The officer held out a remote control, pressed a button. An image came to life on-screen. A face, framed by curtains and family photographs.

The president of the United States, filming from the traditional White House desk.

"Hello, Mr. Nirubi," said the president. "I want you to know that the treatment you have received since your capture so far has ended. Permanently. As I have recently made clear, that kind of abuse will no longer be used or tolerated by this country. We have embarked on a different course, and what I am about to say will represent a major step along that path. In short, the offer being presented to you today has never before been extended to any other prisoner in American custody. It is most extraordinary, and I hope you will consider it in that light. I also trust that you will share my opinion after you've heard what I am about to describe."

Nirubi took a deep breath and glanced about him to the others in the cabin. Perhaps, just perhaps, this was genuine. If so, he had caught a break of truly stunning magnitude. Certainly the man on the screen was no impersonator. It was the president himself. His expression was serious and intense, as though he himself were amazed at the words coming out of his mouth.

"Mr. Nirubi," the president continued, "the United States is undergoing a complete change in the conduct of our foreign affairs. We know that perceived grievances can abound on every side of a dispute, and the War on Terror is no exception. But rather than perpetuate the endless litany of mutual hostility, we want to explore the avenue of conciliation, of goodwill as a way to defuse confrontation. That's why I am making the following

offer to you in the name of the United States and her people. I am
prepared to fully and immediately pardon you of all crimes you
have committed or conspired to commit against this country. For
your part, all we ask is that you publicly renounce terrorism as a
tool of advancing your goals, cooperate in our country's defense
against terrorism in progress, and never again involve yourself
in homicidal or terrorist acts. We know that you have been mis-
treated, and so will need some time to recover and consider this
offer. That is why I have sent Mr. Cahill as a personal escort to
host you for several days of personal time on one of our military
installations. There, we will anxiously await your decision. Should
you decline our offer, by the way, we would have no option but
to immediately try you of all crimes in a military tribunal, and
then swiftly carry out its sentence. I look forward to hearing your
wisest and most considered decision."

The screen went blank, as did the expression on Omar Nirubi's face.

Greg then gave him a sheet of parchment paper from the
hand of one of the officers. "Here it is in writing," he said, "along
with the president's signature. It's yours to keep."

Nirubi received the paper and stared at it without saying a
word. His frown deepened. He continued to discern only sincerity
from this Mr. Cahill beside him—whoever and whatever he was.
The president had proven harder to read. Nirubi still was not clear
as to why he was being handed such an extraordinary offer. As
for the uniformed officers onboard the plane, he had found them
hardest of all to analyze. For one thing, the three men were not
leading the conversation. Instead, they were assisting Cahill.

Secondly, Nirubi had a far different interest in those men
altogether. Ever since boarding, he had watched how they carried themselves relative to their weapons. One exposed hip
and a two-second pause, he calculated, and he would have the

jump on everyone else. However, the cockpit was sealed behind a thick metal door. All that would result was a protracted hostage drama.

He was prepared to die, but the proposal before him did give him pause. He decided to play along and see where this strange mind game led them.

"You will receive complete security and care while you recover from your mistreatment and consider this offer," Cahill said. "If you accept it, you will be granted asylum, along with your family, here in the United States."

Nirubi glowered at him. The very notion of accepting an offer from the United States was enough to arouse his deepest animosity.

"By the way," Cahill said with a nod toward the back of the cabin, "I asked the pilot, and Mecca is in *that* direction. At your six o'clock. You are welcome to use the prayer blanket I brought. I know you have been deprived for several days."

"You are wasting your time," he growled. "I am the worst enemy America has in the entire world, and you insult me with these gestures."

CHAPTER 17

Air Force C-37, the skies behind them

Twenty miles behind the Gulfstream carrying Cahill and Nirubi, another air force passenger plane followed with much of the remaining contingent from Stare Kiejkuty. In a small area of seats turned to face each other, Captain Kilgore sat tensely, pressing a small audio bud to her ear. Beside her, four other officers did the same.

The brute from the CIA turned to her with a scowl.

"You hear that?" he said. "What in the world's he doing? I thought Cahill was supposed to undermine the guy's religion, not support it. What's he doing encouraging him to pray to Mecca?"

She gave him her best glare. "He's trying to establish a point of contact, that's what. I think it's brilliant."

"Oh you do, do you? If that's so brilliant, why don't we fly him straight to the biggest mosque we can find, buy him a brand-new copy of the Koran, and introduce him ourselves to the imam?"

"Islam is the starting point, Major Magnus," said Kilgore. "I didn't mean that he should continue down this path. But it's the obvious place to begin—to start establishing a bond. I happen to think it was a good idea."

She turned to watch the unfolding exchange.

"Remember, he has no script," she added after a pause. "Cahill is instinctively, without even knowing it, following the protocol down to the letter. Just like the protocol predicts, guys like this walk their target down the psychological process like spontaneous clockwork. We have to follow a dozen psychological and interpersonal thresholds and objectives. I grant you that. But those govern our handling of Cahill, not Cahill's behavior toward Nirubi. He knows nothing of those. For Cahill, it's got to be completely spontaneous from the heart, or nothing will work. He has to do it his way, and so far he's doing it flawlessly."

"So, Captain Kilgore, you'd say we are on track so far?" asked another of the officers.

"Perfectly. In fact, I'd say we're ahead of the game."

The lead C-37, 20 miles ahead

Nirubi had just returned to his seat from the rear of the aircraft, his face flushed from the strain of lying prostrate on an unyielding, vibrating floor.

Resting back in his seat, Nirubi turned to Cahill and whispered, "I do not believe this offer."

"That's quite understandable, Mr. Nirubi," Greg said calmly. "At this point in your recovery, I'm not sure I would either. All I ask of you is to give us, give *me*, time to prove ourselves. To earn your trust."

"That will never happen."

"Please remember, much about this situation would be described by veteran observers as impossible. As something that would never occur. Starting with your release from that prison, to your presence here on this plane on your way to a comfortable home in the United States. So why don't we suspend our previous notions of what will and will not happen. Instead, let's start with the one thing we can agree on, Mr. Nirubi. Or at least, *should* agree on." He leaned closer to the terrorist's face. "God is merciful."

Nirubi stiffened, his eyes widening as he recoiled in his seat.

But Cahill did not budge. He smiled and added, "Can we start *there*?"

Air Force C-37, the skies behind them

"Hah! Brilliant!" Kilgore exclaimed, glancing around her for agreement. The officers gave her none. "Oh, come on. You didn't like his initial point of contact, fine. But now he's turned the point into a heartfelt, genuine opening."

"What do you mean?" the officer asked with a shrug. "All he did was paraphrase the leading principle of the Koran. God is merciful and compassionate."

"It doesn't belong to Islam," she replied. "Remember, he said *God*, not *Allah*. The concept that God is merciful is common to all three of the great monotheistic religions. That was a killer segue to talk about religion, and you don't even see it."

"Yeah. All I see is an amateur who's managed nothing more than to suck up to his prisoner. To give a monster more control than he already has over the situation."

"Remember," said Kilgore, "the protocol is very clear. Our witness has to think it's his idea, or there's no way it'll work. Your own research says that Nirubi would spot any duplicity in a heartbeat."

The CIA man held up a hand to quiet her. They all stared into empty space, waiting for whatever would come next.

A low rumble was all they heard.

Then snoring.

Fort Huachuca, Arizona

They landed fifteen miles north of the Mexican border in the middle of the night on Christmas Day, when the only light over this remote stretch of Arizona desert shone from a pale, gibbous moon. At least until its broad, star-strewn desert sky was punctured by landing lights from the low-flying, unannounced arrival. The mystery flight, along with its unregistered jet, landed at a runway that, despite its relative isolation, was actually eight thousand feet long—long enough to make it an emergency landing site for both the space shuttle and Air Force One.

Locals at the nearby town of Sierra Vista called this their municipal airport, but it also bore the name of Libby Army Airfield, a name attached because of the nearby presence of the plane's ultimate destination, one of the army's most scenic, most secure, most controversial domestic installations: Fort Huachuca.

A single army van flanked by two black Suburbans met the taxiing Gulfstream, yet the illusion of a sparse reception was only that—a carefully managed illusion. It was no accident that the fort itself, three miles to the south, featured more concealed surveillance and security technology than any other installation of its kind.

Much of it, regardless of the late hour and the sparseness of the greeting party, was now trained intently on the arriving aircraft and its passengers. Streaming video of the arrival was being watched across the nation. In a fraction of a second the whole site could be cut to pieces under machine-gun fire provoked by a single muttered word into one of a dozen well-concealed headphones.

The three vehicles drove within feet of the parked jet, took on a trio of disembarking passengers, then quickly sped away. By the time they were out of sight, more landing lights appeared overhead. Two more military transports landed in quick succession, this time disgorging several dozen haggard military officers.

Brooding over the scene, a nearby mountaintop bristled with cutting-edge surveillance equipment. It ranged from an aerostatic balloon used for DEA interdiction to long-range thermal sensors, motion detectors, and dishes uplinked to the nation's most sensitive espionage satellites.

Fort Huachuca was home to the U.S. Army Intelligence Center, which provided training in all facets of intelligence, from human to imagery to electronics. It also hosted the army's interrogation school—the place where Captain Kilgore had received her training, along with most of the interrogators employed in the War on Terror—and the Electronic Proving Grounds. It even headquartered the Unmanned Aircraft Systems Training Battalion, which was the reason for a Predator drone silently shadowing the jet's last four miles of final approach.

The three vehicles drove to the farthest reach of the fort's residential area, close to where it narrowed to a single lane that emptied into a mountain canyon. There they pulled into the driveway of a stuccoed bungalow set back from the road by fifty yards. Two minutes later, they had unloaded their passengers and were gone from sight. The neighbors may have thought that one of the street's residents, usually a high-grade officer, had merely been escorted home after a heavy night's partying.

Except for one unusual fact—there were no neighbors. All

nearby dwellings had been summarily evacuated and replaced with surveillance teams. The new arrivals might well have bedded down immediately for some badly needed sleep. But their watching neighbors never slept for even a second. The surveillance continued, relentless and complete.

CHAPTER 18

The Respite House, Fort Huachuca, Arizona—the next morning, 6 days before the attack

Greg awoke in a bed he did not recognize, smelling desert aromas he could not place, stirred by sunbeams streaming through a tall wooden window frame he knew he'd never seen before. The sound in his ears struck him as vaguely familiar.

Yes, he had heard it before. The night before, on a jet. An endless flight, yes.

Omar Nirubi, saying prayers.

He rose from the bed and followed the sound of Nirubi's chanting voice through the wood-paneled rooms of a rambling antique home. Reaching the foyer, he saw that its front door hung open. Nirubi had finished and was out on the front porch, prone on his forehead, facing east.

Greg hesitated for a moment, wondering if his first impulse was offensive or would be considered blasphemous. Then he caught himself, realizing he had no one to answer to in this matter except God. So he knelt a few yards away, bent his head, and began to pray in his own fashion.

Dear Lord, I don't know how I got into this mess, except that I don't think it was my doing. I'm hoping it was yours, God, and that you're going to guide me. You'll have to, because I don't know how to talk to this man. He's so filled with hate, and he comes from a place so foreign to me that I don't—

"What are you doing?"

Greg opened his eyes and glanced up to see Nirubi standing, scowling over him.

"Same as you," Greg replied, trying hard not to sound flippant. "I'm praying."

"Are you a Muslim?"

Greg shook his head.

"Are you mocking me?"

"No. I saw you praying, and I was inspired. It's a beautiful morning and a promising day. I thought I would take your lead and ask God for His blessing."

Nirubi leaned back on his heels and squinted out over a stretch of open lawn separating them from an opposing row of stately homes. He turned back. "So your words to me last night were not just provocation."

"Which words?"

"God is merciful."

"No, they were not. I am a believer in the one true God, the Creator, God of Abraham."

"But you are a Christian."

"I follow Christ, yes. I want most of all to be known as a godly man."

Nirubi gave a shrug. "Me too." He turned to Greg with blazing eyes. "What are you doing here? With me?"

"I'm simply your host. I was asked to be an escort to you, a companion as you spent time recuperating and considering the president's offer."

"And you are not army or CIA?"

"No."

"Then why did they choose you?"

"I'm not entirely sure. But I have a good idea it's because I spend my time being a friend to prisoners. Especially inmates facing crisis situations."

Nirubi drew back, bemused. "You do this with your time? As a career?"

Greg nodded, chuckling at the man's obvious disbelief.

"Where are we?" Nirubi asked.

"Fort Huachuca, Arizona. Just north of Mexico. I told you that you would appreciate the landscape. It's called the Sonoran Desert."

"So this is the West? The famous Old West?"

"Actually, according to my briefings, this is as close to the Old West as you're going to find. This fort was built in the 1800s to fight Cochise and the Apaches. Later, the Buffalo Soldiers, the African-American cavalry troops, called it home."

"It does not feel like a desert," Nirubi said. "It is quite cool."

Greg looked out toward the expanse of hilly brushland that stretched out for miles beyond them. Even now, his old army training was leading him to scan for probable sniper sites, such as the field at far left, the shadowed hedged-off boundary between houses, the space under an old Mustang parked in a driveway . . .

There. He saw one, cunningly concealed. Only the tiniest reflection from a spotting scope had given the man away.

Good, he told himself. *They weren't leaving anything to chance.*

His skin trembled against a refreshing breeze.

"Well, you have to remember that it's winter now. It's

December. We could even have a bit of snow, according to what I was told."

"Am I free to go?" asked Nirubi with a playful arch of his eyebrows.

"You're free to take short walks if you wish, but only after I inform the—"

At that moment, Nirubi skipped down the home's half-dozen wooden steps and launched out for the open grass.

Just as quickly two soldiers in full assault gear appeared from each side, machine guns at their waists. The taller one, a rangy but muscular African-American, looked at Nirubi with a grin of mixed greeting and defiance.

"Sir, please confine yourself to present quarters until otherwise authorized."

He'd said it quickly, with the rote cadence of a memorized phrase.

Nirubi turned back with a knowing smile and rejoined Cahill on the porch. Without hesitation he threw himself on the sitting American, leaping headlong across his open posture. In a moment of wild grappling, he flipped Greg over and gripped his neck in a twitching forearm. Pulling his prey across the veranda, he backed himself up against the wall.

But Greg's arms hung limply at his sides. He was offering no resistance. "Do you think I'm being kind to you out of a position of weakness?" Greg asked in a strangled voice.

"Yes, I do. Americans are weak. They are dulled by unclean living and godlessness."

Shouts now rang out from the houses on either side of them. The same commandos who had stopped his unapproved excursion a moment before were back, storming up the steps, augmented by four others. Together, the team reached the veranda and stopped ten feet away from the pair, aiming their assault weapons straight at Nirubi's head.

"Well, then I guess you read me wrong, Mr. Nirubi," Greg said. And with that, he wrenched his shoulders forward, thrust his hands upward and, with blinding speed, flipped Nirubi around. Wrapping his arms around him, Greg brought himself into the same controlling hold that Nirubi had just exercised over him.

Nirubi winced, then opened his eyes to six gun barrels just inches away.

Greg quickly released him without inflicting pain, even as he waved off the soldiers.

"I am not of the American government," Greg said. "But I have been a soldier, and I know how to defend myself. Besides that, I live a clean life and I obey the one true God. What I offer you, I offer you out of strength, not need or vulnerability. I offer you my protection and my service."

With a shake to clear his head, Greg walked back to his chair and sat down again. Nirubi joined him.

"I even offer you a bit of unsolicited advice," Greg continued. "I tell you this for your own best interest—not mine, not America's. You see, I truly believe that your best interest lies in accepting this offer of clemency. It sounds like your life hangs in the balance. If you reject it, I'm sure they will have no choice but to resume course, put you on trial and carry out the sentence."

"I am quite willing to offer my life to Allah."

"I'm sure you are. But why do so if it's not necessary or even called for? Put American mercy to the test. We have much to forgive each other, our two sides. Let us forgive you your murderous intentions toward us. Then judge for yourself if we're true to our word. At least it's a start."

"You are wasting your time, all of you," Nirubi said. "I would never trust America to keep its promises to me, even if I wanted it to."

"Then can you believe *me*? Because I assure you, my presence here is no subterfuge."

"*Subterfuge*? What does that mean?"

"A lie. A covert tactic meant to fool you."

"Yes, I can believe that *you* are not subterfuge, Greg Cahill. You may or may not be a dupe, but you are honest to me. And you have shown me kindness, even if its motive is unclear to me. For that I thank you. I sense that your kindness is heartfelt, and not easily given. But I still cannot accept that this offer comes without an agenda behind it."

"Of course there's an agenda. But maybe this time it's changing the way we act toward each other."

"You are going to tell me it has nothing to do with a certain New Year's Day attack against your country?"

Greg swiftly turned to him, his eyes locked with Nirubi's for a long moment.

"Oh, so you did not know about that?" the Arab said with a tone of superiority. "Something they neglected to tell you."

"New Year's Day?" Greg asked.

"That is the name your government has given it."

"Where is it taking place?"

Nirubi shrugged, smiling. "Nobody knows. Not even me."

"Well, I can assure you. For better or worse, I knew nothing whatsoever about it."

Omar peered closely at the man's eyes and face. "Strangely, Greg Cahill, I believe you. I do not know what this means concerning your employer's honesty toward you. But I believe you are telling the truth."

CHAPTER 19

The two men lapsed into an uneasy silence. After fifteen minutes, Nirubi stood with a yawn and disappeared inside the home. Greg remained on the veranda, appearing to lounge in the faint sunlight but actually thinking hard and praying even harder. Ten minutes later, he heard footsteps on the lawn and looked down to see Captain Kilgore approaching the steps.

"Hello, Greg," she said in a pleasant voice.

"Captain. I didn't know you were even here!"

"I need to stay out of Nirubi's sight, because it's your turn up to bat. But yes, I'm very much here. And, in case you're wondering, your friend is asleep on his bed. We have audio recordings to prove that he's resting quite nicely. A good sign. It shows he's taking his recovery seriously."

"So I was right about the house."

"What about it?"

"It's wired. Every inch of it."

"Oh, yeah. Don't doubt that we can see and hear everything."

"So what about this New Year's attack?"

She shrugged and shook her head. "One of fifty

threats that homeland security's tracking at the moment. We're obviously intrigued that he mentioned it, but other than that it has no relevance."

"Then how am I doing?"

"You're doing better than expected, Greg. You've gotten right in there and advocated for the clemency offer. And you've told him a lot of helpful and true things. Probably more true things than I've even told *you*, yet."

"Like what?"

"Like when you told him that this offer is delicate and even troublesome for Washington. In fact, it's so true that it's why I have to ask you to step things up, even though you're doing well. There's a lot of pressure mounting against our even bringing him here and making this offer at all. Time for a successful resolution is growing shorter every day."

Pasadena, California

The self-proclaimed Azzam the Younger returned from a hard day's research at Caltech—actually a long day of dreaming about all the infidels his nerve gas would kill. He came home to his apartment just as the sun was starting to kiss the fronds along the highest rows of palm trees. The screen door had barely had time to slap against its frame when the young man focused his eyes and froze in place.

She was sprawled out all cute and akimbo on his couch just as she'd always done back home. Back in his days of high school infamy and aimless, all-American debauchery.

"Vanessa?" he said, still unsure that it was her. It had been years, and the creature before him appeared different in many ways from the on-again, off-again girlfriend of that forgettable epoch of his life.

Her hair was now a neon shade of blue, for instance. The face was leaner, more garishly made up. And her limbs, scantily clad for ample display, were clearly firmer and more muscular than he'd remembered. Still, there was that familiar mischievous gleam in those hazel eyes. It had to be her.

"Surprised to see me?" she asked in her best playful voice, and all remaining question was now dashed. The sound of her musical laugh instantly melted his heart. "It took me forever to track you down."

He stared at her. Truly he'd wondered if he would ever see her again, or whether his drastic change of direction would steer him forever off her path. Ironically, he had pictured her countless times sitting right here, on this very couch. Only in his fantasies, she had been more demure, quieter, and respectful as he launched into an eloquent and persuasive description of his conversion to Islam. The daydreams had always ended a bit hazily, with her somehow embracing his newfound faith and declaring him a hero for the bloodbath he was poised to unleash.

"So, you gonna give me a hug?" she said.

She jumped up with that same coltish awkwardness that had once driven him to hormonal distraction. Reaching out, she clasped him in a bony, angular embrace. One thing, he noticed, that she didn't do as before was to press herself against him in that old suggestive manner. Perhaps it was true that time did impart some measure of self-restraint.

"How did you get in?" he asked, pulling back and suddenly feeling paranoid.

"Same way I used to sneak into your house back in Visalia," she answered. "Or have you forgotten?"

He walked in, seized by an impulse to claim his space. It already felt like she'd taken over, a sensation she'd always provoked in him. "No, I haven't forgotten. It's just been a while."

"Well, are you wondering why I'm here?" As usual, she didn't wait for his answer before launching into her explanation. "I'm coming here to live! Olivia and I are moving to West Hollywood and becoming waitresses. Isn't that cool?"

He stopped and tried to come up with an acceptable reply. In his current state of utter devotion to Allah, the thought of someone, anyone, waitressing in West Hollywood sounded like a one-way ticket to the pit of hell.

"That sounds, uh, right up your alley," he said in the best terms he could manage. "It'll be perfect for you."

"Speaking of which, there's no booze in this place. Have I heard right and you're becoming this totally square, clean-living maniac?"

"Well, I wouldn't exactly put it that way."

"Then where'd you hide it?"

"Nowhere. I don't need that stuff anymore."

"I don't get it, Soapy."

He cringed. Soapy had been his high school nickname, the one he'd traveled two hundred miles to Los Angeles to lose. Even when she'd been his hot-and-heavy girlfriend, she had used it as relentlessly as his worst enemies. His hatred of the name had only endeared it more to her perverse imagination. Now, not having endured the name for over three years, he recoiled all the more at the moronic sound of it.

"Would you not call me that?" he asked sharply. "I've worked very hard to never hear that name ever again!"

"Oh, so should I call you Azzam the Younger?"

He tensed and struggled mightily against an urge to whirl around and launch himself at her throat. "What in the world are you talking about?"

"Well, I've been here two hours, waiting on you. I popped on your computer to check my webmail, and I saw all that weird stuff about Islamic jihad on your browser window. Kind of spooky."

He forced himself to breathe steadily. To exhale the rage along with the carbon dioxide.

She'd already read too much. There would be no telling her about his conversion to Islam now. He had to cover, and fast.

"Everybody's getting the wrong impression about me," he explained in the most convincing tone he could improvise. "I'm doing a major research paper in sociology on militant Islam. In order to get fresh, original data, I've had to make up a meaningful screen name and dig into some of that stuff online. But I do wish you'd have asked me before reading it."

"Oh yeah," she laughed, "what are you gonna do? Get rid of me?"

He looked away, inwardly breathing a sigh of relief. At least she seemed to have bought his cover story.

"Look," she said. "I'm back. Get used to it, honey. And I've heard all about how you've done great at Caltech and gotten yourself hired on to some super-secret government weapons project. I think it's awesome. I'm proud of you."

"Who told you about my job?" he asked.

"Come on. Who do you think you're talking to? This is Visalia here, not Los Angeles. Half the town knows. Besides, your momma's worried about you. Says you never answer her calls and that you've started talking about Mohammed and hanging out with some weird guys."

"Please," he mumbled. "Don't speak of Mohammed."

"What?"

"Nothing. Forget it."

Her eyes narrowed. He felt her appraisal of him adjust quickly, almost imperceptibly, in the same unforced manner that he'd seen skimpy dresses shift themselves around her slim shape with just a shrug of her shoulders.

"Fine. I won't say it again. No need to talk about religion anyhow, if you know what I mean. It's never worth the trouble."

But he noticed that she seemed frightened. Her pupils were dilated oddly. She was holding her mouth in that strange way she always did when upset and not willing to reveal it. The slightest sheen of sweat glittered on her upper lip.

"By the way, I got a Coke out of your fridge. What were all those vials in there? You doing your own experiments?"

It occurred to him, with a dull thud of reluctance, that this was the final straw. She was afraid because she had made the connection. She had come to see him out of prurient, romantic curiosity perhaps, but also from a need to check out the rumors. And now he had gone and confirmed her worst suspicions. If only he'd kept his mouth shut, surely Mohammed would have forgiven him an overlooked slight.

He took a deep breath and took a seat next to her. The decision before him plunged like a ball of dread inside of him, as heavy as a boulder.

"Yeah," he said, "I'm making my own organic supplements. Would you like to try one?"

CHAPTER 20

Respite House, Fort Huachuca—later that afternoon

Following a two-hour nap, Nirubi rose just in time for an early lunch of couscous and roasted lamb, a nod to Middle Eastern cuisine brought over by a pair of staff sergeants in a minivan. After eating, Greg and Nirubi stepped outside for a brief walk.

They walked side by side across the lawn without speaking, the Arab leaning his head back to absorb the sunshine on his face, waving his arms slowly at his sides and taking long strides.

"I cannot see them," said Nirubi, "yet I assume they are watching us."

"That would be a safe assumption," replied Greg.

Nirubi turned and gave him a searching look. "You are different this afternoon. Something has changed your attitude toward me."

Greg responded only with a faint smile. After several more steps in silence, staring down at the grass, he said, "I have ministered to men who were hated by most of the so-called respectable folks. Criminals. Killers. At first, I had my own difficulties, but I overcame them when God reminded me that I too had taken life, that I too am a sinner. But you, Mr. Nirubi, are a challenge far beyond that. Before hearing about the New Year's plot, I found it easy to forget exactly what you stand for, the slaughter you've dedicated your life to. I asked God to help me through my first meeting with you, to give me the strength to see you not as a monster but as a human being. And He answered that prayer. When I walked into that torture chamber and saw you there for the first time, you were a scared, brutalized man staring death in the face. It wasn't hard at all to humanize you and to have sympathy for you."

Greg stopped cold—beneath the shade of a large ponderosa pine—turned and faced Nirubi.

"But you see, my wife, Donna . . . I mean my *ex*-wife, Donna, had a cousin named Darren who died on 9/11. They weren't all that close, and Darren wasn't a shining star of a human being, sort of an artsy New York knockabout. He had a son, a baby boy by an old girlfriend. He was a waiter at Top of the World, the restaurant on top of the World Trade Center."

Greg paused, and his lip began to quiver despite his best effort to still it.

"He was one of those who jumped, Mr. Nirubi. We don't talk about it much, and it's not common knowledge. It's something I learned through my law enforcement contacts. His last moments on earth were so filled with horror that he leaped out into a thousand feet of nothing just to escape the hell you conspired and planned and worked very hard to inflict on him. Darren wasn't political. He was no Zionist, that's for sure. If he had any sympathies at all, they probably would have gone in your favor. It's hard to tell, because he was a complete rebel. But he was a father. And someday his boy's going to learn how his daddy died. There's no way a sane person can call that serving a merciful God.

"You would bring the same horror to me and my little boy, and his mother and a million more like us. You're complicit in a plan to do that very thing, right now as we speak. And who knows? My boy might be one of your victims, because none of us knows where this mass murder is going to take place."

"Neither do I," Nirubi said.

"Somehow," replied Greg, "that's even more evil. The randomness of it. You're willing to kill anybody, just as long as they're American. You just want to pour out as much death and suffering as you possibly can on the innocent and guilty alike. Do you call that mercy?"

Nirubi stepped away and began walking back toward the house.

"Answer me!" Greg shouted. "Do you call that mercy?"

Greg broke into a run and caught up with him.

"We both believe in a God who is merciful and compassionate, remember? So I want to hear you tell me that killing my son, who doesn't know Israel or Mecca from the back of a cereal box, along with millions more like him, is merciful!"

Nirubi quickened his pace, pulled away from Greg and reached the veranda first.

The two men did not speak again for four hours.

Deep in the fort's intelligence complex, Captain Delia Kilgore stood before eight large plasma screens and stared at the grainy image across one of them, transmitted from the rooftop camera of a concealed watcher. The sound of Greg Cahill's final challenge echoed through the room from a half-dozen speakers, degraded by a faint wind hiss and the inherent limitations of eavesdropping microphones.

"I'm glad he decided to grow a spine," muttered the senior officer beside her. "If I was standing next to the guy, it'd be all I could do to keep from tearing him limb from limb."

"That's why he's there and you're not," she responded with a bite to her words.

"So, Captain, in your considered opinion," broke in a younger analyst just in from Washington, "is this a setback in their bonding?"

"No!" she snapped. "This was very necessary. Even the protocol itself has a name and a rationale for this stage, which it considers essential to a true establishment of trust. It's number three on the list, although they're not ranked in order of importance. It's called Conflict Processing. How could Nirubi possibly take him seriously if he didn't process this kind of negativity at some point or other?"

"Good point," said the senior officer.

"What's important now is that Greg not stay here. He has to move on. This isn't about continually throwing the man's sins back in his face. We could have done that back in Poland. The other thing to focus on is Nirubi's response."

"How do we gauge it?"

"That's the big mystery," Delia answered. "He didn't say much, and his body language is ambiguous. Only the next few hours will tell if this honesty had a positive effect or not."

"I just don't see how this will have the ultimate effect of destroying the man's faith, though."

"I agree that it looks murky," she said. "No pun intended, but you need to have a little faith. And patience. Cahill is circling, angling for some kind of opening to throw the subject of faith wide open. I can see it in his body language, hear it in his arguments. He's desperate for a breach in the man's ideology. I just hope he finds it in time."

"It's just so uncontrolled and hazy," said the senior officer with a shake of his head. "I can't believe a major national security objective is hanging in the balance of a conversation between a terrorist and a civilian, who has no clue what's even expected of him."

"I understand," said Delia wearily. "That's why it's a called a measure of last resort."

"Or to put it another way, the Homeland Security forces of the United States are on standby, waiting with bated breath for two men, a terrorist and a complete amateur, to sit and talk about religion."

CHAPTER 21

Respite House, Fort Huachuca—next morning, 5 days before the attack

After an hour's solid prayer on the subject, Greg emerged with nothing more than a powerful dilemma. The first thing he realized was that veering to the subject of the man's sins had been a major deviation from his goal. The government's offer was all about forgiveness. Likewise, his wish to share Christ with his charge was also about reconciliation and redemption, not condemnation.

And yet he kept remembering—there was almost too much to condemn about Nirubi. So much that it was difficult for an ordinary person to rise above it. After all, Greg told himself, here he was playing a glorified concierge to one of the most evil men in the Western world. The greatest threat to the safety and survival of his family, in all of humanity. The twenty-first century equivalent of Hitler.

Still, everything Greg stood for told him that even these things could be forgiven. Even all this man had done and stood for could be wiped clean forever if only the man turned his life over to his Creator. Praying on his knees in his bedroom, Greg felt himself reach the outer limit of his compassion, an almost physical sensation of having run head-on into a solid barrier.

Please, God, give me a bit of your heart, he pleaded silently, *because I don't have it in me to forgive this man, or even treat him like a human being. Help me . . .*

He heard footsteps in the kitchen, telling him that Nirubi was close by. With a quick inward plea for wisdom and the right words, Greg stood and walked through the home's polished veneers to the granite counter where Nirubi stood, hands planted wide apart on the surface as though awaiting orders.

"We need to talk," said Nirubi.

"I agree. But would you let me start?"

Nirubi nodded, his eyes darting over Greg's face and hands as if in a quick effort to discern his state of mind.

"Hearing about the New Year's plot reminded me that I've never met someone whose life was dedicated to destroying me, my faith, my family, my country, everything I hold dear."

Nirubi sighed, then looked down at the counter.

"Even though most of the condemning things I said to you were true, I now wish I had never said them. Primarily because that's not what we're here for. Your presence here, and mine also, is not about trying to make you regret or recant your life's choices, as destructive as they might be. It's about giving you a chance to accept forgiveness and have your slate wiped clean. Turn away from that past, making the kind of fresh start that honors your heritage and your God."

Nirubi nodded as he processed Greg's words. He looked up again.

"So, no more long lists of how evil I am?"

"No more of that," Greg assured him. "Besides, I'm sure I made my point."

"You did, and quite powerfully I might add. But I am not going to try and defend the things I have done or planned to do."

"Why is that?"

"Because I feel somehow separated, estranged even, from my past. After my time in the hands of your interrogation squad, I feel like someone who has awakened from a very long coma. My whole life, up until being captured, now feels far removed from where I stand today. Like an event I can look at from outside myself, with a sense of detachment. I neither reject it nor embrace it. I merely see it lying there before me. I look at those years, and I certainly see cause for hate. I grew up in the refugee camps of Lebanon. I also had a cousin die violently, murdered by Christian militiamen at Shatila in the 1982 massacre of Palestinian refugees. I had nightmares for years about my playmate Irana lying on a sidewalk with her throat slit, and the rest of her family lying on top of her, dead, while her mother was being raped by Lebanese thugs. I had already been taught to hate Israel and the West from the time I could understand language. Condemnation of the infidels was more constant than talk of the weather. So the murder also strengthened my feelings toward all of you, gathering it into a force so potent that I could taste it like blood on my tongue."

Greg saw that Nirubi's eyes had glazed over with the power of his recollection.

"But there is another reason. It is difficult for me to discuss. You see, all my life I have felt a dark cloud of rage follow me everywhere I go. Most of my days I have felt that its presence was normal. It seemed a part of being human. Still, I resented it. I would long for the moments when it would dissipate even the smallest bit. My only relief from its presence came during prayer. That is why I seek out the daily prayers so fiercely. It is devotion to Allah, yes, but also because of the brief peace it offers me. As the years have gone by, and my struggle for jihad deepened, this dark cloud has seemed more oppressive and corrosive to me. Often I resign myself to it and let its blackness fuel my hatred for the West. I seek solace only through action, through warfare. Many days, that is the only way to deal with it.

"When I was captured by your soldiers and taken to that hole in the wall, the rage became so overpowering that I could do nothing but surrender to it. It consumed me. It swallowed me so completely that I thought my own identity had been eaten away in the process. A part of me, what I cared about, was gone, leaving behind only this numb detachment."

Nirubi cradled his forehead in the palm of his hand and sighed loudly.

"Right before you walked into my prison, I had seen the water-board being brought out and I knew that my last moments were just ahead. Silently, I cried out to Allah for deliverance. It was my first prayer in days, as I had not been allowed to pray toward Mecca in the right way. Then there was a flash of light. You appeared. You spoke harshly to my tormentors and took me away from there. For the first few hours I had an overwhelming feeling that you were Allah's messenger, sent by him to deliver me."

"Maybe that's partly true," Greg interjected.

"All I know is that something in you breaks up that darkness. You are an oasis, somehow. Some force inside of you repels the cloud completely. Being around you gives me the longest relief from this rage and blackness I have ever known in my life."

"Well, I take no credit for that. I can't."

"I believe you, and I expected you to say that. I have sensed from your very first words that you not only had compassion for me but that you were being truthful, even if nobody else around you was. That is why I find it difficult to decide about this offer of clemency. I know you are presenting it honestly, but no one else I believe. Nowhere in the character of America do I see a reason why I should expect forgiveness. True clemency. All I know is talk of war and of breaking prisoners' wills at any cost."

Greg hid all the signs, yet inside him a great signal was going off. Here, at last, was the opportunity he had prayed for, the opening he had pleaded about!

"Actually, there's a huge precedent in American life for the clemency offer. It's the heritage of the Christian message of good news we call the gospel."

"Please," Nirubi interrupted sharply. "Let us not bring religion into this, just when we are getting somewhere."

"Please allow me to continue for a moment," Greg said. "I'm not referring to the divisive aspects of it all. Just this one thing. In Christianity, there's one great act you must perform in order to be free of your sin and its condemnation. That is, to accept an offer of forgiveness. Jesus already did everything else. He paid the price for our sins by dying for offenses He didn't commit. He conquered the power of sin and death. All so He could offer forgiveness to humanity. His offer is already out there, extended and waiting. All you have to do is believe in it, and accept it."

"You sound like some American television preacher."

"I'm only explaining how this notion is ingrained in the American culture, and why a clemency offer like the one given to you makes perfect sense. The greatest gifts are the ones freely offered and given, not earned through lists of good versus bad deeds as in Islam."

"So I simply accept this clemency, and everything in the past is swept away forever?" asked Nirubi in a pained voice. "No. It is too easy. Too painless."

"Remember that the one who made you this offer paid a high price to make it. In the case of Christ, He paid the ultimate price. A horrible death and the weight of the whole world's sins upon Him, an innocent. In the case of our current offer, you must remember that the president would pay a high political price for granting you clemency and finding you a home among our population. Most of America wants you dead. It would be a scandal if news of your clemency were to emerge."

"I do not know. It still feels cheap, this easy forgiveness of yours. I trust good deeds, acts actually performed."

"It's not cheap," said Greg. "It's an incredible gift, given by a God who is merciful and compassionate."

"Ah, yes. That first statement of yours. I remember."

"Do you think the gift I spoke of is too much, too merciful for the God of Abraham?"

Nirubi frowned and crossed his arms, bobbing his head forward. "No, it is not too much. Nothing is impossible for God. But I do not believe this is what happened. The Koran does not speak of such things."

"Thankfully, we don't have to decide this now. All we need is to understand that America believes in this gift; it is our cultural precedent. And the foundation for a similar gift being offered you by our government. It's the reason you can trust in this offer's authenticity. It's also the reason why I asked if we could start with an understanding of God being merciful. Because I don't think a merciful and compassionate God would want you to turn away from even the possibility of your enemy offering you genuine mercy."

"Where is mercy in this offer from an enemy who has tried to kill me most of my life?"

"Remember," said Greg, "I'm not a spokesman for my government. I'm just a man here to be of service. But simple logic tells me this. Your being alive right now is far more delicate for the United States than having killed you. America could gain a great deal of leverage from displaying your corpse on international television. If we were being completely mercenary and ruthless, we would have taken that advantage right away. Instead, we have undertaken a more complicated and dangerous route by offering you a clemency we've never extended to a terrorist before. That must count for something—"

"Men, may I interrupt?"

CHAPTER 22

It was a female voice; it came from the back of the room. Both men turned and saw Delia Kilgore, standing in full uniform with a thick folder in one hand.

"I'm very sorry to disrupt your conversation, but I have some news to share."

Motioning them to a nearby dining table, she sat down and opened the folder to a packet of papers that she grasped, ready to give out, as the men sat across from her.

"Mr. Nirubi, I have some grave news for you." She took a deep breath. "Your former colleagues of al-Qaeda, knowing that you were taken by our forces, have reacted in a very vengeful and cruel way. Of course they have been too proud to officially admit America successfully snatched their leader. But knowing we have you in our custody, they have turned against your closest confidants, and your family."

She slowly spread out on the table a series of photographs. Within a split second of seeing them, Greg turned away. His brain's afterimage bore the sight of blood, prone bodies, and lifeless eyes.

Nirubi nearly bolted out of his chair. A strange, urgent cry rose from his chest, and he formed a tight fist with his hand.

"You do not have to look at these," Delia said. "I will be glad to tell you myself, although it pains me. A new faction has taken over, led by your old rival, Khalid Ambali. Your top three lieutenants—Omar Sahab, Ayman Jamal, and Ramzi Zumbayadh—were beheaded four hours ago. But it gets far worse than that." She held up another set of papers, which she held close to her chest. "Your wife and the three children with her were taken from their home in Islamabad yesterday morning. An hour ago their bodies were discovered outside the city beside a highway."

Nirubi leaned back and raised his hands to his face, his mouth open in horror. He covered his eyes, rocking back and forth in the chair, groaning loudly.

Finally he stood and stumbled to the room's far corner, still weeping.

Greg stared at her, suddenly filled with rage. It was the height of cruelty for her to lay down gruesome photos of a man's slain relatives like that. It struck him that perhaps this was a necessary tactic to jolt Nirubi out of his complacency and arouse his emotions. Even so, at that moment it seemed inhuman.

After a respectful pause, Delia spoke again.

"Mr. Nirubi, there is one bit of good news."

He turned and looked at her, his expression hopeful, vulnerable.

"Your eldest son, Daoud, was rescued from the Madrass in Quetta. We took him into our protection and brought him to the United States for treatment. He's at Children's Hospital Boston, still unconscious. As soon as he regains consciousness, we will arrange for you to speak to him over a video hookup."

Nirubi stepped closer to Delia, wiped his eyes with the back of his hand. "That is not good enough. I want you to take me to my son right now."

"Sorry, but that's out of the question," said Delia. "Your being out of chains required a special order from the president. That was already the maximum."

"Take me to him!" Nirubi shouted.

"All right, Mr. Nirubi. Accept our offer right now, and not only will we take you to see your son, but you will be reunited for good."

"But only if I accept your offer?"

"Let me point out for you the current state of affairs. Your old organization wants you dead and has killed your family to make sure the point is clear. You have nothing within al-Qaeda or Islam to return to. Your only path to any kind of future lies in accepting our offer."

"That is no path," he muttered. "It is no life."

"There are still ways that, here in America, you could live on to play a positive role in the world. You can be a voice in exile, speaking out on the issues you care about. As long as you don't take part in terrorism, you'd be perfectly free to advocate your beliefs."

He shook his head, saying nothing.

She looked over at Greg. "Mr. Nirubi, Greg and I are going to give you a little time to yourself. You have our deepest sympathies."

Nirubi spent the next two hours in his room with the lights out.

Delia and her electronics monitoring team in the neighboring house saw on their screens only the darkened figure of a man prone on the floor, accompanied by the sound of crying.

After the two hours had elapsed, Nirubi finally rose and left his room. He found Greg walking along the perimeter of the living room, slowly and steadily, like a man walking in his sleep. He watched while the American turned at one of the room's corners, his steps resembling someone making some kind of measurement. He noticed that Greg's lips were moving.

Nirubi moved forward, curious, and saw that he had attracted his host's attention.

Greg stopped and faced him with a stricken look. "I cannot tell you how sorry I am for your news. I too have a wife and a young son. I can't imagine how I'd feel if they were killed, and in such a manner. My prayers are with you."

Nirubi only nodded. There was a faraway look in his eyes.

"You're probably wondering what I'm doing," Greg said.

"You are marking the room's size?"

"No. I'm prayer-walking. I'm asking for an angelic guard to surround this house."

"You feel this is necessary?"

"I feel it's absolutely imperative. Many forces in the spiritual realm would seek to disrupt any good things taking shape here. Only a few of them are human in nature."

"And you physically walk through the place while you ask this?"

"That's right. It may not be necessary, but many people believe this focuses our prayers. It makes very real to me what I'm asking for. The more concrete and real your prayers can be, the better."

Nirubi turned and gazed out the window. He blinked and quickly looked back to Greg. "Too bad. Instead, you get this blinding fog."

Glancing out the same window, Greg asked, "What do you mean? What fog?"

"That bright white mist outside. I can hardly stand to look at it, it is so intense."

Greg frowned. He looked again, then at Nirubi with a strange expression.

"I'm seeing a clear blue morning," he said. "Hardly a cloud in sight, except for one blocking out the sun."

Nirubi gave him a perplexed look. "You do not see that brilliance pouring through the windows? It is so vivid, I can hardly see those guards standing post. Even though they are incredibly close to us. The brightness makes them appear larger than life."

Nirubi's face was that of a man dumbstruck, one whose entire view of reality had just been stood upside down.

CHAPTER 23

Greg walked over to the window and stared out for a few seconds. When he turned back, he had a strange smile plastered across his features. "Mr. Nirubi, tell me more about these soldiers you see."

"Why?"

"Are they holding guns? Are they wearing uniforms?"

"No, but they seem to be guarding us somehow."

"Take another look. Please."

Nirubi joined him at the window. This time he did not react, but turned to Greg at once. He looked visibly disappointed, even bereft.

"They are gone," he said. "Now I see the same morning you do. And the guards are gone."

"Mr. Nirubi, you have spiritual sight. You saw the answer to what I have been asking for. An angelic hedge of protection."

Nirubi stared at him, processing Greg's words. Something about the ease of his response had once again inflamed his dormant suspiciousness.

"Oh, right. Please do not insult my intelligence.

Those men are agents of your psychological operations. Do not take me for an uninformed fool."

"Really. Tell me, how tall did these men seem to you?"

Nirubi glanced up at the ceiling, estimating. "They were extremely tall. Seven, eight feet, or even more."

"So you think we recruited a bunch of NBA basketball players to come and give you a thrill? Here. Come with me."

Greg led the way through the front door and outside, onto the front lawn. Overhead the sky was becoming grayer, and a cool wind touched their limbs at once. Walking barefoot, they approached the site of the strange apparition. Greg crouched and began scrutinizing the ground.

"Come. Let's look for signs of giant men in strange uniforms, who ran away when you turned your head. See any tracks or anything?"

Nirubi gave a genuine inspection of the grass and the soil beneath it. At length, he shook his head. "No. I see nothing."

"See any evidence at all?"

Again, Nirubi shook his head.

"There was nothing fake or contrived about what you saw. I swear to you."

Nirubi peered at him, and Greg knew the man was studying him through his own powers of perception. They were not friendly enough yet for the terrorist to betray his conclusion, but Greg thought he could discern a barely visible nod of agreement, and an acceptance that softened the man's eyes.

"How many did you see?" Greg asked as they climbed the steps to reenter the house.

"I am not sure" was Nirubi's reply. "I could not bear to look long enough to see more. My second sight has only shown me darkness until today."

"That is why I'm asking for this guard. Great things are

happening here. Or about to happen. And many fighters beyond just the human kind might try to disrupt us."

Once in the living room, Nirubi settled into a thick leather armchair while Greg took a seat on the couch beside it.

"We have a mystical order within my branch of Islam," said Nirubi. "They are called Sufis. Their priests are always dancing, trying to reach the very presence of God himself. You might know them as the Whirling Dervishes."

"How do you feel about Islam right now?" Greg asked. "I mean, knowing what your brothers in the faith did to your family."

He made a heavy sigh and closed his eyes, a picture of extreme emotional fatigue.

"I will admit to you, my loyalties are confused. If this is all the mercy I can expect from my fellow Muslims, to see them slaughter my family just because something bad happened to me, then what good is it? What good is the love and mercy I was told would flow among the righteous?"

"I would never judge a faith by the failures of its followers," Greg said. "Christian history is also full of horrible deeds and betrayals. I try to look at what each faith says about God."

"Yes, and since I am a man of action, I look at results. I look at things like real angels, whom I have never seen before, appearing as a result of your prayers. That is simply amazing. Or a dark cloud which has followed me all of my life, disappearing in your presence."

"How about the fact that your old path offers you nothing but death and rejection. While this new direction offers you forgiveness, clemency, and a whole new start in life. Not to mention a chance to reunite with your son."

Nirubi said nothing but stared ahead, lost in a scowling haze.

"I'm always amazed," Greg continued, "at how much our two faiths have in common, considering how much hatred exists between them. We both believe in the God of Abraham. We both believe Him to be merciful and righteous. We both revere Jesus Christ, even if in different ways. We both ask God to forgive us our sins. We all aspire to live holy lives."

"Still, there are huge differences," Nirubi added.

"Sure. One of the biggest differences we've talked about already. About forgiveness."

"I cannot understand how you can be 'saved' just by accepting an offer of forgiveness. It belittles the cost of sin to make it so easily overcome."

"Just the opposite," Greg said. "We think the cost of sin is so high, we could never pay it ourselves. It's so enormous that only God could pay it for us. So He did."

Nirubi lifted his eyebrows. An idea worth pondering.

"That is too easy. I do not buy it. You just say, 'Thank you, I accept,' and all your evil deeds just fly away?"

"No. I never said that. They don't just fly away; there are still consequences. You still have to accept God's forgiveness. You have to work out your salvation in your life. You have to live with the aftermath of what you've done."

"What does that mean?"

"The earthly cost of our failures."

"Why do you speak like such a haunted man?" Nirubi asked. "You say these things as though you are the worst person on the earth. Instead of someone accomplished enough to be picked for a mission such as this one."

Greg laughed with a tinge of bitterness. "Believe me, I was not chosen for this mission because of my spotless record or my intact life. In a way, I was chosen for the opposite."

"Why? I don't understand."

"I was chosen for my ability to befriend the friendless. To love the most wretched of men. And if there's one thing that makes me capable of doing that, it's my awareness of my own wretchedness. I have killed. I have murdered in the worst way. I have failed in the deepest ways imaginable."

"I do not believe you. Tell me how."

"This time is not about me, Mr. Nirubi."

"No, that is an excuse. You just do not want to talk about it."

Greg met the man's gaze and smiled. Nirubi was right. In fact, Greg *never* wanted to talk about it—least of all now.

CHAPTER 24

Greg exhaled loudly. He stood and swung his arms out like a man who had just made a difficult decision. Returning to his place on the couch, he settled himself back into the cushions.

"I guess I'd better start with how I ruined my career, because that's the cause. I used to be a member of the army's Delta Force. A Special Forces unit I'm sure you've heard of. I was a sniper with them, and my whole life was going great. Married to my college sweetheart, a baby on the way. Until a call came to assist the ATF in a high-pressure standoff in the mountains of Idaho. A white supremacist was holed up in his remote compound with a stash of weapons and six kids. I was flown up there with three of my fellow snipers, and I took up a position a hundred yards from the man's log cabin, camouflaged in a pine tree. I'd been up there for hours when the brass decided to break the silence and had one of our negotiators approach the house with his hands up. It was one of those highly tense moments with at least a hundred gun barrels aimed at the scene. Our orders were 'shoot to kill' at any sign of a hostile action being taken. Then, in a side window facing me, I saw a rifle barrel and the silhouette of a machine gun moving into position. I took aim and fired."

Greg paused and breathed deeply, his eyes closed, reliving the event.

"It was a kid. A nine-year-old, aiming a toy gun out the window, at the strange man approaching. I heard his mother scream at him to put it away just as I pulled the trigger. I tore him apart. My shot provoked a chain reaction as the other snipers and quite a few ordinary officers opened fire on the place. Five of the six children were killed, along with their mother. It turned into one of the biggest scandals in the history of the U.S. military."

Nirubi slowly shook his head. "And you became the . . . what do you Americans call it?"

"The fall guy," responded Greg. "The brass had to offer up someone. I'd obeyed the rules of engagement, but I could have shown more restraint, they said. The thing was, the officer walking up to the house was a friend. I had watched him write a letter to his family the night before, something they would read on the event of his death. So I was a little jumpy, and I made the mistake of admitting that to a colleague during the horrible moments right after the shootout. At my hearing, the army argued that this was a sign of what they call culpable impairment. I wasn't court-martialed, but I was given an immediate discharge and told that if I ever went public with my story or became an embarrassment to the army, my name would be forever held up as the Butcher of Idaho. So I basically washed out into civilian life. I had no particular skills to make it in the outside world. And without the ability to talk about what happened, I became depressed. I started drinking a lot, and became miserable to live with."

Greg stood then and started pacing the floor. The most painful part of the story lay just ahead.

"A couple of weeks later," he continued, "I went on a drinking binge and drove drunk with Robby in the car. I ran a stop sign, crashed into another car, and nearly killed my son. He was still in the hospital when I got out of jail. When I came home, the locks had been changed. She'd kicked me out of the house. Even then I refused to admit my problem, or its inner cause. Three days later, on the night Robby got home from the hospital, I got drunk again and vowed to break into our house. I was dead set on fighting my wife for our child. I got inside and nearly beat up Donna when she ripped Robby from my arms. I ended up hurting her and reinjuring some of Robby's wounds. I was arrested again, and the next day she filed for divorce. The court found me guilty, granted the divorce, and issued me a restraining order against having any contact with either her or my son. I'm not allowed within a hundred feet of my own boy."

He took a deep, ragged breath, vowing not to lose his composure.

"On the first night of that jail stay, I woke up from a nightmare with these words running through my mind. It turned out they were words from my childhood, spoken by a preacher I'd once heard. He said, 'There's always hope. You've never done so much, or sunk so low, that you can't be restored and come home again to God.'

"So I cried out to Him, and I accepted His forgiveness. Instantly I could feel my body being healed. I knew right away that my craving for alcohol was gone. I haven't had a drink since."

Greg stopped his pacing and dropped himself back on the couch.

"Here's why I told you this, Mr. Nirubi. It was to tell you the next part. In the spiritual realm, I'm saved, I'm healed. One hundred percent, head to toe. But in the physical world, I'm still very much dealing with the aftermath of my actions. The restraining order against me still stands. I haven't been clean long enough, and I'm still subject to the law. My divorce is still in effect. I am what's called a noncustodial father, and there's nothing I can do about it until the proper waiting period has passed."

Nirubi looked at him, lost in thought. "Please, go on," he said at last.

"Well, that's why my Christian faith isn't as easy as tossing off a prayer, being forgiven, and living happily ever after. I still have my temptations, my brokenness, and the world to wrestle with. I still have to live out the meaning of my forgiveness to those I've hurt, and those I come into contact with. That includes you. I'm going to tell you something I've told every prisoner I've ever ministered to. Jesus said there's no greater love than a man willing to die for his friends. So I pledge this to you right now: I will protect you no matter what. No matter how this thing shakes out, I will give my all to protect you, even if that includes my life. Got it?"

"No, I do not," Nirubi said. "I do not get it at all. Why would you give up your life for me?"

"Because that's what real love is about—sacrifice and forgiving one another."

Nirubi flashed an angry look at him.

"What's the matter?" asked Greg.

"I have heard enough of your idea of forgiveness, your religious nonsense. I lost my wife and children today, and through no fault of mine. I deserve better than this slick, prepared routine of yours. Give your life to protect me? Please do not insult me with any more of this talk. Let me grieve in peace."

Surprised, Greg rose to his feet. "I'm sorry, Mr. Nirubi, if I offended you," he said, trying to sound as unhurt as possible. "I'll leave you alone now."

He was entering the kitchen area when Delia came walking in, a laptop computer under one arm.

"I was just on my way out," Greg told her.

"Hold on a minute," she whispered. "I'm here to save you." She stepped toward the living room and called out, "Mr. Nirubi? I have something to show you." Setting the laptop on the dining room table, she punched a button. "Would you like to say hello to your son? He just regained consciousness."

Omar Nirubi shot up from his chair as if catapulted by some mechanical device. A second later he sat by Delia's side as a video image popped to life on the screen.

It was a little boy, his face blackened by bruises, with one eye nearly swollen shut. But he was smiling.

The name Daoud flew from his father's mouth. It was the last word Greg understood, for what followed was a barrage of Arabic, passionate and flowing.

Nirubi transformed into a completely different man. Gone was the reserve and the shell of resentment, the drawn mask of shock and trauma. The man speaking to the laptop's screen was a proud father like any other man greeting a beloved son he'd feared dead. At one point, the two wept openly, obviously coping with the deaths of the boy's mother and siblings.

After five minutes, a nurse's face appeared on the screen. "I'm sorry, but our young patient needs his rest. We need to stop now. You may speak again tomorrow."

The screen went blank.

Nirubi turned to Delia, his cheeks quivering and eyelashes batting rapidly.

"My son confirmed everything you told me," he said. "He told me his rescuers risked their lives to save him, with gunfire going off and people dying on every side. He said that as frightening as the situation was, they were gentle and kind to him the whole way to America. Please thank everyone for me."

Delia nodded, clearly unsure whether she would pass on the thanks of the world's number one terrorist.

"I want to be very clear," she said in a stern voice. "Your son is not a hostage. For the moment he is still a seriously ill child. And we both know that if you decline the president's offer, you will not be in a position to resume custody of him. You will be on trial. But if you accept the offer, we will reunite you two as quickly as humanly possible. And now I'll leave you to your leisure."

She smiled, got up with a military briskness, picked up the laptop, and left the room.

Greg turned back to Nirubi, feeling a renewal of purpose surge within him.

"It seems your choices are becoming obvious," he said. "Remember that if you accept the president's offer, you won't be caving in to the West. Instead, you'll be positioning yourself as the driving force behind a whole new way of handling Islamic and Middle Eastern issues."

"And if I refuse the offer?"

Greg paused, wishing he did not have to be so blunt. But he had to describe matters as they actually stood.

"You will rot in a maximum-security prison for the rest of your life, or very possibly face execution. Either way, you'll never see your son again."

CHAPTER 25

Pasadena, California

Driving his former girlfriend to the campus of Caltech, the man known to America's intelligence community as Azzam the Younger felt abruptly pulled down by a weight of sluggishness, a sudden feeling of dread.

Visiting the school had been *her* idea, he reassured himself.

But he knew her too well. Back at his apartment, he had steered their conversation to the subject of his wonderful school. He shared how the things he'd learned and the people he'd met there had virtually saved his life. He told her how, in spite of his surfer's appearance, his professors had quickly recognized his prodigy-level aptitude for chemistry and biology. Showering him with scholarships and fellowships, they had quickly channeled him into projects so top secret and important that they boggled the mind.

Azzam knew that after five minutes of such talk, her curiosity would gain the upper hand. She would beg him to take her there.

"But I can't show you anything," he had insisted.

"Why is that?"

"Like I said, it's top secret. I'm working on a project that's so off the books, if I told you—"

"You'd have to kill me?" she interrupted. "Oh, please. Drop the secret agent stuff. I know you. You'll always be Soapy to me."

Seized by a perverse wish to rock her world, he had reached under his tiny dinette table and yanked out the Glock revolver he kept taped there. With one swift, sweeping motion of his right arm, he thrust the weapon in her face and cocked the hammer back.

"Don't ever call me that again," he had warned her with just enough menace to convey his seriousness, yet just enough levity to not freak her out completely.

After her eyes had returned to their normal state, he had suggested a ride.

And Vanessa, true to form, had suggested Caltech.

Now, as the school's elegant Spanish archways and manicured lawns swept into view, the temptation before him reared up and overwhelmed his thoughts. For the first time ever, her beauty did nothing for him. Instead, he felt like vomiting from sheer frustration.

What's the matter with you? he thought. *For months you've been planning the killing of thousands, maybe millions. Now you're all queasy over a single one?*

But this wasn't just anyone, he reasoned with himself. It was Vanessa. His first. A girl whose every inch of female form was forever imprinted on his fevered subconscious. A girl, moreover, he'd once thought he loved.

An infidel, argued his sterner Islamic self.

He forced himself to ignore this internal debate and shifted his mind into robot mode. No thinking. Just move forward.

They parked as far away from the lab building as he could and then strode together across the freshly cut grass.

"It's so pretty here," she said, glancing around at the graceful facades and the lushly maintained lawns.

"It should be. Caltech has less then two thousand students, but an endowment of over two billion dollars."

"Whoa. That's two million a student!"

"Yeah," he taunted, shoving her gently. "You figure that all by yourself or have you got a calculator hidden somewhere?"

She laughed. "So, you gonna take me?"

"I did take you. We're here."

"You know what I mean. Your lab space. Where you do your allegedly important work."

"I told you—"

"I know. You'll have to kill me. Well, that's a risk I'll have to take . . . Soapy." She laughed again, and all the half-buried fright and suspicion left her eyes.

How like her, he reminded himself. He'd seen the doubts flicker in and out of her features. Now she'd just put all the bad stuff out of her mind and steeled herself for the next adventure. He'd once loved her all the more for that very quality.

Feeling once more like a man five times his weight, he led her to the Kerckhoff Laboratory of Biological Science, a square stone edifice whose second and third stories of windows were framed by ornately wrought millwork.

He took her hand, led her inside, and steered her through the public areas' thin flow of after-hours student traffic. Finally they came to a discreetly placed door with a narrow blue frame. Reaching up, he placed his palm flat on the frame's surface and held it there while a white light swept across it, illuminating the tips of his fingers in a bright, translucent pink.

"Is that James Bond enough for you?" he asked with a grin.

"No. Not near enough," she said, taking the bait.

"Then look at the screen."

She leaned forward and stared. The small display read, *Level Z—access log erased.*

"Look," he said. "Level Z. You know what comes after Z?"

"Nothing?"

"Exactly. Nothing higher. It means my clearance is so high that as soon as it knows it's me, it erases all signs of my presence. No entry log. All security cameras turn off. No one else allowed inside without equal clearance."

"You mean no one knows we're here?"

"No one. I could do whatever I want."

She flashed him that smile again, only this time a tiny bit less confidently. "Okay, Soapy. I'm impressed now."

They approached a flight of stairs leading downward, the whitest and most immaculate set of stairs Vanessa had ever seen. Almost one hundred steps later, he punched open a side door, only the third they'd encountered, and entered the basement floor.

The room they stepped into was large, anemically lit, and crowded with lab equipment new and old from the floor almost to its nine-foot ceiling.

"Here it is," he said.

She looked around. The fact that they were alone seemed to somehow embolden and subdue her all at once. Her grip on his hand tightened, and she pulled him abruptly to her.

"Okay, so what is it you do in here exactly?"

"I can't say. I'm serious."

"Tell me or I'll scream and make a scene and get you in big trouble."

"Remember, no one can hear us," he warned. "Nobody even knows we're here, or ever would know."

She smiled mischievously. "This doesn't look like the kind of place that would look kindly on its people taking home lab samples to keep in their personal refrigerators. If they were to find out, I wonder how they'd take it. . . ."

He felt the blood leave his face. That was it. The final provocation.

"Okay, I'll tell you," he heard himself say in a strange-sounding voice. "But you're never going to repeat this to anyone. Ever."

"Of course."

"That wasn't a question, Vanessa. It was a statement of fact. See, what we do here is develop the most sensitive nerve gas agents in the world."

"For who?"

"Who do you think? The ACLU?"

She laughed heartily at that.

"So, for Uncle Sam?"

He didn't answer.

"You mean . . . to kill people?"

He smirked. "I know more about how to shut down the human respiratory system than about how to change the oil in my own car."

"You guys don't do those awful experiments on innocent animals, do you?"

He smirked again and opened a side door, nodding. "Come. I'll show you."

She stepped into another large room, its walls lined with cages, most of them occupied by monkeys and small dogs.

"What?" he said. "Did you think we would experiment on *people*?"

"No, although there's some people I would gladly volunteer for something like this, especially over a cute puppy."

He laughed. "Me too, now that I think of it." He led her to a clear enclosure that vaguely resembled a walk-in shower, except for the rubber gaskets sealing its outer edges. "Here's the killing chamber."

Frowning, she asked, "Why is it so big? Do you kill primates too?"

He nodded. "Sometimes. And sometimes . . . I'm not supposed to tell you this." He paused, looked around. "Sometimes we actually do experiment on people."

Her mouth fell open in shock. "No way! You're playing with me."

Remaining poker-faced, he said, "I shouldn't have told you that. Forget I ever said it."

She stared at him as if trying to gauge whether he was being truthful.

"What kind of people?" she asked. "Convicts? Really horrible prisoners?"

"That I can't tell you. Except to say they're certainly not innocent."

"Yes, but what does that mean? I mean, I'm certainly not innocent."

Finally he gave her a playful smile, then gave the chamber door a small shove. It swung open with a barely audible click. "Exactly," he chuckled. "So I guess you better get inside."

He pushed her on the shoulder—just enough to knock her off balance and send her through the open door. It gave way and she tumbled in, nearly falling.

Still smiling, he quickly pulled the door shut behind her. She cursed him, clearly failing to appreciate the stunt. Soon she began yelling and beating her hands on the clear surface, but her voice did not carry through the enclosure.

He shook his head, turned, and flipped a switch on the wall nearby.

". . . me *out* of here!" she said, half shouting, half sobbing.

"But you said you weren't innocent," he teased.

". . . not funny! I'm getting claustrophobic . . . I can't breathe!"

"You shouldn't have looked in my fridge," he said, his voice lowering to a growl. "By doing that, you made yourself my guinea pig."

"Why . . . You're going to kill me?"

"Not me, exactly. Think of it more as Western apostasy killing you, as jihad killing you. You're to be the first of maybe a million people to die from my invention over the next few weeks. Come to think of it, I might name it after you. Kind of an honor, don't you think?"

"Stop messing with me, Soapy!"

He snarled, suddenly launching himself against the plastic enclosure. "Call me Soapy again and I'll experiment with slow doses. A couple molecules at a time. You'll die the most painful death in history, you hear me?"

"Please! It's not funny . . ."

"No, it's not. But it is too late. Not to sound like a comic-book cliché, but you already know too much."

"I don't know anything!" she screamed. "Soapy, what's happened to you?"

"They killed my dad, that's what. They shipped him off to die, for Zionism and Big Oil."

"But that was years ago! Before we even met!"

"When I got here, I started asking questions. I found out why Washington threw away his life. I found the truth."

He walked over to a shelf, took out a dark-colored ampule, and began flicking it with his middle finger.

Something about the way he performed the task seemed to

convince her that he was serious. She slumped against the wall and slid to the floor.

"It's nothing personal," he said. "I needed a human trial, and you just happened to walk into my apartment, without permission if I recall, providing me with one. You've practically begged for it."

"Stop! You're scaring me!"

"That's an unfortunate side effect. Believe me. I have no wish to torment you. Think of this: in less than a minute it'll all be over."

"I'll become a Muslim if you'll just let me out!" she panted. "I'll convert. Just tell me how. . . ."

He chuckled. "Too late for that, Vanessa."

She shouted even louder now, followed by her hyperventilating.

"That's good," he said. "The heightened respiration will jack up your pathways and speed the absorption process. Kill you a little quicker. At least in theory."

He fed the ampule into a custom-designed vaporizer and flicked another switch.

"You're going to be famous. You'll go down as the first victim of the Great American Holocaust. Someday American kids will study you in history class. That is, after their Koran lessons."

"You're crazy . . ." she slurred, eyes partly closed. "There's still time to stop . . . you can stop, and we can just call this a bad joke. . . ."

"Not anymore. I just released the first dose. You should start smelling something like almonds in the next few seconds. Oh, I almost forgot." He snatched up a stopwatch and clicked it.

She bobbed forward, her eyes glazed over in unbearable horror, just as the first convulsion hit. She began inhaling hoarsely, violently shaking.

"I'm sorry," he whispered when she had stopped moving. He clicked the watch again with an exaggerated jerk of his hand and then peered forward, staring at her with his hands on his knees.

He could not stifle a smile. Despite his conflicting emotions, he had just proven the efficacy of the poison. Truly he was every bit the genius his professors had touted him to be.

"Twenty-three seconds!" he said to the body. "On New Year's Day, your fellow victims won't even get that much warning."

CHAPTER 26

The Surveillance House, Fort Huachuca

"What's the status on our unorthodox yet orthodox operation, Captain Kilgore?"

Thomas Little, the deputy assistant secretary for homeland security, chuckled on Delia's high-definition monitor, then swiftly replaced the grin with his usual inscrutable mask.

"All systems positive, Mr. Secretary," she replied. "Our moderator is doing an excellent job of moving the conversion forward and keeping our subject off balance and pliable. He has moved the subject of religion to the forefront no less than seven times, today alone. Both their rapport and their discussions have progressed solidly according to the schedule."

"Frankly, Captain, I'm confused about what timetable you're using. How many more days do you think this process will take to complete?"

"I estimate another three or four days. That's excellent progress by the protocol's timetables."

"Well, that may be, but then we may not have three

or four days left in the National Security scenario. Furthermore, I seriously doubt that Washington's patience for this idea is going to last that long. Is there any way to speed things up?"

"I suppose so, yes. A specific step can be taken to accelerate the process. It comes at a great price to the results' reliability, but—"

"I suggest you take that step, Captain Kilgore," interrupted Secretary Little. "And I urge you to keep additional steps in mind as well. The clock is ticking, you recall."

"Yes, I recall," she said while keeping her professional smile intact. *What a jerk . . .*

The National Mall, Washington, D.C.

It was a rare balmy day for so late in the year, bright with atypical late-autumn weather. Mild temperatures and clear skies had brought hundreds of Washingtonians out to practically swarm the National Mall. At midday the nearly two-mile stretch was choked with joggers, tourists, and simple working people out for a breath of fresh air.

Among other things, it was the perfect day and the perfect place for a covert conversation. No chance of bugs, little chance of being overheard, and plenty of exit routes should the meeting go south.

The CIA agent arrived in the guise of a tired jogger who had just reached the end of his run. Approaching a hot-dog stand on the sidewalk adjoining the Federal Reserve headquarters, the agent paused, bouncing as he stretched back on his left leg in an improvised hurdler's stretch. To gain balance, he leaned forward and caught himself on a nearby park bench.

There, in a seeming coincidence, sat Nathan Terrell, chief national security correspondent for the *New York Times*.

"Is that you, King?" the journalist asked, too wary to look over his shoulder.

"It is. You wanna walk while I recover?"

The newspaperman did not answer, but stood and followed him toward the nearby Vietnam Memorial.

"You can attribute this to an unnamed source in the intelligence community," the CIA agent offered with the efficiency of an experienced leaker. "You'll be met with a full denial from the White House, of course, but at least you can satisfy your bosses that due diligence was done."

"I'll buy that."

"Yeah, you will. This is the story of the decade."

"Sure. That's what they all say. Prove it."

"First of all, the rumors you've been hearing overseas are true. Special ops seized Omar Nirubi three weeks ago."

"Why wouldn't the administration want to shout that from the rooftops?"

"Because this sort of thing is complicated. You know that. Following capture, he was transported someplace safe."

"You mean *renditioned*?"

"I mean transported."

"Suit yourself. That's your whole story?"

"No. It's just the beginning. Here's the meat. Because of an urgent national security mandate to debrief him completely, the army has opted for a bizarre form of interrogation. More like a mind flush. Something sanctioned by neither the Geneva Convention, the UN, international law, nor the U.S. Constitution."

"Some kind of torture?"

"Not quite. More like a systematic attempt to brainwash him into abandoning his Islamic faith and converting to Christianity."

There was a pause. To any onlooker, it would have seemed

Terrell was somberly pondering the flat black surface of the Vietnam Memorial. In reality he was trying to process the dozens of
questions swirling around in his head.

"But . . . why would we do that?"

"To remove the primary source of his resistance to interrogation."

"This has been given the go-ahead by the National Command
Authority?" Terrell asked, whispering now.

"Let's just say it's a subject of great controversy throughout
the Pentagon and the national security establishment. Many
officials have strongly opposed this experiment from the start.
Still, it was agreed on at the highest levels."

"The president has officially approved it?"

"Not officially. His plausible deniability has been preserved.
That's why we're meeting like this. But he gave a preliminary
thumbs-up."

"You realize I'm going to have to confirm anything I write with
at least one other source. Maybe two, given this bombshell."

"I know. That's why we wanted to give you a heads-up. Pry
your sources, and this story will fall out like cockroaches from a
rotted ceiling. It won't take that much effort, either."

"And what's this national security mandate?"

Nathan Terrell turned, but the CIA man was gone, jogging
casually toward the Lincoln Memorial.

CHAPTER 27

Respite House, Fort Huachuca

Evening had arrived, a light soup and sandwich dinner had long been eaten, and the two men had retired for the night, exhausted. Greg had drifted off while pleading with God to help him to somehow break through the wall of resistance surrounding this man he'd been called to reach. Finally, after forty-five minutes of pleading, he awoke with a jolt of fear. His muscles instantly flexed for a fight, jerking him upright in the bed.

A perfectly still, gray silhouette faced him in the gloom.

"Mr. Cahill," came a low masculine voice. "You need to come with us. Quietly."

Greg focused his eyes and realized the man was wearing camouflage and holding some kind of pistol in his hand.

He rose shakily, rubbed his eyes and yawned. "Can I have a minute to get ready, throw on some clothes?"

"Just a minute, sir."

He pulled on a pair of jeans and a T-shirt, fumbled through lacing up his sneakers, then followed the soldier on tiptoe through the dark house. Following what Greg noticed was a route farthest from Nirubi's room, they left the house, climbed into a Humvee, and drove for several minutes across the base. They stopped in front of a three-story house and hurried inside.

It took about ten minutes and four ID verifications, ranging from electronic badge at the outermost to a retinal scan before the final barrier, to reach their ultimate destination. Greg looked around the room and reared back in surprise. What awaited him was a full-scale electronics command center, with multiple wires crisscrossing the floor, monitors of every shape and size filling the space, and technicians wearing headphones and earpieces, all of them talking at once.

Greg shook his head in amazement. He knew they were being closely watched, but he had no idea of the technology involved.

Delia Kilgore walked up to him, her hand extended.

"Sorry to wake you from a deep sleep, Greg," she said.

"How do you know how deep I'm sleeping?" he said. "Or shouldn't I ask?"

"You shouldn't," she answered with an indulgent smile. "If you asked, I could give you a reading on the volume of your snoring during REM sleep, down to four places past the decimal point."

A male technician wheeled back from his screen, hitched up his headphones, and faced Greg, snickering. "No kidding. We're got more electronic surveillance on your house than I've ever seen in my career. That's no exaggeration about the mikes. Plus cameras covering every inch of the real estate. We have filament sensors in the flooring that tell us if one of you so much as goes to the john. Even weight readings and length-of-stride measurements to identify exactly which one of you is walking. They're so sensitive that when you're through in there, I could tell by your weight loss whether you went number one or number two."

Greg broke into laughter. "You think maybe that falls under the realm of too much information?"

"Yeah, don't tell the ACLU," the man chuckled. "They'll have a Bodily Function Privacy Act in front of Congress by day's end."

"Seriously though," said Delia, "it's the only way we could justify having the world's most wanted terrorist walk around in anything less than leg irons. The situation demands that much security. Outside, we've got snipers covering every angle of the exterior. Inside, if he ever attacked you, we'd have gas and non-lethal weapons deployed in under two seconds. Armed response within five."

"I suppose that's comforting," Greg said.

Delia stared at him. "You're alive, aren't you?"

He shrugged. It was hard to top that argument.

"Follow me, please," she said.

Captain Kilgore led him deeper into the house, opening the door to what had clearly been a grand dining salon. It was now a functional conference room. Two men in uniform awaited them, seated at the table's far end. They nodded glumly at Greg's entrance.

"Greg, there's something more about this operation I need to tell you," Delia said.

Greg nodded. "You mean all this time, I wasn't being told everything. Man, what a surprise."

"Right. Well, I'm glad we're not bursting your bubble. Here's the scoop, Greg. Something else has come to light, something we became aware of as a result of the raid to capture Omar Nirubi."

She glanced at the other men in the room as though the

decision to tell Greg was not yet final. Receiving no signals from the operatives, she forged ahead.

"That New Year's threat Nirubi mentioned just became relevant. New word is, there's going to be a massive attack on the United States. Soon. New Year's Day, to be exact. It's being organized and carried out by al-Qaeda."

One of the men turned and met his eye. "All we know at this point is that it's some sort of nerve-gas attack. We don't know where in the U.S. it will strike, what delivery mechanism it will use, or what kind of team is carrying it out."

"You see, Greg," Delia continued, "in spite of the biggest intelligence-gathering campaign in American history, every attempt to gain more intel on the plot has failed. Our human assets have gone silent. Our foreign targets have stopped emailing each other. Everyone's talking about this plot, but nobody is sharing details."

"Somehow it feels like this is coming around to *me*," Greg said.

"That's absolutely right," said Delia. "It's come down to this. You and this road you're on with Nirubi are, at the moment anyway, our only hope of stopping the plot in time."

"No way," Greg said, shaking his head emphatically. "You can't lay something like that on me."

"I'm sorry. We have no other choice."

"Then I quit. I came here to share my faith with Mr. Nirubi, and to try to convince him to accept the president's offer of clemency—not to have the fate of the country dumped on my shoulders!"

"Your resignation is not accepted," she said flatly. "And quite frankly, Mr. Cahill, I'm disappointed. I took you for more of a patriot than that. Look, we're not asking you to do anything other than what you've been doing all along. Only now to continue with a greater sense of urgency."

"You've known about the urgency of this threat for a while, haven't you?"

"Yes, but we weren't so desperate until this morning. Now there's no choice. You must succeed, and soon, because many leaders are opposed to this new approach of the president's, along with his hiding Nirubi's capture."

Greg shook his head as this new reality sank in. "You guys haven't been honest with me. Nirubi's knowing more than I do has seriously undermined my ability to come off with any authority."

"I don't agree. It reinforced for him that no matter what he thinks of Uncle Sam, you as an individual are a straight shooter, someone without an agenda."

"A straight shooter who has been kept out of the loop. Who doesn't know the facts. Besides, I *do* have an agenda. I want him to accept the offer. More than that, I want to lead him to salvation in Christ."

"That's still priority one."

"No it's not!" he shouted, suddenly enraged. "Stop lying to me! Your agenda is national security. You've played me for a pawn. I lay aside a lifetime of grievances, lies and betrayals, my whole life's destruction even, all to help my country. And still you managed to use me."

"That's not true," Delia countered. "Nothing about the offer would have worked if you'd been an operative fully briefed on what was at stake. You had to have another motive, one that was sincere and idealistic. That was our only chance of success."

He took a deep breath and closed his eyes. "Fine. I see what you're saying," Greg grudgingly conceded.

"Please," she insisted, "we need you more engaged, more

onboard than ever before, to crack this guy's defenses before thousands of people get killed."

"What if he brings it up to me? Do I acknowledge that I know about the plot?"

"Yes. Continue being transparent at all costs. You know about it, but that has nothing to do with why you're here with him."

"Does it play a part in the president's motives for making the clemency offer?"

The nearest operative spoke up. "Under no circumstances are you to speculate about the president's motives. However, you can offer a personal observation that under our new policy toward terrorism, transparency and candor will be the order of the day."

"Speaking of candor, is there anything else you're not telling me?"

Delia smiled. "Oh, Greg, you know there's always some wrinkle being hidden from somebody. Hidden from me just as well as from you. But nothing of real importance. The only truly significant fact is that time is short. Whatever overtures we're going to make for him to accept the offer, we have to make soon. The longer we take, the less time we have to save the lives of thousands, perhaps millions of innocent Americans."

"Millions?" Greg asked.

"Depending on where it strikes."

Greg thought of Donna and Robby, and felt his insides turn to ice.

"All right. I'll see this thing through. But don't ever lie to me again."

"I promise," she said.

CHAPTER 28

Greg awoke once again to the sound of Nirubi offering his prayers in the front parlor. He glanced at the alarm clock: 5:15 a.m.

He showered and dressed for the day, then walked out to join his guest in the kitchen area. There, a large breakfast platter sat on the counter, covered with fruit, nut bread, croissants, and a variety of cereals in bowls.

"Morning," Greg said.

"Good morning," said Nirubi in a clipped voice. "Listen. I do not wish to waste a moment today. I want to hold my son as soon as possible. I want to take the next step."

"The next step toward . . . the president's offer?"

"Yes. The forgiveness offer, as you put it."

Amazing how quickly things can turn, Greg thought with a weak smile. Obviously the surfacing of Nirubi's son had made a great impact on the situation. As well it should, he reminded himself. Nothing cuts deeper than parental love.

Then he remembered. Nirubi might dearly love his own son, but was he still willing to kill Robby or thousands of other American sons to advance his goals? He recalled the old cliché that even Hitler was kind to his dogs, and even the Auschwitz Kommandant had children waiting for him at home.

"I would offer to get the papers for you," Greg said, "but we both know how many people are privy to every word we speak. I would bet that before—"

"Gentlemen," interrupted Delia, out of breath from exertion.

"—a minute has passed, someone will bring them to us," he finished with a knowing grin. "What is it, Captain Kilgore?"

"This," she said, already placing on the dining room table a set of documents and pulling out a fountain pen. She held the pen out for Nirubi to use. "If you'll sign this first page with your complete signature, we can just initial the subsequent pages."

Nirubi drew back, his eyes darting across the room, assessing what was taking place. His gaze landed on Greg, taking in his conflicted body language.

"Please leave the pen there," Nirubi said. "I will sign in due time. But first, I have some things to discuss with Mr. Cahill."

Delia stopped and looked up, her eyebrows raised, the pen still in her hand, suspended in the space between herself and Nirubi. Finally she withdrew in a frustrated manner. "Okay then," she said, dropping the pen onto the table. "I'll leave you to it." With that, she swiftly exited.

"What is it?" Greg asked him.

"This seems too easy, somehow. I want to hear you swear upon your life, and the lives of your family, that this offer is no trick."

Greg started to speak, but then thought back to Delia's revelations the night before. Especially their final exchange and her tacit admission that led Greg to believe there could be more in the offer's fine print that he wasn't being told about.

"I swear," he said after chasing these thoughts from his mind.

But the damage was done. Nirubi's face underwent a sudden transformation, twisting from open and seeking to a dark and suspicious demeanor.

"You are lying," said Nirubi. "The honesty I usually see in your eyes is not there."

Greg sighed. "The offer is real," he said. "Yes, I'm conflicted about many things. You've picked that up early enough. But it has nothing to do with the clemency terms. And I do swear on the life of my—"

Greg reached the word *wife* and found his throat constricted. He tried to unblock his speech, but some unseen force would not let him continue.

"It is true—you struggle with more than one conflict."

"Yeah, I'm a conflicted man," he answered with a glib smile.

But Nirubi was in no mood for levity. "So you say. And still this whole thing rings false. It is too easy. I simply reach out for forgiveness, accept it, and it is done?"

"Yes, but remember what I've told you. The forgiveness may be free, but it's come at a very high price. For both you and for us. It's like I told you before about accepting and following Jesus Christ. His forgiveness may be free for the asking, but that's only because He paid the ultimate price for it."

Nirubi dismissed the argument with a wave of his hand. "But what about your story? I did not hear much of forgiveness there."

"Quite the opposite. Christ has forgiven me everything—"

"Stop it with the Jesus talk," Nirubi interrupted. "I am talking about you. Greg Cahill, the human being. All that divine forgiveness has not helped you find any peace. You should have seen your eyes when you told me your story."

"You're right. It's still very raw to me. Maybe I find it easier to share forgiveness with others than with myself."

"Then it is meaningless!" shouted Nirubi. "You are so willing to give out this love and forgiveness to others, but why can you not accept it for yourself? How can it be true if you are the one person in your world who does not get it?"

After those last words, Nirubi did something shocking. He spun around to Greg and shoved him hard against the chest.

Fort Huachuca Command Post—that moment

Nearly two dozen people—clustered around plasma monitors inside the Fort Huachuca Command Post—recoiled in unison at the landing of Nirubi's blow.

The lieutenant colonel in charge of operational security jerked his neck toward Delia. "Should we intervene, Captain?"

She gritted her teeth, then shook her head. "Not yet," she replied. "But have your men ready at a second's notice."

On-screen, Greg looked like he was about to burst into tears, or tear off Nirubi's head, or both at once.

"Come on!" Nirubi shouted. "Have the strength of your own beliefs! How can you possibly ask me to give up my life for forgiveness when you are not willing to give up your own miserable existence for the same thing?"

Greg now looked stunned, standing utterly still with a dazed look on his face.

Nirubi struck Greg again, even more powerfully. Greg stumbled backward and almost fell over. "Show me what you say is true! Why has it taken you so long to accept this forgiveness, while you expect me to embrace it in a day or two?"

"I don't know!" Greg shouted back. "Because there were consequences! Because people got killed! Children got blown apart! Because people I love got hurt!"

"Oh, please," Nirubi said, now strutting in circles around Greg. "You do not expect me to swallow that pathetic reasoning."

Now behind Greg, Nirubi gave him another shove, this time in the back.

"I haven't gotten over it," explained Greg, "because those actions ruined my life. I paid a high price for learning those lessons, so I need for them to matter."

"What? So you think these events did not matter because they were soon forgiven? Is that the kind of drivel you are asking me to accept? That forgiveness makes the loss trivial? Then forget it! I reject it, and you, completely."

Nirubi then delivered what looked like his most painful blow, a slap across Greg's face. Still wearing the same dazed expression, Greg took the hit like someone receiving a long overdue punishment and then crumpled to the floor.

The camera operator turned the lens downward, zooming in on Greg's face. The heaving of his chest and clenching of his neck muscles did not lie. The man was sobbing.

Finally, after several moments, Greg got up off the floor and turned with an intense gaze directed straight at Nirubi.

"All right," he said. "You made your point. Let's find forgiveness together."

"Fine," said Nirubi. "Where do we start?"

"Right now. Right here. I've just forgiven myself."

"Just like that?" Nirubi asked, incredulous. "That quickly? That easily?"

"No, not just like that. Like we always said, it's a process, a journey. But the first step is the most important one in any long trip. The hardest."

He reached out with a lightning-quick gesture aimed at Nirubi's collarbone. The watchers recoiled again, expecting another round of bewildering roughness. But rather than striking the man, Greg grasped Nirubi's shoulder in a friendly manner.

"Let's you and I find forgiveness," he said. "Together."

Captain Kilgore looked around at the tightly gathered group of uniformed men and shook her head. Laughing, she said, "Well, gentlemen, I think we've got our breakthrough."

CHAPTER 29

"It's your turn now," Greg said, smiling. "If I recall, this whole thing started with you turning away and leaving on the table the most historic offer of forgiveness in the last hundred or so years."

"Yes, and the fact that I do not quite believe it."

"As you just demonstrated," Greg continued, "the burden of making such an incredible offer believable falls not on the one making it, but on the one receiving it. Accepting it takes more courage and humility than most people possess. That applies to you too. Men have died to give our president the leverage to make this offer—freely or not. The question is whether you can bring yourself to accept it."

"I am sorry," Nirubi said. "I am a very instinctual man. I operate on what you call the 'gut level' more than anyone I know. And this still does not sit right. Until it does, I cannot accept it."

"What would you give to understand it?"

"Right now, almost anything."

"I guarantee you one thing," said Greg. "If you accepted the one offer that's greater than this one, the greatest of all offers, you'd be able to understand. You'd understand . . . instinctively."

Nirubi turned to him with a wary look. "Knowing you, it must be something about Jesus Christ."

"That's right. And why shouldn't it be? You're a Muslim; you claim to follow Jesus of Nazareth just as I do. But if you claim to truly revere Him, you can't just ignore His words. He said that if you put your trust in Him, He'd wipe out your sins, your guilt, your evil deeds. They'd be gone forever. Not just sitting in some huge pile that waits until your dying day to be counted against your eternal fate. That's what He said, and no follower of His can dismiss that part of His message. You dismiss that, you dismiss Him completely."

"You forget who you are talking to," Nirubi said, the volume and pitch of his voice rising. "Do you really expect the leader of al-Qaeda to suddenly become an apostate, the most pathetic of human beings, a convert with no rights, subject to being legally beheaded under Shariah law? An outcast among the people who once adored him?"

"Yes, I do," Greg responded. "I expect you to lead the way for your people, into a place none of them knew existed."

"You are crazy!"

"Remember, you're not making such a leap from the foundations of Islam. We both claim, at least, to worship the God of Abraham, right? So we share a similar history. Doesn't the Koran affirm that the gospel is from God? And doesn't each of us hold up Jesus Christ as a divine gift?"

"Yes, but the God you talk about is not my God! I do not recognize this God of forgiveness, and His wanting to journey with me through life. I know about righteousness and justice and revenge. I know the God who will avenge every betrayal I have ever suffered—from the Maronite pigs who massacred my kin to the

Zionist dogs who stood by and let it happen and exiled my family to a life of poverty, to the rich American demons who manipulate the world and claim moral superiority over everyone else, to the weak-willed half Muslim, moderate infidels, so-called brothers in arms who betrayed me. Allah knows the wrongs I have suffered, and he will give me strength to avenge every one of them!"

"What about mercy?" Greg asked. "If you remember, that's where we started. Allah is merciful, yet I don't hear any of that just now."

"Perhaps someday," said Nirubi. "I have not yet lived that kind of life. Perhaps someday there will be the chance of mercy."

"Maybe *someday* is today."

Looking down, Nirubi shook his head.

"No. It is too much," he said, his voice suddenly soft and plaintive. "I cannot convert to Christianity, and accept clemency from my sworn enemy, all in the same day. It is too far to go for one day."

"But think of how far you've come already," Greg implored. "You're already so far from the man taken from that rooftop in Pakistan. You've told me about how the hole changed you, how the time in interrogation gave you a sense of distance from who you used to be. And now you're cut off forever from your own following—not because of America but because of your brothers' murderous betrayal. You've tasted mercy—from our president, but most importantly in the sight of God and also His angels.

"I'll tell you what," Greg continued, "don't put a label on it. Don't call it Christian or Muslim or apostate or anything. Just call it mercy. You've never known the mercy that's supposed to lie at the cornerstone of your faith and now you're tasting it for the first time. Just accept the offer, and see where it leads you."

Nirubi looked up, stared at the ceiling, and a few seconds later closed his eyes.

"Remember what you felt when you looked out that window and saw *them*," Greg added. "Angels from heaven. Did you feel anger? Hatred? Revenge? Or unconditional love, touching you like a warm wind?"

Opening his eyes, Nirubi said softly, almost inaudibly, "All right."

"What did you say?"

"All right," repeated Nirubi with a smile. He turned to face Greg squarely. "I accept. Is that all there is to it?"

Too stunned to think clearly, Greg muttered, "Well . . . many people make more of a statement out of it, but that doesn't mean . . . I don't suppose you'd want to form it into a prayer, to tell Him you accept—"

"Can I say it in my own form of prayers?"

"You mean . . . ?"

"The *adhan*. The prayers I have said since I was a boy."

Greg froze in thought. Indeed, it seemed odd to encourage a man converting to Christianity to do so from the face-first posture of an Islamic prayer.

But was it heresy? He thought of what the Scriptures taught on salvation, trying hard to remember the words.

"A broken and contrite heart, O God, you will not despise . . ."

"And what does the Lord require of you? To act justly and to love mercy and to walk humbly with your God . . ."

". . . that whoever believes in him shall not perish but have eternal life."

Nothing of what he recalled concerned exact body posture or the phrasing of prayers. It was all about the posture of the heart, of childlike belief.

"Yes," he heard himself say. "Of course you can say it in your own form of prayers. It's the humility of your heart and your desire for mercy that God is looking for."

Nirubi stared at him, and two things occurred to Greg at that moment. First, that tears were beginning to stream down the man's face. And second, that he was genuinely stunned at the answer Greg had given him.

Greg watched as the Arab sank to his knees and adopted the familiar posture of supplication, touching his forehead to the ground. *Can this really be happening?* asked a skeptical voice inside his head.

"Dear God, I accept your offer of forgiveness through Jesus," he heard Nirubi pray. "Please forgive me of my sins and lead me further into the truth."

Greg knelt down beside his new brother and friend, silently thanking God for this day, this miracle.

CHAPTER 30

Fort Huachuca Command Post

In the command post, the news traveled—just as every twist in this bizarre operation had traveled—at the speed of light. Those of the U.S. intelligence community who had been monitoring the two men's conversation were thunderstruck by what they'd witnessed. All of them were rendered speechless, except for the odd, usually profane exclamation of amazement.

Finally, once the initial shock had passed, the expert voices began to clamor again.

Bedlam erupted as Captain Kilgore punched the air with a victorious "Yes!" nearly striking a nearby colonel in the mid-section. She glanced around to see upheld palms awaiting her high five, then spent the next minute swatting down every one of them.

She'd done it. The whole dim-witted notion had worked, she told herself as wave after wave of sweet relief washed over her. She felt her muscles relax, her spine straighten, and the almost palpable sense of a heavy weight fall from her shoulders. Only then did she realize just how much stress she'd been carrying for the last several days.

And why not? She reminded herself that entire departments of the federal government had been peering over her shoulder, breathlessly waiting for her to make the smallest mistake or miscalculation. That, and the fate of thousands, maybe millions, of her fellow citizens hanging in the balance.

Now all the sideline skeptics watching so closely had been treated with her utter vindication. A complete triumph.

Or at least complete for this stage of the game.

It remained to be seen whether Omar Nirubi's conversion would lead him to give up the New Year's Day plot.

White House Situation Room

In the subterranean gloom of the Situation Room, Deputy Advisers King and Little stood side by side before a direct feed and shared somber looks. Neither one had seriously considered the chance that this ridiculous attempt would ever make it this far.

"Unbelievable," whispered King. "Do you think he's faking it?"

Little shook his head. "As much as I don't want to admit it, it doesn't seem that way. Of course, I'd love to see a full biometrics workup on him."

King nodded. They both knew that in several intelligence agencies, biometric analysts would be poring over footage of the event to examine every detail of Nirubi's incredible concession. Shifts in body language, signs of sweating, the speed and angle of head motion, changes in the direction or speed of his focus and size of his irises. But most of all, the stress patterns in his voice that might indicate deception.

Given that the video was high-definition, more sophisticated machines might be undertaking other tests, such as zeroing in on the surface of his skin or the capillaries of his eyes to detect a pulse as well as any sudden variations in its rate.

Longtime operational men like Little, however, who had put in their time in military intelligence, would argue the value of old-fashioned human instincts. And those instincts told him that the Arab's emotions had been genuine. Whatever happened, whether he had truly converted or not—for what was conversion, anyway?—the emotions that had led to the man's prayer had struck Little as unforced and sincere.

Before he had the chance to answer, King's phone vibrated in his pocket. He checked it and then flashed Little another knowing look.

"José wants to talk," he said with a smirk.

Union Station, Washington, D.C.

The CIA Clandestine Service chief met with King and Little at a bench inside the colossal lobby of Union Station, Washington's largest and busiest transit center. Most of the people milling around the trio were forced to speak just below a shout so as to be heard above the roar of thousands of their neighbors echoing across the marble. This made the voice of Matthew Snipes not only harder to hear but safer to listen to.

"The word is out. Don't ask me who leaked it, because I don't know yet. When I do find out, that person will wish he'd never been born. Anyway, we're monitoring a half-dozen newspapers currently rushing around trying to corroborate an exposé on Project Forgiven. Not just the op itself, but Nirubi's capture and his role in the whole thing. The story will be public within days— that is, unless you guys can figure out how to plug it up. And by that I mean the whole stinking thing. Because if you don't, the New Year's plot story will be next. And if that monster gets out, we'll have wholesale civil unrest, coast-to-coast."

"José, do you really care if Nirubi gives up the intel?" asked King.

"Of course!" he snapped. "Don't you ever question my patriotism. It goes without saying that I want to put an end to this plot. But whether he gives up the intel or not, the outcome for him and the op's managers remains the same. You have to go maximum containment." José stopped, leaned in closer to the two men. "Do you understand me?"

Both of them nodded, and immediately King regretted it, for he got the strange feeling they were now taking orders from José. And here they were with the White House, for goodness' sake. The administration didn't take orders from the CIA. For some reason, José had the cart way out before the horse.

"I hear you," King said, yet he wanted clarification. "You're recommending *maximum containment*."

Which in the black ops vernacular meant that no one got out alive. All signs, all traces of an operation's incriminating roster disappeared forever.

"Affirmative," said José. "See that it's carried out."

CHAPTER 31

Respite House, Fort Huachuca—3 days before the attack

The document detailing the agreement lay unsigned on the dining room table, exactly where Captain Kilgore had left it, along with her pen.

To Greg, and to everyone else watching on video, the document seemed to dominate the house like the proverbial elephant in the room. Everyone wanted to take the next step as soon as possible, but no one wanted to ruin the chance by rushing things. Nirubi's signing the clemency agreement, while also giving up the operational plans of al-Qaeda, had to come across as an unforced consequence of his conversion to the Christian faith and the new worldview that, hopefully, accompanied it. Otherwise the whole operation would be for nothing.

In the hours following Nirubi's prayer, Greg had felt completely inadequate. He had treated Nirubi with the delicacy of a highly sensitive houseguest, someone who might crumple to pieces if mishandled. After rising from their prayers, Greg gave him an awkward hug and welcomed him as a brother in Christ. Nirubi seemed dazed, blinking and standing unsteadily. Greg felt compelled to warn him that while some people experienced wondrous and supernatural things upon their acceptance of Christ, most did not. And that was all right. Following Jesus wasn't about spiritual fireworks, although that was never out of the question.

Greg handed Nirubi a copy of the New Testament, reminding him again that the Koran held it up as God-given. Nirubi had received the gift with a still-shaken demeanor and promptly began reading it, taking a chair by the window.

The next morning Greg arose to find the document still unsigned on the table, with Nirubi asleep in that same chair, his New Testament open in his lap to the book of John. Moving quietly, Greg took a seat in a chair opposite Nirubi, closing his eyes to pray.

Moments later, he felt Nirubi's stare even before realizing that his companion was now awake.

"Good morning," Greg said.

Nirubi smiled and gave a little nod.

"I see you did a lot of reading during the night."

"Yes," Nirubi replied, yawning.

"I want you to know that what you did yesterday was the most important act you'll ever perform. However, our hosts are anxious to find out if it has shed some light on your understanding of the clemency agreement."

"The clock is still ticking toward New Year's Day," Nirubi said. "I understand. I did not suddenly lose all my common sense, you know."

Greg chuckled at that. "No, no one expected that to happen. Least of all me."

Taking a deep breath, Nirubi set the New Testament on a side table and then stood.

"As much as I hate to succumb to everyone's wishes," he said, "I must admit that in light of my decision to accept Christ's forgiveness, I now see other things differently as well. After my reading last night, I think I understand the power of grace and atonement somewhat better."

He walked over to the dining room table, picked up the pen still waiting for him, and signed with a flourish. He turned to a corner of the room and held out his arms in a grandiose posture. "To our friends watching by way of video," Nirubi said loudly, "I accept the clemency of the president of the United States. And I look forward to being reunited very soon with my son."

Then came the sound of someone clearing his throat. Both men turned to see a trio of orderlies holding up large, steaming platters of food. Greg carefully gathered up the document to make way for plates of eggs, potatoes, and pancakes.

Greg smiled. A good old-fashioned, all-American Sunday breakfast. Someone had not missed the irony. He tried to imagine the logistics required to prepare such a meal and transport it all over here and within minutes of its readiness. Somehow the thought impressed him even more than the intricate arranging of people and aircraft that had brought him to Arizona.

They both sat down, famished as it happened, and their devouring of the American food gave Greg a perfect opportunity to introduce Nirubi to life in the West. The topic struck him as appropriate as it subtly reinforced the full meaning of Nirubi's choice. The man had done more than repudiate terrorism or the jihadist creed. He had also just cast his lot with America herself. Talking about the Southern tradition of frying eggs—and of frying nearly every other food that could be placed in a skillet—Greg was welcoming Omar Nirubi to a whole new culture.

Then, about halfway through their meal, Greg decided to make his abrupt transition.

"Do you feel like talking to me about New Year's Day?" he asked, his voice higher and more tentative than he would have wished.

Nirubi raised his head and fixed Greg with a surprised look over a forkful of eggs held before his mouth. Lowering the fork, he dabbed his lips with a napkin and nodded.

"I wondered how long you would take," he said. "Actually, it took great self-restraint on your part. Almost twelve hours you waited. But tell me the truth, is this the reason for all of it? Hosting me here, the talk of clemency, the talk of Jesus—was this all a tactic? All to reach this moment, and then get me to talk?"

Greg felt something like lead tug at his stomach. How quickly things could turn, he reminded himself. He had to handle this correctly or else everything—no matter how many milestones they'd just crossed—could all go up in smoke.

Leaning toward Nirubi, he said, "Please believe me, Omar. I was never instructed to bring my faith into this. I was asked to do it because it's who I am, and I was told that was fine. Remember what you've told me about sensing my sincerity and truthfulness. The New Year's Day plot is very important in the here and now. But what you did yesterday, that's for all eternity."

"I was only asking," said Nirubi, "because it all seemed so logical, so neatly lined up in front of me—everything, one after the other, boom boom boom."

"It's more of a coincidence," Greg assured him. "Although yes, we're hoping you'll disclose the New Year's Day details as an outgrowth of a reborn conscience perhaps. You've just repudiated violence, so why not take action to prevent this attack? A display of good faith?"

"Excuse me, gentlemen."

Surprised, Greg looked up. There, standing at the entrance to the kitchen, stood Delia. "Captain Kilgore, hello . . ."

"I hope I didn't startle you, but we have no time to lose if we're to stop this thing. So we might as well—"

Nirubi stood and turned toward her. "Yes, but a personal appearance, Captain Kilgore? Are the hidden microphones not working so well this morning?"

Her face darkened at Nirubi's jab. "I thought it might be jarring to hold a conversation with a voice coming from the ceiling. So I came to you."

"New Year's Day," began Nirubi abruptly, not bothering with preliminaries, "will be carried out using the world's newest and deadliest nerve agent. One so concentrated and powerful that a tall glass of the stuff, if properly aerated and released, could wipe out all of Los Angeles. Only in this case, if my memory serves me correctly, the city in question will be Miami. Your intelligence people probably know as well as I do that we deliberately operate a decentralized, loose-knit organizational structure. So I do not know everything. But I do know the Miami cell is responsible, and they plan to deploy this thing during something called the Sugar Bowl. I remember because when I first heard about it, I had to be told the meaning of it. It sounded like someone was going to pour nerve gas into a spice shaker or something."

Delia looked taken aback, her mouth half open. After a brief pause, she said, "Thank you, Mr. Nirubi. That's very helpful. But can you give us any details about the men's identities? Anything at all?"

"I know that the group is on your radar, because one of them was interrogated once by your Homeland Security people. The leader is a young man named Jamal. I believe he works in the computer field. Trained in India." He shrugged. "That is all I know."

Captain Kilgore couldn't help glancing up at the room's concealed camera. "Thanks again. I'm sure that will be enough for us to act on," she said, her smile of triumph hidden beneath a mask of tense facial muscles.

CHAPTER 32

Before Delia had taken her leave and walked out of the house, already intelligence techs hundreds of miles away were busy checking out the latest intel and had narrowed the Miami cell leader's identity down to a single name.

Without necessarily intending to, Nirubi had given them perfect search parameters for the profile of the American government's database.

Knowing that one in the group had been interrogated by Homeland Security reduced their search to within 173 encounters in the Miami-Dade vicinity. Being from India, as well as a member of a suspect group, narrowed it down to 24.

In what was left, the name Jamal turned out to be a dead ringer—unusual enough to offer up the full name of one Jamal Kaljir, with an address in Miami's Little Haiti neighborhood.

A series of keystrokes punched into a Langley computer instantly beamed the information into geo-synchronous orbit over the North American landmass, where a U.S. spy satellite nudged slightly and began zeroing in over the Magic City, burrowing through block-sized swaths of urban imagery.

Three seconds later it had beamed back down to

waiting task forces a crystal clear, up-to-the-minute aerial photograph of a ramshackle three-story apartment building.

Miami, Florida—one hour later

Officially it was the dead of winter in south Florida. Although the term didn't imply the same level of cold and bitter forecasts that often occurred in northern regions of the country, it did bring with it decidedly cooler and stormier weather.

On this particular day, a wave of thunderheads had swept in over Miami's Little Haiti neighborhood, bringing with them not only rain but strong winds with an unusually chilly bite.

As a result, the exuberant local population, which on an average day might have been out on the streets in droves, now huddled indoors. And the low rumbling of helicopters, which might have typically drawn all eyes skyward, now blended perfectly with the rolling basso profundo of distant thunder.

And so most citizens missed the first sign of the raid completely, until the four Black Hawks flying "nap of the earth"— racing at three hundred feet over the city, shattering federal and local noise regulations—banked sharply, right over their heads.

The Spectre gunship that lumbered overhead, moving above Little Haiti in wide, lazy circles, represented an extraordinary invasion of airspace. Fighters and transports from nearby bases often crossed the horizon, but rarely this close. Frantic calls from air traffic controllers at Miami International went unheeded, even though the gunship's circling pattern brought it dangerously close to the airport's busiest approach lanes.

But nobody in charge seemed to care.

And nobody on land seemed to notice the small black cylinder protruding from the aircraft's front fuselage—a six-barreled rotary cannon that turned an ordinary cargo plane into the world's deadliest gunship. If pressed into action, these whistling barrels could, in less than a minute, kill every person within a three-mile radius, whether hiding indoors or not.

The ground assault had already raced past in half a dozen black Humvees, red lights blazing from their rooftops as they flew through intersections electronically switched to give them all green lights.

Nobody seemed to care, or to know, but the appearance of apathy was of course an illusion. The local FBI office, which held jurisdiction over domestic terrorism issues, was coordinating with every other arm of the Homeland Security umbrella to keep a close eye over the city.

For that very reason, the special agents were watching their own aircraft, and not the skies, when the intruder arrived in the raid's midst.

It was a news chopper, garishly painted with its station call letters, somehow already airborne when the raid had begun. Attack parameters had called for complete radio silence in a media-saturated city like Miami, but the helicopter had over-come that precaution. It enjoyed the advantage of already being in flight, in the right place at the wrong time, when everything went down.

All over Miami, viewers of a nationally televised football game were startled to see their gridiron disappear, replaced by the famil-iar *Breaking News* screen, followed by the grainy, jumping image of a frantic reporter shouting into his microphone.

"All residents of Little Haiti should stay indoors and seek cover," the man panted, as though he'd just run a mile to reach the camera, "as a large-scale raid seems to be under way there. And by raid, I don't mean the kind of SWAT team, local police force operation. I'm talking about armed forces aircraft, both fixed and rotor wing. . . ."

Little Haiti, Miami—that moment

The cell phone reserved for al-Qaeda contacts rang, and one of the men scooped it up in a swift motion. It was customary not to speak any kind of salutation, out of fear that American listening posts might recognize his vocal pattern. But after only a few seconds, he whirled around to the other three, who were dumbly watching a soccer match on satellite.

"Turn it! Now!" he screamed. "The local news! Channel 4!"

Hearing the panic in his voice, and seeing he was holding a dedicated phone, caused the others to comply quickly. Soon the same frantic newscaster filled their screen as well.

". . . the activity seems to be centered around the intersection of Fifty-Seventh and First, so if you happen to be in that vicinity, please take precautions and stay inside. Repeat—stay inside, as there appears to be . . ."

All three of the men leaped to their feet and lunged into the small apartment's spare bedroom, where four cases of automatic weaponry lay waiting. At first they paid no attention to the weapons, but began pulling on heavy body armor and clipping helmets to their heads. After they were fully covered in black, one of them began barking orders in Arabic while filling his arms with banana clips and tossing the ammo into the main room.

As though they had rehearsed the procedure a hundred times, one of them crawled through the apartment to a sliding door and edged it open with one hand, a large-caliber gun in his other hand. He slithered out onto a tiny covered deck, reinforced from the inside with layers of sandbags.

One of the men busied himself stringing a fuse to the front door. The one shouting orders seemed to be in charge of nothing more than shoveling armament into the living room by the armload.

The gunner on the deck did not betray his position to aerial surveillance but stayed glued to the apartment wall, waiting for the right moment to fire. The shouting one, now finished with his task of transferring weapons, picked up a shoulder-launched missile and inched up beside his companion.

Finished with booby-trapping the front door, the last man punched through a trapdoor to the attic's crawl space and pulled himself through with the speed of a man who practiced by doing three dozen pull-ups a day. From the small black square came the ratcheting sound of rounds being chambered.

Thanks to the news station's heads-up, they were prepared.

CHAPTER 33

The assault team saw nothing on their way in. The voices in their headphones gave no indication of any problem other than a bicyclist wandering down the street in front of the address.

And the nuisance of a pesky news chopper obscuring the Spectre gunship's sight line. It had been warned away with threats of lethal fire and yet persisted in crowding the free-fire zone. They would soon learn their mistake when the firing started and they were forced down within an inch of their lives.

Had this been the usual sort of operation, without a horrific time constraint over its head, there might have been hours, perhaps days of prior surveillance to gain precious intelligence about the target. The number of occupants at the site would have been carefully counted and described. The lanes of ingress and egress would have been mapped out, printed on oversized boards, and discussed in briefings. An official strategy would have been ironed out, debated, and then approved with clear lines of accountability and oversight.

In this case, the directive had come down from Washington that not a single minute could be wasted. Some of the men had smirked at that announcement as they shrugged on their gear. In their experience, "not a minute to waste" usually meant plenty of local agents to waste—inferring that cops' lives were more expendable than ticks on the timetable of some government bureaucrat.

Other than that, it was a smooth drive and, for the lack of planning, a fairly well-timed convergence. The firepower for this raid had been cobbled together from the ranks of FBI, ATF, and local police SWAT, and in the choppers a Special Forces detachment from a nearby battalion of Florida's Army National Guard.

The Black Hawks flew into position, a perfunctory distance away from the drop zone, just as the Humvees cleared the last intersection and came within firing range of the target building. The vehicles formed a perfect fan-shaped barricade before the entrance and began disgorging camouflaged gunmen even before they had come to a complete stop.

The second that boots hit the pavement, ropes plummeted from the helicopters, struck the rooftop, and soldiers began streaming down their lengths.

The first sound to disturb the strangely muted street front was that of a thirty-pound mallet striking the building's locked door.

When the shriek of shattered wood rang out, all semblance of the expected outcome splintered apart with it.

A missile screamed down onto the crowd of men clustered behind the door-knocking team. It exploded with a gaseous roar that was immediately drowned out by the metallic thunder of the large-caliber machine gun opening fire from the deck position. Men already sheathed in fire began to fall like mannequins to the street, their Kevlar vests no match for the military-grade rounds hurling their way.

The Humvees' mounted guns opened fire, and the apartment shook under the impact of explosive bullets. But the al-Qaeda men remained impervious, huddled behind their reinforced deck front and the shelter of their own impossibly thick body armor.

Simultaneously, the third man hidden in the attic opened up on the Special Forces men, now exposed along the roofline. Five specialists found themselves within the machine gun's pounding sights and went down in the first three seconds. Only one was able to take shelter behind a brick chimney shaft and return fire.

By the time he began shooting, the terrorist had ducked inside and traded his machine gun for his own Stinger array. A missile flamed skyward and exploded the nearest Black Hawk in a blinding ball of fire. Seconds later, the machine returned and began peppering the other two, which were wheeling wildly into firing position. One began pouring smoke from its tail rotor and limped away. The other, apparently called off for its own survival, sped off into the distance.

A man's voice, never to be identified but just as certainly never to be forgotten, shouted out over all frequencies, "It's a bloodbath!"

The cry registered not only on the operation's frequencies but was somehow apprehended by the microphones of a national cable channel. Its affiliate station had a second media helicopter stationed just yards from where the Black Hawks had perished.

Delia Kilgore in Arizona, Matthew Snipes at Langley, Deputy Advisers King and Little in D.C., along with their companions in the whole debacle, were watching the raid unravel on the usual oversized screens.

As horrible and bloodcurdling as it appeared on-scene, in many ways the raid was more tragic to watch from this vantage point. From the perspective of the nearest Black Hawk, and a patchwork of watching media choppers lurking along the perimeter, the observers could easily see what the men on the ground could not. They watched unwitting soldiers walk bravely into the gunfire, only to be torn apart by exploding rockets. Worse yet, they could see the wounded writhe in pools of their own blood, still exposed to the terrorists' sight lines.

Two thousand miles away, Captain Kilgore turned aside. Behind her, a camera whirled across the scene showing a horizon worthy of war-torn Beirut in the 1980s, its skyline bisected by knotted columns of smoke, towering above streets scattered with a mixture of debris and human remains.

Feeling intimately connected to this raid and its culmination of her hard work, she rushed to a nearby restroom to throw up.

It took over an hour—including evacuation of the apartment building and a virtual shredding of its upper floor by the Spectre gunship's titanium-tipped bullets—to bring down the well-shielded terrorists. The outermost, window-sited gunman went down first. The leader, crouched behind him, followed within seconds, felled by a massive gun burst that would turn the wall behind him into a canvas of carnage. The third perished in a fireball created when the entire roofline was detonated by answering Stinger rockets.

By now, the "bloodbath" was playing live and in high definition on nearly every television screen in America.

By the time the fighting ended, nineteen members of the assault team had been killed, along with three innocent bystanders struck by falling aircraft and stray shrapnel. The terrorists would later be identified by forensic teams with cotton-tipped swabs and needle-nosed tweezers, protective white masks over their mouths.

CHAPTER 34

The smoke had hardly cleared before network talking heads began asking what they considered the hard questions. Why had such a raid been carried out so recklessly, with so little regard for collateral damage and proper planning? Why had the minds of American viewers been seared with these gruesome images in the first place? What possible law-enforcement objective could have been worth all that?

As though yanked out of their hiding places by the streams of agitated pixels, FBI and mission leaders soon made appearances behind microphones and podiums of their own.

"This mission had to be undertaken in a lightning-fast manner," said the special agent in charge, "with the planning and deployment attendant to such an assignment, in order to attack an identified cell of foreign terrorists. These men were not only preparing operations in our country but actively planning a raid that would have soon taken the lives of many thousands of our citizens. We will have additional details in the hours to come, as I would remind you the incident is still only three hours old."

National Counterterrorism Center, McLean, Virginia

King and Little glanced around at the crowded conference room table, seeing there the most tangible proof yet that their private project had finally left the coop in a major way. The director of national intelligence sat at one end of the table, the secretary of homeland security at the other. Every other inch of table space was occupied by someone's firmly planted elbow and a packet of pages stamped *Top Secret* in red ink. Matthew Snipes was but another formidable name among many, unable to secure for himself an end-zone seat.

Both of the cabinet secretaries held their information packets in the same prim, vengeful manner, which, along with their pinched expressions, seemed to strike their minions as a mixture of thinly veiled rage and the bureaucrats' petty demand for an explanation.

Clearly this promised to be a *there will be blood* sort of a meeting.

"Preliminary results?" called out the Homeland Security secretary, ever anxious to plant his flag first and establish his supremacy.

A midlevel FBI official pulled out a sheet and began to read nervously. "The apartment's contents were a near total loss, but crucial evidence has nevertheless been recovered. Three vials of an unknown liquid were taken from an elaborate cache within the apartment wall. They are at USAMRIID being evaluated as we speak."

"And we're thinking it may be a nerve agent?"

No one would answer.

"I'm assuming that's why we got Fort Detrick involved, would anybody agree?" he asked, glancing around sullenly.

But those at the table were loath to agree with his points,

only to have their support thrown back in their faces when he was invariably found incorrect. Fort Detrick, most of those in the room knew, was the installation which housed USAMRIID, the nation's clearinghouse for biological and nerve weapons.

Finally, a lowly undersecretary nodded. They could now move on.

"Well? Any proof they were terrorists?"

"Oh yes. Considerable scraps of al-Qaeda material were recovered on-site. Also, I might add, three seats at the fifty-yard line to next week's Sugar Bowl."

A cell phone chirped and was immediately silenced. The Homeland Security secretary held it up to his ear and bent his head to signify a worthy caller. A minute later he ended the call. He appeared to have lost most of the blood in his face as he did so.

"My friends, we have a preliminary assessment from Fort Detrick." He paused, took a deep breath. "The substance in the vials was found to be a previously unknown, highly potent and concentrated nerve agent, just as we were led to believe."

A strange noise circled the table, a combination of some gasping in shock, with others breathing out in relief. Which sound emerged from which mouth depended on which government agency the person was employed with.

"Good work, folks," said the other secretary, now tapping his fingers on the packet of papers before him. "We dodged a big one there."

People began to stand, although King and Little appeared rooted to their seats by some dark intuition.

So did Matthew Snipes. As everyone filed out of the conference room, the three men remained, saying nothing, looking everywhere except at each other. When the area was clear, Snipes turned to the pair.

"Okay, fine. We got some actionable intelligence off the man.

But everything else I said still applies. Even more urgently now. This story's going to grow legs, I've been assured. Right now it's just a heroically avoided terrorist strike, but by the next news cycle it'll pick up the name of Omar Nirubi like a sticky snowball rolling down a mountain."

King adjusted the knot of his tie and turned to glare at Snipes. "Not that it's your business for the next eight hours, but I'm at liberty to disclose, to you alone, that Project Forgiven has officially been suspended."

"Even before the nerve gas was identified?"

"Like you said, the raid's success, and the veracity of Nirubi's disclosures, are both irrelevant. The point is that authorities have determined his continued role to be against the interests of national security."

"May I ask from how high the authorization came?"

King gave him a little smile; he was going to enjoy delivering this bombshell to the pompous fool. "No, you may not. But suffice it to say, it came from beyond your pay grade."

As it happened, the name Omar Nirubi entered coverage of the Miami raid long before the ensuing news cycle. Within three hours, the various Pentagon and intelligence correspondents of the major networks had begun to add long-simmering rumors of Nirubi's capture to their reporting mix.

In the West Wing, the president soon became aware of the reporting and quickly called for an explanatory briefing from his National Security staff. Advisers King and Little, flanked by their respective bosses, found themselves in the Oval Office, each trying to flick stray droplets of sweat from his forehead with discreet swipes of a finger and tiny shakes of the head.

"Are we going to be able to put a lid on this?" the president asked.

"We should, sir," answered King. "The cell has clearly been destroyed, and their cache of nerve agent recovered. The plot in question must have certainly been eliminated along with them."

"But where did it come from?"

"That, Mr. President, is definitely our next order of business," replied King's boss, the National Security adviser. "We're working with the FBI and USAMRIID to engage a full task force by day's end. Nevertheless, that's an ancillary issue, even if an important one. The threat, along with the need for everything that uncovered it, has clearly passed."

The president rose from his desk and walked over to the adviser. Bending over, he spoke softly in his ear.

The official nodded and spoke in a whisper. "Yes, I already ascertained that audio and video recording are turned off for this meeting, sir."

"Good. So what about the crazy operation that led to all this?"

"Nonexistent, sir." King had said the words in an exact, carefully parsed manner, a time-neutral choice of words. *Nonexistent* did not presuppose whether the entity in question had ever existed. That was the point.

"And what's the story regarding the fate of Mr. Nirubi?"

The secretary consulted a pristine sheet of paper, marked with a single line of printing. "I believe the release will state, and I quote, 'was killed in the crossfire of a surgical military strike, carried out by American military personnel to apprehend him.' "

"Shall I make the announcement?"

"Well, we had thought to shield you from all involvement in any stage of the issue. It was slated to be given by our Pentagon spokesman."

"But surely I can be allowed to gloat over this thing a bit. Lord knows we've had few enough things to crow about in this awful mess. A few *I told you so*'s broadcast from the Rose Garden?"

"It's up to you, sir. But we'd advise in favor of your staying as far away as possible."

"Oh?" said the president, his eyebrows rising. "Are there lingering doubts of success?"

"No, sir. Just preserving your deniability. The safest way to do that is to keep all possible distance."

CHAPTER 35

Pasadena, California—6 hours later

Sprawled out on his ratty secondhand couch, the code-named Azzam the Younger watched the evening news, kneeling before the screen like he had done only hours before in the direction of Mecca.

This present posture was not, however, an expression of worship or adoration. It was an absentminded reflex of his restless limbs, which only recently had begun to lose the fine muscle tone and tanned appearance of his daily surfing habit.

Listening to the anchorwoman, he began to rise, moaning softly.

"No!" he cried, raising his fists toward the ceiling.

He then sank to the floor and began flailing at whatever items lay within reach: the coffee table, scraps from his last fast-food meal, the sofa cushions.

"I'm so proud of our boys," declared the president on-screen, dripping with satisfaction, "who risked their lives to take out such a dangerous terrorist. Of course we tried to take him out alive, as we've always done with even our worst enemies. But his own side refused to protect him by stopping their fire. He was killed by an al-Qaeda bullet. And in case anybody is wondering just how dangerous a man this was, we've seen proof with the awful shootout in Miami earlier today, along with the breaking up of an attack against our very own Sugar Bowl. Let all those who question our presence in Afghanistan and Iraq remember this day."

Each word spoken by the president afflicted Azzam like a solitary droplet of acid. By the statement's end, he'd done enough contortions on the dirty carpet to call his survival into question.

Yet he was very much alive, and in fact quite physically healthy.

His emotional state was not as intact, however. Curled up now against the sofa, he hugged his knees like an overwrought teenager. He moaned and struck the sofa with his fist as hard as he could.

What a horrific day. He felt betrayed by everything he knew— by life, by fate, even by the cause to which he'd sworn his life. It was as if someone had siphoned off all the joy, the hope, and the beauty he'd known in the world since turning to jihad.

First, his idol, Omar Nirubi, had been reported killed. Normally, if such an account had been fabricated, a denial would have quickly been communicated by his al-Qaeda superiors, usually by email. He'd kept a constant vigil on his in-box, and nothing had arrived.

He could hardly bear to think of it. Nirubi was one of the chief reasons he had identified so completely with his jihadist brothers. A lowly refugee kid from Beirut, selected because of his smarts, and later his success at Oxford. There he had excelled, even as he had supplemented his education with Islamic studies at some of Kilgore's most radical and secret Madrass schools. It was Nirubi who had given a famous speech, calling on all the orphaned sons of American soldiers to rise up and avenge their fathers. The very invitation he had embraced on the spot.

In a second cruel blow, his Miami team, recipients of all his hard work, had been wiped out, their cunning plan along with them.

He gritted his teeth, tried to marshal the strength to overcome the sense of defeat that threatened to crush him. Without some kind of outward intervention, he felt certain he would simply sink into the earth and disappear from sheer misery. Asking Allah for help, he struggled to organize his thoughts.

Finally it came to him, and he knew what to do. The audacity of it made him shiver.

He would brew up a new batch.

Of course. What else was there to do? Wait for the FBI to come and arrest him?

Yes, he would show his resiliency and initiative by putting all his energy into producing a whole new batch of the gas.

When the dose was ready, he would shock the world, Islamic and American alike, by delivering it himself.

Someday his jihadist brothers would admire him, hold him up high for his dedication and perseverance, right up there with Mohammed Atta and 9/11 itself.

It was common knowledge that al-Qaeda cells operated in a self-governing, autonomous manner, he reminded himself with a smile. Well, now he would prove it. He would carry out the whole thing himself and right here in his own corner of America.

Yes, the countdown to New Year's was back on.

CHAPTER 36

Fort Huachuca Command Post

At first, as the operation's electronic jungle had been unceremoniously dismantled and carted away around her, Captain Delia Kilgore had sat glued to the televisions, watching the news like an unrepentant junkie.

Footage of the disastrous Miami raid had struck her with equal parts horror and satisfaction. Despite the carnage and loss of life, the raid's outcome had proven that she had helped to expose not just al-Qaeda terrorists but the most dangerous ones at that. These were no wannabes, no disaffected teenagers or terrorists-in-training. They had been the real thing.

The subsequent discovery of the nerve gas had bolstered her affirmation even further. She'd taken some of the worst pressure and political infighting someone in her position could endure and had been proven resoundingly right. Ridicule had been heaped upon her psy-ops project, yet it was vindicated beyond her wildest hopes.

If only someone had been there to share it with her.

Even her commanding officer, her ever-present guide and mentor during the Polish portion of this operation, was now off in another corner of the world. He would have loved this. Sure, he would have had a hard time expressing it, as the man had always found outward expressions of sentiment difficult. He'd chosen the right field in the military—a great place for the emotionally constipated.

Oddly enough, she now sat less than a quarter mile from her ex-husband, a man whom she'd worked hard to distance herself from. The thought of it—of him—pained her like a knife in the side.

Captain Kilgore's quarters, Fort Huachuca

While nursing a scotch three hours later at officers' quarters, riding her bliss late into the night, she saw a headline crawl across the bottom portion of her muted television. Its words made her blood run cold.

> Omar Nirubi, al-Qaeda chieftain, confirmed dead in Pakistan crossfire . . .

Every impulse that had occupied her mind and body fled from her in a flush of pure rage. The self-congratulations, the long-delayed relief, the pleasant tingle of the alcohol—all of them disappeared in an instant.

She was still a soldier, and now every nerve ending in her body told her to brace for combat.

It took only a split second for the truth to burst upon her mind like a continuation of that dreadful scroll on the TV screen.

Thinking it through, she felt like a complete idiot for having believed them. For having trusted that even though the clemency offer was unconventional and burdensome, it would be in the nation's long-term interest to honor it.

Honor . . . the notion now tasted bitter to her.

Now, she realized, her danger was at its peak. Before entering her peculiar field of specialty, she had hardly dared dream that her government was capable of such dastardly deeds. Crimes needing to be covered up, not justified or debated behind closed doors but buried forever.

Well, now she knew different. Worse yet, she was standing dead center in one of these affairs herself. A sense of panic rushed through her, increasing her heart rate, the frantic pace of her thoughts. She felt like she could hardly breathe.

Could she do anything against such forces? Should she just sit there and wait for a trumped-up court-martial, a one-way ticket to career oblivion . . . maybe even a premature death? Or should she attempt to do something to save herself, to fight against this thing?

She glanced outside and saw nothing but blackness pressing against the windowpane. The dark night caused her to think of the evil intent and malice surrounding her, which then caused her anxiety to double.

She needed help.

And there was only one, highly unlikely source from which to beg for it.

Lt. Col. Dale Scheer's quarters, Fort Huachuca— 20 minutes later

Lieutenant Colonel Dale Scheer stepped off his front porch, intent on grabbing one of the last possible outdoor runs of the year, even though it was much later than his usual time.

It was well into December, and at most of his other postings, the season for jogging would have been long past. This remained one of the few solaces of living here near the Mexican border—a climate so mild that only during the final weeks of the year did outdoor activity become uncomfortable.

He'd heard that morning that true winter was finally on its way. A snowstorm had been forecast for Fort Huachuca, with lows below freezing, several inches of snow, and a good day or so of socked-in cloud cover. He smiled in the darkness. Another good thing about a climate like this was that you didn't resent the few days of genuine winter when they arrived. Instead, you looked forward to the change.

Taking his time in getting up to speed, he turned onto Hines Avenue with the idea of running through the Old Fort section, where many of the old bungalows and homes were inhabited by the men to whom he answered—full-bird colonels and generals.

He chose this way to avoid the cordon of heavy security surrounding the parklike stretch behind him. On his last run, he'd come upon a sniper, who had waited until the last second before revealing himself. Stepping out from the bushes and planting himself in front of Dale, he'd demanded with his rifle held high that Dale state his business. Although a good soldier, the man had barely made captain. And as a lieutenant colonel, Dale had enjoyed stating his name, rank, and serial number.

"What in the world is going on here, Captain?" he had asked once his identity and purpose were established.

"I'm not at liberty to answer that, sir," the sniper said with a good-natured grin. "Except to say it's some pretty serious business. If I were you, I'd do my running on a treadmill for a while. Right now you're liable to get shot out here. Step into the wrong area and it's 'shoot on sight.'"

Dale whistled in amazement. In fact, the base was abuzz with rumors about the strange operation that had commandeered the oldest and most picturesque portion of the reservation. He'd even heard a vague mention of his ex-wife having shown up, landing on some phantom flight in the middle of the night.

No telling, he grunted to himself. After the bizarre call he'd received from Poland, anything was possible.

Of course, he hadn't altered his jogging course by much. He'd been running the route for years, and nobody short of God would make him abandon it altogether. Instead, he'd decided to resurrect his old stalking skills from childhood and his early military training. Forcing himself to run silently and stick to the shadows, he compared himself to Cochise or Mangas Coloradas, Apache heroes whose adventures had, ironically enough, taken place in these very mountains.

On his first covert run, he'd observed the tightened security cordon and spied two snipers. Truly something extraordinary was afoot for these kinds of precautions to take place here, deep in the Sonoran Desert. Jails had been built around here because of the isolation. He tried to imagine what kind of scenario would warrant such security, but after thinking about it awhile, he couldn't come up with anything plausible.

After all, he went running to empty his mind of all anxiety, to leave the military behind and, for a few minutes at least, enjoy a little peace and quiet.

Tonight, though, he noticed far less activity. The cordon of security was only a shadow of its former self. He saw a single sentry and only one sniper. The barricades were gone and the support vehicles had thinned considerably.

Truth be told, he found the canyon far more interesting. The rigors of running silently brought back to mind the old cowboy and Indian games of boyhood. He had never wanted to be John Wayne or any of the cowboys, but rather an Apache scout, invisible and one with the land, blending from one location to the next in little more than a breechcloth, leather boots, and a very cool headband.

Soon the pavement gave way to gravel, followed by packed dirt. The desert, which held sway for over a hundred miles, was only too willing to yield its barren soil and flat surfaces in favor of fragrant grass, towering pine trees, and the hint of a mountain incline to come. Passing through these riparian transition zones always thrilled him, awakening a primeval call of the wild deep within him.

He began thinking of himself as a real Apache Indian, running the actual path of his heroes. According to legend, Apache youths were given a mouthful of water, told to run forty miles through the desert and back, then on their return to spit out the contents of their mouths. Those who swallowed the water had failed the challenge.

He doubted whether such a challenge could pass the biological truth test, yet he appreciated the spirit of the story just the same. It didn't prevent him from lugging along a canteen of water, but it helped him to remember that, despite his being physically fit, there would always be ancient predecessors whose heritage and exploits would forever elude him.

His thoughts zoomed on ahead from adolescence to adulthood, including thoughts of the woman whose face always seemed before him. It shamed him to think of her as anything so final and so dark as his ex-wife, although legally that was what she was to him now. They had parted badly, with great anger and shouts of hateful spite. The regret of those moments stung him so sharply that he could hardly bear to think of them.

He preferred to keep the image of her face—when laughing, during the early months of their courtship—somewhere on the periphery of his mind. As time went on, the image had ascended to join that eternal audience he felt watching his every moment, a beloved group made up of his mother and father and favorite high school teacher, those people whose approval he sought with every act of his solitary life.

Three hundred yards beyond the pavement, his adopted Apache instincts kicked in. He felt a presence of something travel up and down his spine like the tiniest of breezes.

Dale was being watched.

He broke stride, not intentionally but from the raw indecision over what to do next. Where was the intruder hiding? He could feel that he was being watched, but had no idea as to its point of origin.

All at once he caught sight of a faint motion. To his right, behind a line of ponderosas. Without thinking through the consequences, he charged off the path and in the spy's direction. As he ran he pulled out the snub-nosed Colt he always carried with him on his runs.

With a great leap he burst through a barrier of pine boughs and into a small clearing, the gun brandished before him.

"Who are you?" he snarled. "Show yourself!"

Scheer was primed for a fight, but rather than a threat, a figure emerged. With each tentative step, it changed from foreign to strangely familiar to a recognizable silhouette, and then a face he beheld with astonishment.

The woman pulled back the hood of her sweatshirt. Yes, it was her, a ghost straight out of his darkest regrets, not only stalking his thoughts but now kicking through the layers to pierce the outermost shell of his waking life.

Delia.

CHAPTER 37

He staggered back, his charge blunted by shock and bewilderment.

"Dale, I'm sorry to give you a scare," she said in a voice that
to this day throbbed seductively in his dreams. "I didn't know
how else to talk to you in such a secure place as this."

"Looks like you managed pretty well," he said, feeling the
old reserve set in.

"Please, will you talk to me? I know I don't deserve it. I didn't
deserve the help you gave me a few weeks ago when I called from
Poland. I know the way I left was awful and incredibly painful.
I'm sorry, I should have told you long before now, but I realized
some time ago how immature and impulsive that was."

"You were young," he said, his tone wavering somewhere
between forgiving and remote. "And I was set in my ways."

It was the best he could do. But then he'd never spent much
time psychoanalyzing himself. Maybe if he had, he realized now,
he'd still be married.

"But I was smart too, as you always reminded me. Smart
enough to know better. Our careers weren't mutually
exclusive. I know that now."

Tucking the gun away, he looked around, taking stock of their conversation's odd location. "That's great to hear, Delia, but I don't get it. You had to come all the way out here in the forest to tell me these things? You think the officers' club isn't safe enough for this kind of talk?"

Her face fell as the sound of his old defiance met her ears once more. He felt a bit remorseful at the sight of her hopeful countenance now darkening.

"No, Dale. It's something else—the op you helped me with earlier. That's the reason I'm here."

"I heard a rumor that you were involved in that strange business over on Bungalows Row."

"I'm in huge trouble, maybe in danger for my life."

He looked her in the eyes for signs of delusion or levity, but saw none. If anything, he recognized the signs of her sincerity better than any other man she knew.

"What are you talking about?"

She described for him the events surrounding Project Forgiven in an impassioned torrent of words. Then she gave him the ominous final chapter. "There's only one explanation. The whole thing was a psy-ops ploy from the beginning. They never intended to honor the offer of clemency, or to reconcile Omar Nirubi with any surviving family members, or resettle them in America. His usefulness ended as soon as he revealed the New Year's plot conspirators. Otherwise he never would have survived capture back in Pakistan. The A-team would have had instructions for him to fall under 'friendly fire,' or the crossfire of his own men, as the news reports are now saying. How stupid, how naïve I've been. I'll bet there's a black ops team on its way over there right now, getting into position to take them out."

Dale placed a comforting hand on her shoulder. "Listen, you

haven't been naïve or stupid. Your heart is pure, and if you ever read the Bible, you'd find that's a pretty good thing."

"You read the Bible these days?" she asked.

"Yeah, a little."

"First, I have to ask you. Do you think I'm personally in danger?"

He looked up at the starry sky, thinking. "Could be, depending on how quickly you show back up at work, and whether you give them any reason to suspect your allegiances. I'll bet within a day or so, someone's going to offer you a nice promotion in exchange for your hard work and your discretion. That will be their cue as to whether you're going to be a team player or not."

"Well, I'm definitely not a team player here," she snapped. "I'm not going to stand by and let those two men, one of them completely innocent, get killed because of me. And that's why I need your help."

"Anything," he said, surprised to hear the words come out of his mouth. His last official stance toward her had been implacable hatred and resentment. At least that was what he'd told the boys over at the officers' club bar late one Friday night, before calling a cab for a ride home.

Her face brightened, equally shocked by his reaction.

"I'm going over there right now," she said, "to try and spring them loose. It's a gamble, but I think it might work. Will you help them get away? After all, you know these backwoods behind Fort Huachuca like nobody else. You even know where the old Apache hideouts and all the old mines are located."

"Well, let me think about this. You're asking me to help the head of al-Qaeda and a disgraced child killer escape from the United States Army? It's hardly something that will wind up boosting my career."

"They've both turned over new leaves," she pleaded. "Really.

Omar Nirubi has genuinely converted to Christianity, renounced violence and jihad, and voluntarily gave up the identity of a terrorist cell about to kill innocent civilians. He signed a document accepting clemency from the president, who's now going to wash his hands of him, I'm sure of it. He's a different person, Dale. A new man."

"And what about Greg Cahill?"

"Cahill is the most broken, transparent guy I've ever met. He's just trying to put his life back together, reconcile with his wife and son, and do as much good along the way as he can. He's a man of deep faith now."

"What exactly do you want me to do?"

"Just meet them somewhere out here that's safe, and apply all that knowledge bouncing around in your head so they can have a fighting chance. You know how much technology is about to be used against them. They're innocent, Dale. You may hear otherwise in the days ahead, but they're one hundred percent innocent, just as I am."

"I believe you," he said, staring at her, still not believing she'd come to him like this. "Meet me at the Reef Townsite, and we'll think of something."

Delia leaned forward, hesitated for a second, then broached the remaining distance to plant a soft kiss on his cheek.

"Thank you," she whispered, looking every bit as lovely to him as the midnight ghost she seemed to be.

"You take care," he said as she started toward the four-wheeler he had noticed only moments ago. Shivering from a sudden gust of frigid wind, he called to her. "There's a storm coming, you know."

"I know," she said, revving up the engine. "It's the only reason they have even a snowball's chance of surviving."

CHAPTER 38

Respite House, Fort Huachuca—that moment

For Greg Cahill and Omar Nirubi, the previous hours had passed in a daze of gratitude and sweet relief, the glow of a new day dawning for both of them.

As soon as Delia had called with news of the successful raid, it finally occurred to Greg that he now stood an overwhelming chance of having the entire veil of alienation and disapproval lifted from over his life. At least that had been Captain Kilgore's offer, and he'd done more than hold up his share of the bargain.

He tried to picture himself approaching Donna and Robby, walking close enough to embrace them. And when Donna warned him about coming too close, for violating the restraining order, he saw himself whipping out a letter of clemency signed by the president himself, declaring him a father who was free to spend time with his son again.

He saw himself walking through life straighter and prouder than ever before, secure in the knowledge that his innocence was no longer in danger of attack, that his terrible secret was buried as deep as his oldest sin. He could be a true father once more. Maybe even embark on the long road toward being Donna's husband again, with an unshakable grip on the last remaining strand of her trust.

He was forgiven now, he knew it. He had known it ever since the climactic shouting match and near fight with Omar. He felt it in the gleam of his eye, in the angle of his upheld head. Who would have thought the most hated man on earth would be the man to help him experience God's unfailing love for him?

And then there was the wonder of Nirubi's own conversion. The thought of it blazed in his mind like a dawn so splendid and bright that he could hardly stand to look at it for very long. He could hardly believe it on several fronts.

First, despite his stubborn faith and determination, a large part of his fallen self refused to believe that a man like him would ever turn away from the path for which he was so infamous. No matter who attempted to dissuade him from his murderous version of jihad, he never would have thought it capable of succeeding.

Secondly, he never would have believed that he, Greg Cahill, a disgraced man on the ultimate downhill trajectory, would have ever been used to carry off such a far-fetched victory.

And now to know that not only had he succeeded on the spiritual front, which had mattered most to him, but he had also succeeded in saving the lives of possibly millions of Americans.

The abundance of this whole happy consequence threatened to overwhelm his faculties.

He stood on the home's front porch, gazing out into the deepening night and thinking these thoughts, when a cell phone rang in his pocket. He looked down and frowned. Then he remembered; Captain Kilgore had slipped the phone into his pocket as a way of communicating without Omar's knowledge. He had only used it once.

He fished the phone out and flipped it open.

"Greg, are you alone?" asked Kilgore, her voice thick with urgency.

"Yeah, why?"

"Where are you?"

"Out on the porch, getting a breath of fresh air before turning in. Looks like it might snow. It's kind of fun feeling a whole season blow through in just a few minutes' time."

"Great. Go and sit on the bottom step and casually cover your mouth when you talk to me."

"What's going on?" he asked as he moved down the steps and took a seat.

"Listen to me very closely. The world media is reporting that Nirubi was killed in a Pakistan shootout a month ago. That means only one thing. You and he are in mortal danger. The project you've been a part of—it's a sham, a ploy straight out of psychological operations. Please don't get mad at me, because I wasn't in on the betrayal. I thought the clemency offer was good, that it would be honored. Look, the stakes were real. The subject was real. But your role and the clemency offer were more than a covert experiment in order to get Nirubi to cooperate. You've got to get out of that house as soon as you can, and then disappear for a while. They're not going to waste a moment."

Reeling with a sudden storm of fury, Greg slammed the phone down. Within seconds he remembered the precautions Delia had insisted on and realized the foolishness of his action.

Fort Huachuca Command Post—that moment

Delia put her cell phone away and continued walking from her parked four-wheeler to the office where she had spent most of the previous four days. A part of her felt insane and suicidal to reenter that building, given what she now knew. Yet she realized the wisdom in Dale's recommendation. As evil as they were, the cover-up men couldn't kill everyone who'd ever been associated with the mission. If she could project a lack of alarm and a willingness to go along, she'd at least survive the next few hours.

Which was the amount of time she'd need to carry out her plan.

She had only decided to use the secure cell phone between her and Cahill after remembering that most of the surveillance equipment had already been removed from headquarters. Had there been a listening device on the line, which she assumed was the case, it would likely have been disabled by now. And that made the phone her only safe way of communicating the truth to him.

Passing through the remaining layers of security, she tried to think of Cahill and what he was going through at that moment. In a few whispered words, he'd been whisked away from a night of well-earned contentment and hope, into a nightmare of danger laced with the bitterest form of betrayal.

She hoped he could take it. Granted, he had already absorbed a lifetime's worth, a fact he'd already demonstrated when she was forced to dole out the truth to him in measured portions. But he'd also been a soldier, had known for years how to rule himself through sheer military discipline. Hopefully those virtues would resurface and give him the mental and emotional fortitude to calm himself and figure out an escape.

Just as she reached her desk, she saw them. Two men wearing ordinary gray suits, trying hard to look inconspicuous. To Delia's trained eye, that made them stand out even more.

She felt the blood drain from her face and her cheeks go suddenly cold.

This was it. The strike force she'd anticipated.

Here in the command post with the two men, it struck her with a double dose of cruelty that she could lose her life, or at least her freedom, and that if she wanted to live she would have to do something extraordinary, something unprecedented. She'd have to beat Special Forces assassins sworn to kill her.

Not about to give her misgivings away, she nodded at the men and pretended to pick up some stray items from her desk.

Then she reasoned that maybe they hadn't been given the order yet, or they would have taken her out from a distance, before she'd even entered the building. The men seemed to be waiting for something. She could see one of them turning away from the other, looking as if he was mumbling to himself. It could be he was speaking into some kind of microphone, hidden on his body.

She had only minutes, then. Until the order came, they'd only be tasked with keeping her in sight.

Without hesitating, she began to fiddle with the back clasp of her military skirt while walking briskly for the women's restroom. Once in its small vestibule she turned away from the inner door and toward a second door, which opened to a janitorial supply room. While setting up the operation several days before, she'd helped the custodian pull a folding table from the room and remembered seeing the outline of a door on its outer wall. Maybe, just maybe, it would lead to . . .

She approached the door, pushed against it, and felt the door give way under the weight. Cold air met her face. She quickly stepped outside onto a cement walkway that led down to a Dumpster.

She broke into a run, moving as fast as her legs would allow— away from the windows and in the opposite direction of the men.

Thankfully, she'd hidden the four-wheeler in an alley not far away. Unfortunately, though, it was quite loud, and in a pursuit would alert anyone within half a mile of her location.

Trying to stay to the shadows, she lengthened her strides, feeling the distance increase behind her. Seconds later she heard a metallic noise, consistent with outer doors being swung open and allowed to slam shut.

A male voice rang out. Her courage quailed within her.

The chase was on.

At least she had managed to gain a substantial headway. If only she were back at the respite house, or better yet in the vicinity of the canyon where she had met Dale. Then escape would have meant a quick turn into the forest, where soon she would become untraceable. Her greatest danger lay in these brightly lit streets, lined by fences and security barriers.

Delia knew the men would have guns and only required a brief view of her figure, even from a distance, to make quick aim and shoot her. So she needed to find a place of concealment and then stay there.

She ran to the end of the base's Montessori school and stood in the parking lot, beside a pair of transport vans. Looming just ahead was a strip of wooded land. Freedom. She felt her leg muscles twitch in anticipation of how quickly she might lose her pursuers if she went that direction.

Then it struck her. That was precisely what they would expect.

She glanced around. Instead of sprinting ahead, she got down on her stomach and crawled beneath the nearest van. Trying to still the thumping of her heart and the runaway rhythm of her breaths, she prayed and waited.

She didn't have to wait long before she heard the sound of fast-approaching footsteps.

The steps halted with the slapping sound of arrested momentum, close by her head. She held her breath.

"Where?" came a deep male voice, panting.

"Had to be that way," said the other man.

"You go right, I'll go left. And be careful."

The running steps resumed, then faded into the distance.
Delia felt relief flood through her, along with the air from her
first breath in several long moments.

Fighting the urge to leave her hiding place too soon, she
stayed put. She closed her eyes as a cruel wind came whistling
underneath the vehicle, chilling her now sweaty limbs.

After waiting another fifteen minutes, she peered out from
under the van and at first was confused at what she saw. A flurry
of white flakes floating to the pavement.

Surprised, she realized it was snow.

Then it struck her. Snow meant tracks.

She needed to move.

CHAPTER 39

Respite House, Fort Huachuca—2 days before the attack

Trying desperately not to betray alarm through any outward sign, whether facial expression, body language, or speech, Greg Cahill reentered the house and began going through the motions of preparing for bed.

Halfway through brushing his teeth, however, he was overcome by a desire to speak with Captain Kilgore again. Pulling out the cell phone, he closed and locked the bathroom door. Here, at least, he had been told there were no cameras. He switched on the overhead fan for its white noise, then opened the phone and redialed Kilgore.

It rang, and continued to ring five more times. Finally a dull-sounding voice came on to announce that he'd reached her voicemail. With a shaky intake of breath, he closed the phone and struggled to process what this meant. It meant trouble, he decided.

He tried to adopt the mind-set he'd once lived in for months at a time—that of a soldier in a tactical situation.

What might follow next? A squad of men? Coming with the intent to kill?

No, he realized. Black ops would want Omar alive, perhaps for more interrogation, and later to kill him somewhere that was easy to sanitize. Furthermore, too many people knew of the unorthodox operation taking place here. And there was the risk of forensic evidence being left behind, such as Nirubi's fingerprints, which were all over the place.

Instead, he reasoned, what lay ahead was a commando snatch-and-run, using nonlethal weapons and grenades. He tried to inventory what each soldier would carry. For one thing, this late at night, he knew they would be using night-vision goggles.

That could very well work in his favor. The dim outline of a plan began to take shape within his frenzied mind, although the complete formulation proved difficult. It occurred to him that he sat smack-dab in the middle of perhaps the most heavily surveilled home, wired inch-by-inch with the most sophisticated technology, known to man.

Still locked inside the bathroom, he took a few more moments to think, to allow the plan to mature. When satisfied, he left the bathroom and walked to the kitchen, pretending to look for Omar. After searching all the common areas, he realized that Omar must have gone to bed.

He returned to the kitchen. Reaching for a teakettle, he placed it on a burner, turned it on, then fumbled in the cupboard for the box of tea stored there. Finding it, he took the box down, and while carrying it to the stovetop, let the box slip from his grasp, its contents spilling out onto the tiled flooring. Rolling his eyes with feigned exasperation, he knelt with a loud sigh and began gathering the dozen or so tea bags.

Moving his body between the room's open space and the site of the spill, he pretended to search the crevice between the lower cabinet's edge and the wall. When his bulk had obscured the location of his right hand from any possible camera angle, he reached in.

The day before he'd spotted a stretch of old piping that led from the gas stove to where it entered the wall. Quickly he grasped it and yanked hard. It pulled free at once. The hissing sound that escaped from the pipe was too faint for anyone to hear but him. He yelled "Ow!" and raised his finger to his mouth, feigning an accidental cut. Keeping his thumb firmly between his lips, he rose, grabbed a napkin, and pressed it to the thumb to hide the lack of blood.

He removed the kettle from the burner and switched off the heat, seemingly giving up for the night.

He headed off to bed, turning off the lights behind him.

After climbing between the sheets, he wondered how to make sure he was considered asleep by those watching. Should he begin snoring? Bury his face in the pillow?

He remembered the control room he'd seen when summoned to Captain Kilgore's side. One screen displayed the interior of his bedroom, but did it show any kind of infrared or night-vision capability? Or did they rely instead on the filament sensors to convey movement in the room?

Something Captain Kilgore had said came to his mind, when she'd called him to relay the news about Miami. The operation had been deemed a success and was in the process of being canceled. Workers were coming to haul away a great deal of the electronics.

Then it hit him. If someone was coming to harm him, then surely whatever surveillance remained had been shut off. Nobody wanted to leave an incriminating record.

Assuming there was some kind of building-level microphone,

with the cameras shut off in his room, he began to carefully, slowly, pull back his covers in the darkness. The furtiveness of his motions reminded him of being a kid again, when some clandestine "mission" had called for him to sneak out of bed. Despite the danger, a long-ago sensation of childlike secrecy fluttered through his senses.

Taking nearly a minute to do so, he left his covers, arranged them to look like they were still occupied, and began to plan his ambush spot. He looked around and saw that, like many old homes of its period, this one bore a substantial height of ornamental wainscoting, set off nearly an inch from the plaster. At the floor's edge, the baseboard protruded another full inch over the floor.

Feeling with his toes, he found the baseboard's lip, measured its solidity with a strong push, and settled his full weight against it. The edge cut into his toes, though not unbearably. He let go of the bed and rammed his fingers into the vertical grooving at his waist, moving sideways away from the bed. Passing a nightstand, he reached out and plucked a matchbox left there. Placing the box between his lips, he resumed his slow progress toward the room's corner, a space hidden behind the door leading to the common area.

In the corner stood a coat rack. Sliding himself behind the open door, he stepped onto the rack's wooden base. Even though he knew this would convey added weight to the flooring, he also knew that however meticulous the technicians might have been, they would not have wired underneath furniture but around it. Remembering that, he placed both feet on the coat rack, leaned his back against the corner wall, and waited.

It was a nerve-wracking and increasingly agonizing wait. The effort it took to stand motionless and quiet in that position, feet perched on the base of the coat rack to avoid motion or friction, soon became a chore. Forcing himself to remember the privations of combat, Greg gritted his teeth and bore the discomfort.

To distract himself, he forced his mind to think of his surroundings. Outside, he could hear the wind howling, and could see through the far window that it was snowing, the white stuff sticking to the windowpanes. Winter had come with a vengeance, he told himself. If only he'd been allowed the luxury of a night's rest, he might have enjoyed this weather. He'd always been one to lie in bed and relish the sound of rain pelting the roof above him, the wind gusting, pushing against the siding.

As the minutes passed, an odor reached his nostrils and he remembered the gas—leaking and spreading throughout the house.

Greg was trying to think of what to do next when he heard the outer door let out a soft creaking sound.

CHAPTER 40

Feeling the same uncontrollable shivers of a kid seeing a ghost, Greg tensed his muscles and readied himself for the next phase of his plan.

Another squeak reached his ears. No doubt about it, entry into the house was being attempted by someone.

And with all the electronics in the western hemisphere behind him, all the measures and countermeasures shown to him the other night, no alarm was going off anywhere that would ensure his safety.

That, more than anything else, confirmed his worst fears.

A surge of cool air told him that indeed the outer door had been breached, most likely by a three-man team. He strained his ears for the sound of footfalls, of straining floor. Finally he thought he heard a groan.

Dread settled on him like an evil fog. The thought that he had only a slight chance of living through a perilous chase began to eat away at his hope of survival.

At least he was well concealed behind the door.

How long, he wondered, would it take for them to smell the strong odor of gas and realize his plan? He knew that the open outside door might have dispelled lingering fumes near the exit. He slowly raised the matchbox, readying himself to strike a match against its side.

Sensing if not hearing the steps of someone approaching, drawing closer to his position, suddenly it galled him—the thought that his own government, his brothers in arms, were attempting to murder him!

He steeled himself when he saw the shadow of a commando moving slowly through the doorway. He risked a better look and noted the man was wearing night-vision goggles. He held his breath while the soldier took two more steps toward the bed, thankful that he'd remembered to arrange the blankets to form the semblance of a human occupant.

As quietly as he could, he slid the match head against the side of the box and tossed the small flame to the floor. Pressing his back into the corner, he lowered his head and shut his eyes.

Whoosh!

Rather than exploding outright, the pooled gas thumped into a blinding wall of flame that flared upward for a second, then fell back just as quickly.

But groans and frantic footsteps told Greg that his trick had worked. The night-vision equipment, which magnified ambient light several hundred times, had temporarily blinded the men with a flash beyond what the human eye could tolerate.

This was his moment. Leaping from his hiding place, Greg jumped onto the nearest soldier's back and began wrestling him to the floor. Already disoriented, the man fell down quickly. With a hard punch to the face, Greg knocked the man out.

Groping for the contents of the soldier's weapons belt, he ripped away a small grenade, followed by the belt itself. He tossed the grenade into the now day-bright common area, toward the figures of two more soldiers struggling to pull the goggles from their eyes.

The flashbang grenade, typical of a nonlethal raid, went off with a deafening noise and a series of blinding strobelike lights. Dazed, the two remaining intruders collided with each other.

Greg picked up the soldier's weapon, realizing from its light weight and unusual shape that it was a sonic weapon. Perfect. He had guessed correctly. He aimed the device at the two soldiers and shot straight in their direction. High-impact explosions knocked the attackers to the floor, both unconscious. Greg bent over, groaning from the sheer chaos of even standing next to the weapon when it went off. Even though it was designed to stun only those struck by its sound blasts, just being nearby was painfully loud.

Reaching down, Greg began yanking at the fallen soldiers' belts and assault vests. Their weapons and equipment would be sorely needed. All around him, flames from the gas explosion were beginning to surround the room. Soon the entire house would be on fire.

He shrugged on a coat, then a pair of sneakers, quickly and without socks. He ran through the house looking for Omar, checking each room. But he was nowhere to be seen. Dreading that he might somehow have taken a bullet during all the confusion, Greg continued searching the house with growing panic. Then he ventured a look to the front porch and found Omar standing outside, eyes wide with terror as he stared up at the house, now engulfed in flames. Seeing Greg approach, Omar nearly fell down in shock.

"Let's go!" Greg shouted.

The two men rushed out into the night, and into six inches of new-fallen snow.

Turning cold from the frigid air, they halted to take in their surroundings and decide on their next move. Greg had already determined they would flee to the nearest mountain that dominated the southern skyline. But now in the middle of a snowstorm, and in the dead of night, finding their way wasn't going to be easy. The only light came from flames rising from the house burning behind them.

"That way!" Greg shouted at last, pointing to their right.

They sprinted off into the blackness. Without help, they were—

The whine of an engine rose in the night, its revving growing louder and louder. Greg and Omar turned in its direction, desperate to discern friend from enemy.

It was a four-wheeler, with Delia at the controls, her blond hair bouncing in the wind and swirling snow.

Pulling alongside them, she shouted, "Jump on!"

The remaining seat space was intended for one, but the three of them managed, happy to have a means of escape. With a lurch and a strain of the overworked engine, the four-wheeler surged ahead, its headlight carving a white slice of snow-filled night before them.

CHAPTER 41

Almost invisible in the driving snow, the three raced up the route Dale had jogged earlier—up Hines Street and into Huachuca Canyon. Greg was grateful for every foot of distance added between them and the site of his close brush with death. He thought of the men back at the house, and he felt a twinge of sadness, wishing he could have come up with a better way to get himself and Omar safely out of there. True, he'd started the fire, yet he sure hadn't started this conflict they were now embroiled in.

Before long, they could see the broadness start to narrow, the valley compress into a wooded canyon. *Great*, thought Greg with a rush of relief. They were making some headway into the wilderness.

A mile farther in, the path on which they were traveling began to look more like a hiking trail, with the ground turning rougher, the incline steeper. An inexperienced driver, Delia pushed the throttle too hard to compensate. The four-wheeler reared its nose like an enraged bronco, its engine racing out of control. Greg toppled off, clutching his leg, while the vehicle threw the other two aside and then flipped over on the trail with a loud crunching sound.

"Are you all right?" Delia asked Greg.

For the moment all he could do was roll in the snow, groaning in agony. Omar took hold of the four-wheeler, trying to right it again.

Finally Greg succeeded in standing, just as the other two managed to wrest the four-wheeler back into position and get it running again. The vehicle had sustained a nasty dent in one side, but nothing more. When Greg stepped in front of the headlight, his injured leg greeted him with a saucer-wide bloodstain across the upper thigh.

"You did not suffer that in the fall just now," Omar said.

"You're right," Greg replied, nodding and wincing at the same time. "It looks like I got some kind of knife wound back at the house. I can't believe I didn't even notice."

"C'mon. Let's go," said Delia, who had climbed back on the four-wheeler and was impatient to continue on.

But Greg shook his head, still clutching his leg. "I don't think I can. It's hurting pretty bad."

"Well, we're not going to just leave you here," Delia argued.

"I'll be all right. You go on. I'll stay here and deal with anyone chasing us. That way, you and Omar can get away safely."

"Absolutely not!" Delia cried. "They'll kill you just as quickly as either of us."

She hopped off the four-wheeler, giving Omar a knowing look, and the two of them helped Greg back on the vehicle. Gritting his teeth in pain, Greg hung on as they raced ahead.

For several minutes they drove through an eternity of falling snow and winding mountain path. Every so often, Delia would brake to a stop, pull out a handheld GPS unit and a map, and take a reading of their exact location. Farther up the mountainside they drove, thankful for the track-erasing snowfall even as they cursed the freezing temperatures.

Then, just as it seemed their endurance could carry them no farther, she came to a stop, turned off the engine, and motioned for them to follow her. A tiny flashlight came on in her hand. To their left loomed a high rock face. A battered sign beside it, half crusted over with snow, read *Reef Townsite and Mine*. Moving past it, Delia led them into a shallow depression, which seemed to be taking them straight into the rock itself. Suddenly they were walking through a narrow fissure in the stone and into a cave. Its uniform shape soon identified it to Greg as an abandoned mineshaft, burrowing deep into the mountainside.

After progressing nearly a hundred feet by the feeble glow of Delia's flashlight, the walls fell away and broadened into a large chamber. A flickering light awaited them, as well as the figure of a man bent over the flames.

At the sound of them, the man jumped up, rushed over, and gave Delia a hug.

"Men, this is Dale," she said, pulling back. "He's been waiting for us. He will be your guide now." She turned to face him. "You were right, Dale. They didn't waste any time. They were waiting for me back at the office, and almost got me. Two hours later, a team of three men snuck into the house in full gear. I don't know how these guys got away, but I picked them up near the house just as it went up in flames."

"Good thing you were there," Dale said. "Well, let's get you guys warmed up." He pointed to Greg's thigh. "Hey, is that blood on your leg?"

Greg nodded. "I'm all right," he said, shrugging off the man's concern. He sank to a sitting position and pulled as close to the campfire as he dared.

"I need to know what has happened," said Omar with a stunned look on his face. "One moment I am drifting off to sleep, happy that I have been granted forgiveness, or clemency, and knowing that I have helped protect America against one of my own teams. I am thinking that everything is wonderful, I have kept my word, and will soon see my son again. My future will begin in the morning, bright and hopeful. I then hear an explosion, look up to see fire everywhere, so I run out of the house to keep from burning to death. The next thing I know, I am outside, it is snowing, and Greg is pulling me away into a mad escape. I do not understand. What are we escaping from?"

Delia sighed. "Mr. Nirubi, I'm the one who owes you an explanation, although I'd rather cut off my own arm than have to tell you. But it turns out that your suspicions at one point were correct. Greg's so-called hosting of you, and his introducing you to Christianity, was just an elaborate army protocol to secure your cooperation. Back in Poland, you were growing more and more entrenched in your Muslim faith. We saw this as the only way to stop the New Year's Day plot in time."

Omar turned to Greg with a look of shock and revulsion. "So . . . everything you told me—"

"Now, wait a minute," interrupted Delia. "Greg knew nothing of this. I'm the one who misled you, and the United States government. He was totally unaware of the operation. All he knew was that you were a prisoner in need of friendship and direction while you recuperated from your wounds."

"Do you expect me to believe he *accidentally* led me to betray Islam and place my faith in Jesus Christ?" he bellowed.

"Omar, I share the gospel of Jesus with others about as accidentally as I breathe air," Greg said. "Give me another minute and I'll be sharing my faith with Dale here, even though I just met him and know nothing about him."

"I already believe," Dale said with a smile that earned him an immediate second look from Delia.

"Since when?" she asked.

"Not that it's any of your business, but since about a year ago."

Cocking his head, Greg pointed at Dale while still facing her. "You guys sound like you're—"

"Divorced." Delia shook her head. "Some years back." She turned back to Omar. "I'm so sorry things turned out this way, Mr. Nirubi. But as you can see, I've gone against my superiors to try and make this right. I had no clue they would attempt to terminate . . . I mean, kill you, when the operation was over. I know this must confirm for you the very worst things you've always believed about America."

"No, not America," Omar corrected. "Only some of those in your government. It has always been this way. But I have also learned a great deal about America's people in the last few weeks. You have far more of a conscience than I ever expected. Even, it appears, more than some of my own so-called brothers," he said, referring to his family's massacre.

"That part is the truth, I'm afraid," she said.

"I do not understand you Americans sometimes," Omar confessed. "One minute you are lying to me, trying to trick me to give up my knowledge, and the next you are sacrificing your lives and your careers to save my life."

"Do you remember what I told you the first day you arrived?" Greg said. "That I would protect you with my life, no matter what? That pledge came from Christ. No love is greater than that of a man willing to give his life for his friends. Without Him in my life, I never would have been able to do it. And now He's in your life too, and you're capable of the same thing."

"So that part was not a lie? The show of kindness, the willingness to forgive?"

"Again, the offer of clemency *was* a lie," Delia explained. "But Greg wasn't in on it. He was completely excluded from the deception, at least until days after the two of you met. He then did everything he could to make things right."

Omar let out a sudden bitter laugh, and then leaned forward and grabbed Dale's revolver, which was lying on his backpack in the dirt. Seething with anger, he aimed the weapon at each of them in turn.

"It does not matter," he growled. "None of it matters, because my prayer of asking Christ for forgiveness was also a lie."

CHAPTER 42

Greg closed his eyes, instantly grief-stricken.

"I only spoke those cursed words to lower your guard and to buy myself some time. Time to figure out an escape, which you and your hateful masters so easily arranged for me."

Equally dismayed, Delia shook her head in disbelief. "And the men in Miami? Were they dupes? Because certainly they were terrorists."

"Martyrs of war," Omar proclaimed. "Yes, they were brothers of mine. Proud al-Qaeda warriors ready to give their lives at my request. And my false confession was exactly that. A command that they lay down their lives for the sake of jihad."

Delia took a half step forward. "Wait. Are you saying you didn't compromise the New Year's Day plot, after all?"

Omar thrust the revolver in her face, cocking it. "Stop asking so many ignorant questions, woman. Whatever I did, it worked, did it not? It motivated you fools into taking me out here and at the risk of your own lives."

He now spun on his heel and aimed the barrel at Greg's forehead. "If you want to live, my so-called friend for life, then convince me why an American would forgive a terrorist sworn to destroy his country. And then offer to risk his life in return. That makes no sense at all."

"It makes about as much sense," Greg explained, "as a righteous God, who by all explanations should just get rid of His faithless, disobedient creations, but instead humbles himself to come, give His life to pay their penalty in full, and embrace them to himself."

"Would you stop your preaching for even a moment?" spat Nirubi. "That did not convince me one bit. I have half a mind to send a bullet through your head."

"The only person you would harm would not be me but a beautiful six-year-old boy, not unlike your own son, who would go fatherless, as your son probably would. I've already told you that I shot a boy, accidentally but through carelessness. After my life fell apart, alcoholism stole my family and my career, but I found forgiveness in Christ. Except not having forgiven myself, I was craving forgiveness from someone, and I wasn't getting it from my wife. So I tried to think of the next person I had wronged almost as badly. I could only think of the dead boy's father, who'd been sentenced and sent to jail. So I went to the federal prison to speak to him, and convinced him to give me ten minutes of his time. I don't know what he expected of me, but he certainly did not wish to talk to me. I wasted no time begging him to forgive me. I didn't even share my faith with him at that time. All I was after was his knowledge that I'd repented of my actions and to ask for his forgiveness."

"And of course he gave it to you," Omar said, rolling his eyes.

"Actually he didn't. Not at first, anyway. The first words he spoke were a question. He asked me where I had gotten the guts to come and face him like that. That's when I told him it was the power of the One who had forgiven me of all my sins. Not only did he grant me his forgiveness on the spot, he asked to learn more of the source of that kind of strength for himself. It wasn't long before I led him in the same prayer you said, Omar. Today he's out of prison and a content man at last. And he's become a good friend."

"Just like that?" Omar said. "No revenge? No justice?"

"Remember when I told you that it's not that easy? That the offer of forgiveness may be freely made, but it's been paid for through a great sacrifice?"

"What about back at the house, did you lie about forgiving yourself?" Omar asked. "Or was that just the most cunning part of this whole mockery?"

"I never lied to you," Greg insisted. "And whether you were truthful or not, God used you to lead me to a forgiveness I had been too stubborn to give myself."

"How noble of you to forgive yourself. But how about those who have harmed you the most? Starting with your wife?"

"My ex-wife." Greg paused and exhaled, gathering his strength. "That's a perceptive question, I must admit."

Nirubi waved the gun in his face. "Stop stalling or I will kill you. You are, after all, injured and a hindrance to my escape."

Greg looked Omar in the eye, took a deep breath, and forged ahead. "Fine, you want to hear it? Here it is, then. My wife not only left me and ended our marriage, but did something else as well. As it happened, right around the time I destroyed my life with alcohol, Donna discovered that she was pregnant. She confirmed the pregnancy two days after signing the divorce papers. So for her, carrying the baby to term was an intolerable thought."

"So she . . . ?" Delia said.

Greg nodded. "Legally I had no say in the matter, although I was so pickled with booze at the time that I probably would not have fully grasped what she was threatening. But yes, one day she had a friend drive her to a clinic, where she paid to have our baby killed."

Still wincing from the pain of his injury and now the agony of his words, Greg slumped forward, weeping.

Still holding the gun on them, Omar said, "I suppose she has not forgiven you. What an endless cycle. What you talk about so incessantly, you cannot seem to demonstrate in your own lives."

"You're absolutely right," Greg said weakly. "My inability to extend forgiveness to myself poisoned my ability to forgive her. Now I know about forgiveness from all sides. The healing power of receiving it, and the destructive power of withholding it."

"So now we come to me," Omar said. "Have you forgiven me for all my supposedly evil deeds against America?"

"Yes, I have. I can say that because I spent hours the first night here, begging God for the strength to help me to do it. And He gave it to me."

Omar seemed to consider his reply. "And would you now forgive my deception, knowing my prayer of conversion was only a trick to get you to lower your guard?"

There was a long silence. "Yes," Greg said at last. "I feel betrayed, angry, and a little disillusioned, but—" Greg stopped, replaying the man's question in his mind. "Are you asking me for my forgiveness?"

Nirubi shrugged. "Sure. Why not?"

"Then I give it to you. I would still die for you, Omar. But more important, so did Christ."

The answer enraged Omar. He stepped forward and pressed the gun barrel hard against Greg's temple.

"Do *not* say such a thing if you do not mean it!" he screamed. "I will blow your head off right here if you are not completely truthful with me! I have had enough of your lies!"

CHAPTER 43

"I do . . . I do mean it," Greg said, wincing against the gun poking his head.

"Of all your insipid preaching and your mind-numbing talk about forgiveness, this is all I really care to know. When I pull this trigger, will you still forgive me?"

His eyes wide, Greg paused for a split second, then nodded his head.

"It's okay," he whispered, shutting his eyes as if anticipating the bullet. "If that's what it takes. If that's what finally settles it for you—I told you, I'll gladly give my life for yours."

Omar Nirubi exhaled loudly and pulled back the gun barrel. He shook his head, his eyes now shining with tears.

"Is it morning yet?" Omar asked, peering down the length of the mine in the direction of the entrance.

"No," said Dale. "It's four o'clock. Dawn is still hours away."

Omar's mouth went slack, then opened wide. "Then why are those same white-uniformed soldiers out there at the tunnel mouth, guarding this place?"

The others swung around to see, and only Delia shook her head in disbelief. The other two men stared in awe.

"There's nothing there," said Delia, turning back.

"Oh yes there is," Greg and Dale countered in unison.

Greg turned to Omar. "You would not be seeing the angels if God was not dealing with you."

"Are you saying you know?" Omar said.

"Yes," said Greg. "I do."

After a long stare into Greg's eyes, Omar shook his head, uncocked the revolver, and handed it to Dale. "I am sorry," he muttered. "I should never have taken that."

"You wouldn't have hurt us," Delia said.

"I thought I would. But now I know better. Greg, do you forgive me all this?" he asked, his voice shaking.

Greg nodded. "Of course I do. But I'm not really the one whose forgiveness you need to accept. You did it once, out of false pretenses, but I wish you would ask Him again. For real this time."

Without answering, Omar got down on the ground and leaned forward onto his forehead.

Greg and Dale glanced at each other, then bowed their heads in silence, praying.

After several minutes Omar rose to his feet.

He was beaming.

Cocking his head, Omar looked over at Greg. "What is that feeling?" he asked.

Greg could only laugh. Dale, still taken aback by everything—the intense conversation, the angels, you name it—just stared into the fire and chuckled to himself.

"It's all gone," Dale told Omar. "Gone forever. You're free now."

"What's gone?" asked Delia.

"His sins," answered Dale. "All the crud separating him from God. It's disappeared forever."

"This is all getting to be a bit too much for me."

The three men turned to her.

"Well, you started it!" laughed Greg. "Remember collaring me in a penitentiary parking lot?"

She joined him in laughter. "All right, you got me there. Now, if we're through with all the spiritual hand-wringing, Mr. Nirubi, I have a question to ask you one more time. If the information you gave authorities was contrived, why was a real terrorist cell destroyed in Miami?"

"Because al-Qaeda is designed with an accordion-type attack structure," Omar explained. "If one cell is taken out, the next in line takes up its own plan. In this case, the man who developed their nerve gas will probably carry out an attack that is just as devastating. Only now he will do it all by himself, a solo killer. Your government's worst nightmare."

Delia gasped. "Do you know where to find this operative?"

Omar shook his head. "That is the genius of it. Most of the specific knowledge ends within one layer in either direction. The Miami crew knew all about him. In fact, one of their men recruited him."

"So what you're saying," Dale said, frowning now, "is that even though Washington thinks it's eliminated the New Year's Day threat, it's actually more potent and alive than ever? And you, us, the only people who know the truth, don't know enough to stop it?" He paused, whistled. "Either way, we're too busy running for our lives to prevent the thing from happening."

Greg faced him and shrugged. "That's about the whole of it."

"That's your reason to keep running," Dale said, his voice thick with conviction. "If you can somehow figure it out, help get the word out, that's worth everything. Didn't you both say you were fathers?"

The very sound of the word seemed to startle both Greg and Omar from some kind of lethargy, and they both stared at him.

"I mean, I'd give anything to have a boy," Dale continued. "I'd give him the boyhood of a thousand lifetimes, if only I had the chance. And if I knew he was in harm's way, or even the remotest chance of it, you'd have your hands full trying to stop me."

"I did not say I knew nothing about the maker of the nerve gas," said Omar. "I have a few hints, nothing more. I do remember that he was a non-Arab and a brilliant student at a prestigious research school."

"It's a start," Greg said, sounding hopeful. "Now, Dale, do we have a realistic chance of getting out of here?"

"What do you want first? Good news or the bad?"

"The bad news," Greg replied. "I'm more familiar with that variety."

"All right. Well, as it happens you are in the middle of the most heavily monitored, most high-tech listening post and surveillance facility in the world. The army, which can track a jackrabbit across the desert without lifting a finger, has chosen to research and develop all those miracles of science within a twenty-mile radius of where we stand. And for sheer redundancy of the system, as soon as you think you've beaten one of our barriers, another layer takes over. There's no beating them."

"So what's the good news?" asked Greg.

"Well, it's quite fascinating actually, and very powerful, especially on a morning like this. First of all, one of the reasons they develop all that technology out here is because it hardly ever snows and the sky is almost always clear. After all, it's a desert. All the imaging systems and weapons navigators capable of steering unmanned aircraft and the like—they prefer clear skies to do their business. And what we have outside at the moment is the thickest cloud cover this region has seen in eight years. That's the first part. Second is that this area has one of the most legendary hiding places and escape routes in the West. It's where some of the most hunted men in history—men like Geronimo, Cochise, and Mangas Coloradas—came to escape the regiments of cavalrymen pursuing them down to Mexico and beyond. The legendary stronghold of Cochise is just a few miles to the east of here. When we leave this cave into the daylight, you'll see what I'm talking about. We're not just on top of a mountain; we're surrounded by strange rock formations that could hide an elephant. I can show you ways of escaping this area that not even Uncle Sam's hottest reconnaissance bird could ever find."

"Sounds like we may have a plan," Greg offered.

"It's our best hope," added Delia.

"And it starts with you staying alive, honey," Dale said with a wink. "This whole mess reeks of plausible deniability. The president's ability to truthfully deny he knows anything about it. And you know who has some of that deniability right now? You do, Delia. All you've done so far is to obey orders and evade a couple of murderers. You escorted the men in your charge to a place of safety. You couldn't get court-martialed for that in a thousand years, and we need to keep it that way. As for these men, I'm guessing they're going to be on the run for a while. They'll need some backup, both transportational and computational. That's cars and computers, in plain English. Now, the snow has given us some time. Delia, I suggest you use it to get yourself back to the base, find some wheels, and hit the road. You're still in cell phone communication, right?"

She shook her head. "Greg, you don't still have the cell phone I gave you, do you?"

Greg looked down at the assault vest he'd taken from the downed attacker. "I do, but won't that be picked up too easily?"

She smiled and reached out her hand. Receiving the device, she flipped it open and quickly snapped a picture of Greg and Omar. "It's the camera I wanted."

Scheer chuckled. "Great call, Delia. There went the president's deniability."

Greg pulled out a pair of telephones from one of the vest's pockets.

"Those are satellite phones!" Delia said. "Way to go, Greg. And look—the numbers are stenciled on the sides. We're in business."

"Good," said Dale as one of the phones flew through the air and struck Delia's open hand. "Then get on out of here. These men and I have some hiking to do."

CHAPTER 44

Pasadena, California

The young man, who now thought of himself only as Azzam the Younger, walked aimlessly along the sidewalks of downtown Pasadena, lost in the throes of his dilemma. As a scientist he had relished the challenges of bringing his stunningly lethal concoction to life. But mostly, he was compelled to admit, his genius ended there. The logistics of dispersing the poison over a large crowd of people now seemed to elude him, to exceed his vaunted intelligence.

Buoyed by the cool air and its bracing relief from the confines of his apartment, he cast a glance about him, hoping for a random stroke of inspiration.

Blue sky, palm trees, streetlights—nothing seemed to help.

Until the raid on the Miami cell, he hadn't counted on this task falling to him at all. He had thought of himself only as the lone scientist toiling away in obscurity, leaving all other issues to the operational men. Now his sworn mission of carrying out the attack by himself left him reeling under a barrage of questions he'd never entertained before.

Security. Concealment. Disguises. Even the apparatus necessary to disperse the deadly mist. He had jerry-rigged the apparatus needed to carry out his research, but that had been elementary and small scale. What the raid required was massive and elaborate. And there was no longer time for leisurely design and construction.

Al-Qaeda was depending on him.

Finally, he looked up and saw, waving from a streetlight banner, the bright red shape of his answer.

Of course, he thought to himself.

The solution came to him as perfect and complete as an email from heaven.

The infidels would die like flies.

Miller Peak Wilderness, Arizona—that same moment

"One of the great things about military installations," said Dale Scheer as they followed his flashlight beam down into the darkness, awkwardly straddling a small channel of clear running water between their feet, "is that they keep things well maintained. Even, if it serves their purpose, old and decrepit things like hundred-year-old mineshafts and crumbling waterworks."

"Why in the world would they keep something like this place maintained?" Greg asked, grunting with the effort of keeping his feet dry.

"Because as it turns out, the mountain above us is riddled with hidden and not-so-hidden monitoring and electronic testing sites. And if you'll look up here . . ." Dale aimed the flashlight at the shaft's ceiling. Reaching up, he grazed with his fingertips a bundle of brightly colored cords mounted along the low-slung ceiling. "That's one thing," he said, lowering the beam again to point their way, much to his companions' relief. "The mining tunnels provided a perfect conduit for all the power and guidance wiring that was needed. Secondly, about half of the support equipment has pretty major cooling needs. That's the reason this water is still running free and clear. Most tourists brave enough to come this far think it's a miracle spring of some sort. But it's actually the army's sheer stubbornness."

"Where is this going to lead us?" Omar asked with a tinge of apprehension in his voice. "It was my predecessor who loved caves with such a passion. Me, not so much."

"The short answer is that it's going to lead us out of the mountain many miles from Reef Townsite or Huachuca Canyon, which is the first place they'll look when the snow clears. The more precise answer is that we'll exit back into daylight in three hours, about six miles from here, although I've never measured it exactly. The location will be the Huachuca Peak watershed, otherwise known as Cochise Creek, approximately four miles southeast of Sierra Vista, Arizona."

The other two whistled in admiration.

"You certainly know your stuff," said Greg.

"This is my playground," Scheer chortled. "It's what I have instead of a family life."

The statement elicited a pause, punctuated only by the sound of footsteps on stone and the gurgling of water. They walked on for several interminable minutes, after which Scheer spoke again.

"Gentlemen, this is where I leave you. I'm expected back on base today, and although I'm allowed sick days and time off, given what all's happened at the base, today's not a good day to take off unexpectedly."

With that, Scheer turned to his left and shined the light down a side shaft, which suddenly appeared there, headed downward.

"This is the fun part of the tunnel system," he said. "This, my friends, is the Cochise Creek chute. It was bored separately by the Army Corps of Engineers a few decades ago, using some of their most specialized equipment. Its path through the stone is so smooth and regular that you're going to ride it straight down to freedom, right down to the desert floor. The ride's more thrilling than anything you'll find at the best amusement park. And you'll have no need of a flashlight, because it's seven o'clock in the morning now. Once you get to the bottom, there'll be plenty of daylight."

Greg peered down the chute, lit only by the pale gleam of Scheer's flashlight. He could see no end, and no sign of any sunlight.

"You're sure it's not plugged up anywhere?"

"If it was," said Scheer, sealing off its water flow with a metal barrier hanging from a chain, "it wouldn't have that water running down its length, now, would it?"

"We just slide down through the freezing water?"

Scheer pushed the barrier down to the bottom, sending all the water down the main channel before them.

"Not anymore. It'll be a bit damp, but clean as a whistle."

Omar took a deep and reluctant breath, turned to give Scheer a handshake, then looked back to the chute's entrance. Stepping over the barrier, he grabbed both sides of the passage, eased himself down, and let go. A "Whoa!" rose to mark his fall as his body disappeared from sight.

Now came Greg's turn.

"Thanks for your help," he told Scheer with a smile. "I'm sorry we didn't meet under better circumstances. I'd love to hang out again sometime, and have you show me the area."

"Me too."

"And maybe see you and that beautiful woman back together again."

Dale Scheer didn't respond with words, but instead gave a nod.

Greg, imitating Omar's entry, carefully lowered his backside onto the stone, then let go.

All at once he was flying through darkness, the stone at his back almost impossible to feel. Cold air rushed up and over his hands and face, the only discomfort in an otherwise exhilarating plunge. Only the smallest imperfections gave him the feeling of stone under his·body as tiny cracks and channels sped past his legs. Far below him, he could hear whoops and shrieks of delight. Omar was certainly enjoying himself, if that was any comfort. Sliding on through the long seconds, he began to experiment, first sending his body high on the right side, then the left, alternately weaving all over the chute's passage. He was trying to imagine just how fast he was going when it hit him. He was a child again, flying through outer space at warp speed, on his way to some epic interplanetary battle.

He laughed out loud, perhaps the first time in years that he'd done so. The last time had been with Robby, who would have loved this.

Finally he began to see a faint glow emerging through the gap between his feet. Suddenly fearful, he began shouting to make sure Omar had cleared well out of his path. What would the landing be like? Scheer had definitely seemed to have a glimmer in his eye when he'd described the experience.

Before he could speculate further, the end rushed up to meet him. An eyeful of blinding daylight and a brief, savagely brisk flip into the air came next. He twisted midair, tumbling. Then he struck a stiff coldness, hard.

That was it. He'd been tossed skyward at the bottom of a tiny opening in the mountain, then crudely deposited back onto the earth.

Which just so happened, on this particular morning, to be amply covered with new-fallen snow.

CHAPTER 45

In an instant he was upright again, unwilling to soak any more of his body than he had to. Glancing ahead, he took in sixty miles of winter desert, stretching on as far as the eye could see. Omar was doing the same thing, standing before the view and staring.

It was the most beautiful landscape either of them could remember seeing. Lit by a warm shade of pink and purple by the rising sun, the desert spread out as a vast painting, overwhelming and heartwarming.

Greg felt like the king of the world, as if he were gazing out at this marvelous planet's first appearance. He bowed his head and whispered, "Thank you, Lord."

Now, after hours of crouching and walking in darkness, followed by a few minutes of virtual free fall, it was time to run. And running in the open air felt good to the two men. The once hard-baked earth was now soft and moist, yielding to their steps and allowing them to propel themselves forward with great momentum. Far to their right ran a long strip of road, the only sign of civilization for miles. Greg pointed to it and called, "That way!"

Just a few feet away, Omar suddenly dropped to the ground, stomach first. Confused, Greg did the same.

"What is it?" Greg asked.

Still prone, squinting from the sun, Omar pointed. In the sky to their far left a trio of helicopters was banking hard toward the mountains to the north. Huachuca Canyon.

"Do you think they can see us this far away?"

"Maybe," Greg answered. "But that's the beauty of Dale's escape route. It put us far away from the nearest known exit point. They'd never think we would come out so far from familiar ground."

Just seconds later the choppers disappeared behind a line of foothills. Greg and Omar leaped to their feet and resumed their running across the desert tundra, toward the highway that was still way off in the distance.

For two hours they continued their trek, keeping the highway constantly in their sights. At last, as the cloud cover began to dissipate and the rising temperature melted the snow, the road grew rapidly in size. Soon they were upon it, feeling its hardness with their feet.

"What do we do now?" asked Omar, sitting and resting on the pavement's edge.

"We wait for someone to come by and offer us a lift."

"Well, from the looks of it, we may be waiting for quite some time," Nirubi said.

"You're going to eat those words," Greg said with a hint of gloating in his voice. "Look. Down there." At the bottom of an endless incline, an eighteen-wheeler was laboring to climb toward them.

"I wonder what's wrong with it?" Omar said.

"In these kinds of conditions, there's no telling."

Strangely, the truck seemed to move even more slowly with every foot it approached them. The incline was almost to the point of nonexistence, yet the massive truck appeared close to expiration at the brink of reaching the road's summit.

"It doesn't sound like the driver's shifting gears," Greg observed. "Just in case, we better hide before it reaches us."

The two huddled behind the only thing available—a couple of large cactuses. Finally, shuddering and groaning as if its engine was about to seize up for good, the truck inched its way toward them. Gradually the driver came into view. He was a young man, twenty or so, squinting out through tiny slits for eyes, a malformed cigarette dangling from his lips.

They heard the pounding of fists against metal coming from inside the trailer.

Greg turned to Omar, gave him a signal that said *let's go*. Together they stood and took off sprinting, heading for the accessible platform attached to the trailer. Greg was the first to jump on, Omar following him a mere moment later, leaping up onto a thick metal grate.

The pounding was undeniable. There were people inside the trailer and they were desperate to get out. Hanging on tight, Greg glanced down at his newly acquired assault vest and spotted his salvation: a curved Ka-Bar commando knife. He pulled the knife from the vest and plunged it through the trailer's outer skin, burying the blade to the hilt.

"Watch out!" Greg yelled to whoever might be standing beyond the hole.

But the pounding continued. He yanked the blade upward, expanding the tear, and then sideways until he had a sizable section cut out. Immediately brown hands began to poke through, heedless of the blade's danger.

He took the flap's upper edge in his right hand and pulled, peeling it back like a banana. The screaming grew louder, and now he could make out the language.

Spanish.

The odd picture was starting to make sense. With more

cutting and yanking at the trailer's skin, he opened a hole big enough for Greg and Omar to slip through.

The first thing to greet the two men was the stench. The smell of human waste mixed with vomit and sweat. The second thing was the mass of hands, all of them waving frantically. Greg and Omar exchanged appalled looks.

"Human trafficking," Greg said. "Illegal workers, packed in here like sardines. Some look like they're near death."

"But before we can help them," said Omar, "we must deal with the driver."

Greg looked around them—at the highway, at the warming desert as it crawled past. He nodded his agreement. "You're right. First thing we do is take him down."

Greg exited the trailer and inched his way forward to the cab, careful not to be seen in the truck's side mirrors. Reaching the driver's door, he gripped the knife as he peered into the cab.

"Hey! Scumbag!" he shouted. "What's up with the cargo?"

Without a second's hesitation, he threw open the door, reached inside, and grabbed the young man by his shirt collar, launching him out onto the desert floor. With a swerving leap he was inside the cab and behind the wheel. Thankfully he'd driven a moving truck to help pay for college, so he understood the gearshift—probably better than the driver did. The cab's air was saturated with the sickly sweet aroma of marijuana.

The transmission, however, was jammed in second gear. Yet it took only a firm stomp on the clutch and several wriggles of the shifter to loosen it enough and slip it into third gear. Easing forward, he adjusted the rearview mirror and glimpsed Omar through the torn opening in the trailer, doing his best to comfort the people inside.

Greg smiled as he pulled ahead. Something had definitely happened inside that man.

CHAPTER 46

Reaching highway speeds now, Greg drove the truck beyond the desert valley and into a series of low hills. There, a turnoff sign indicated a nearby rest stop, surrounded by trees and thick bushes.

Pulling into the most secluded parking spot he could find, he brought the truck to a halt and leaped down from the driver's seat. Taking the keys with him, he raced to the back of the trailer and began trying keys in its oversized lock. Four tries later, he felt the key slide in and turned it with a click. The lock fell away, as did the chain it was holding. Greg jumped up, unfastened the bolts keeping the door shut, then pulled hard on the door.

The stench that now rolled over him was twice as strong as before. The smell clung to human bodies, which poured out of the enclosure, prisoners fleeing for their lives. Unable to do more than step back and let them proceed, he greeted Omar with a sympathetic look.

Anguished voices flowed out in Spanish, assaulting the men's ears with their pleading, though otherwise incomprehensible.

A moment later a few stragglers peeked out from the trailer, pointing back toward two motionless bodies.

Greg reached up and pulled himself to the trailer floor, wincing at the sudden reminder of his injured thigh.

The first face had the ghastly paleness of a body that had been dead for days. He indicated that Omar should tend to the man while he turned to the second one, which wasn't as pale as the first. Just to make sure, he felt the neck for a pulse. The man kneeling beside him jerked at the sudden motion, clearly still fearful for his life.

"No, no . . ." Greg began, searching his memory for the precious few phrases of Spanish he once knew. Tapping his chest, he repeated, *"No mal. No mal. Amigo."*

Anxiously looking him in the eyes, the man nodded and visibly relaxed.

"¿Está muerto?" he asked.

That phrase, sadly, Greg understood. He moved closer, feeling for the smallest sign of life.

There it was. A delicate flutter across his fingertips.

"No. No muerto," he said with a smile to the one waiting, who by his devotion must have been either a relative or a close friend. *"Muy enfermo."*

The man was probably dehydrated, as well as oxygen-deprived. Greg checked his vest, but it held no water. He thought of the truck's cab and remembered seeing shiny cylinders bouncing around on the front seat and floor. The mere thought of it, with this man dying of thirst back here in the trailer, made him want to drive back into the desert, find that driver, and beat him to a bloody pulp.

He looked up to where Omar was tending to the other victim.

"Any luck?" Greg asked.

Omar shook his head, saying nothing.

Greg leaped down and ran to the cab, flinging open the door.

Inside, he found bottles of mineral water strewn across the floor. Grabbing them, he hurried back to where the group of thirty or more Mexicans lay resting on a patch of grass, listless, like a bunch of spent marathoners at the finish line. He handed out all but one of the bottles, then climbed into the trailer to care for the unconscious one.

After the first trickle of water down his throat, the man's cheeks began to quiver. Slowly his eyes opened.

Holding the bottle to the man's lips, Greg took stock of their situation. "What's the date, Omar?"

"I think it is the thirtieth."

"Less than two days to find a mass murderer and stop him, and here we are nursing wounded in the middle of the Arizona desert. It doesn't look good, my friend." Greg looked up to the ailing Mexican's friend, a lean man. "*¿Inglés?*" he asked.

The man, wearing a sheepish smile, held up his thumb and index finger. "Little bit," he said.

"How long have you been in this trailer?"

"Three, maybe four days. Hard to tell in the dark."

Greg shuddered. "Where were you going? *¿Adónde en América?*"

He nodded. *"Al Norte de California. Valle de San Joaquin."*

"Northern California? The San Joaquin Valley?"

The destination made sense. The San Joaquin Valley was a dense agricultural region, widely considered the breadbasket of the West Coast.

"Nuestras familias . . . our families. They wait for us. Now fear us dead."

Greg nodded, for their families had every right to fear. Every few years, a truck was pulled over in this very region, its trailer full of dead bodies, usually from asphyxiation.

As he was thinking about their next move, the satellite phone rang at Greg's waist. He snatched it up and checked the caller ID screen. It was Delia.

"You two okay?" she asked breathlessly.

"We're fine, and so was Dale, last time we saw him. He escorted us to the middle of the mountain, and then had us slide the rest of the way ourselves."

"That's his favorite spot," she said. "Listen. I've been doing some checking and most the cities hosting a New Year's bowl game also have major research universities. And Pasadena, home of the Rose Bowl, has Caltech—not only one of America's most elite scientific schools, but they also conduct research on nerve gas for the Pentagon. Hear that? Nerve gas."

That was it! It had to be.

"Delia, don't ask me how, but I think we have a way to get there. Just hold on and I'll call you back soon."

He shut the phone and turned to Omar. "What about Pasadena? Does that sound likely?"

"Pasadena? California?" He smiled. "Yes, I think I have heard that name before. And there are many mosques in California?"

Greg nodded.

"Then, yes, Pasadena must be the place!"

Thanking God and apologizing for his faithlessness all at once, Greg remembered his lament of just a moment before. Here he was, in a unique position to stop the attack, despite being in the humblest of circumstances.

That's God for you, he thought.

After giving the immigrants time to wash up and recover a bit, as well as to bury their loved one, Greg approached his translator with a message.

"Tell everyone I will drive."

"California?"

"Yes. I will drive all of us to California, and then I will leave you with the truck."

The man translated to the group, which immediately broke out into clapping.

"And soon we will stop for food. *Comida!*" Greg shouted as he turned and headed for the cab.

Unfortunately it was more than an hour before they finally found a food market. Parked at the rear of the store for maximum concealment, Greg had everyone stay put in the trailer while he and Omar discreetly entered the store to get food for everyone. He paid from a thick wad of bills he'd found stuffed in the cab's glove box. On returning to the truck, he and Omar passed the food through the back of the trailer to the famished immigrants.

That done, they headed out again, following Interstate 10 through Phoenix and across to the California border. Greg followed the farm workers' instructions for avoiding rigorous border inspections by leaving the interstate and tracing a little-known mountain road across the desert. The precaution added an extra four hours to their journey, but it was a welcome comfort to Greg, who had made the crossing before and wondered how he would do it without the necessary papers or legal cargo.

It was late that night, under a starry sky, when he stopped the truck outside Palmdale in the high desert just inland from greater Los Angeles. After handing the truck keys to his translator, who claimed he knew how to drive the rig, Greg and Omar said their good-byes to the immigrants and then started walking away.

Not thirty seconds later, Greg heard a sound behind him and spun around to see what the commotion was all about.

The immigrants had returned, converging on the pair with hugs, slaps on the back, and hearty handshakes, crying *gracias*

MARK ANDREW OLSEN

over and over again. The outpouring was so overwhelming that Greg and Omar were forced to wait and watch the truck leave, finally disappearing as it entered the interstate.

Breathing a prayer for their safety, Greg turned back with a smile of satisfaction.

"I like it better when you preach with your actions," Omar said, grinning at him, "than with all your talk."

"I'll remember that," Greg laughed.

"And now where are we going? We have no transportation and very little money."

"You'll see soon enough."

CHAPTER 47

Cahill residence, Palmdale, California—New Year's Day

Robby Cahill was playing alone in his backyard. It wasn't that he had no friends. More than anything, it was the mothers. After the debacle at his last birthday party, complete with cops and a screaming birthday boy and a father who had shown up as G.I. Joe, little Robby had fallen from his classmates' Most Wanted guest list.

He hadn't been invited to any parties, even the obligatory ones with his class, in longer than he could remember.

Christmas had come and gone, and had proven equally disappointing. His father had disappeared with some vague promise and failed to produce even a card. And his mother had bought him a popgun as a gift, not the powerful BB gun he'd really wanted. But Robby didn't want to hurt his mother's feelings, so on this day he finally had taken the popgun outside for a test hunt.

Aiming down the barrel's narrow groove, Robby was preparing to take out a bad guy masquerading as a dragonfly. He aimed, squeezed the trigger, and heard the *pop*.

Then he saw a light. It blinked at him from the back hedge, not once but twice. It was the signal—the one his father had taught him, and had used to great mischief at his birthday party. But this time Robby learned his lesson. No more sudden outbursts and sprints across the lawn.

As he began to walk casually toward the hedge, Robby thought back to yesterday, when he and his mom had received a visit from a very friendly man in a nice suit. He gave his mom a tiny card that said *FBI* on it, saying he was an agent.

Rather than tell stories about cops and robbers, the man had come to tell them that Robby's dad was in some dangerous trouble. The FBI could help Daddy a great deal if only they could reach him. Mommy had assured the man that she hadn't spoken with Robby's father in months. The FBI man asked his mom to call the number on the card, letting him know if there was any contact, and then he'd left.

Robby felt like a real secret agent when his dad's signal appeared. He continued to wander toward the bushes, pretending to aim and shoot at things around the yard just in case his mom was watching him from a window.

He could see his dad now. He was crouching down in the underbrush. Close by was a strange-looking man, someone Robby had never seen before.

At the sight of his father's face, all pretense of secret agent coolness vanished from the young boy's mind.

"Daddy! Daddy!" he cried, trying in vain to hug his father through the hedge.

"Robby, I'm so glad to see you finally," said Greg with moist eyes. "I'm sorry about Christmas. Remember, I told you that I was going away somewhere special? Well, there was no way for me to call or write. I just couldn't, even though I wanted to every day."

"That's all right, Daddy. I forgive you."

"Now listen, Daddy has to talk with Mommy real bad, and right away. But I need your help to do it."

"Okay, Daddy."

A few minutes later, Robby rushed back into the house, calling for his mother.

"Mommy! Mommy! You have to come see what's in the backyard!" Without waiting for her, he ran out again. But his mother was following close behind. Robby had not been this animated in months.

When Donna Cahill came within ten feet of the hedge, Greg's voice floated out from the bushes, low and nonthreatening.

"Donna, it's me. Please, whatever you do, let me explain. I have to talk to you. And believe me, it's important."

She froze in place, not only from surprise but from an instant wariness at what her ex-husband had to say. These days nothing, no matter how carefully phrased, ever seemed to turn out well.

"Donna, what I have to say isn't about me, or about us, or even Robby. But if I don't get some help right away, tens of thousands of people may die today."

She rolled her eyes and grimaced. "Yeah, right, Greg. You're the savior of the world, hiding out in my backyard bushes."

There was a commotion in the shrubbery, and Omar stepped forward, slow and smiling.

"Hello, Mrs. Cahill. I am here with your husband, to help him and to verify that he speaks the truth. Do you recognize me?"

After recovering from the shock of this man's sudden appearance, she said, "I do recognize you, but I'm not sure from where."

"I am Omar Nirubi."

The kitchen scrubber in her hand fell to the grass.

"But . . . isn't that the name of the al-Qaeda leader?"

"It is. And I am he."

"But they said you were dead. I saw the president on TV talking about it just the other day."

"As you can see, I am not dead, nor am I a terrorist any longer. Please, your husband is on a mission of the highest urgency, and we alone can save thousands from a horrible death."

"New Year's Day? I don't get it. I thought the New Year's Day threat was stopped days ago."

"There's another one," said Greg. "Only nobody will believe us until we prove it. Will you take us to Pasadena, the Rose Bowl?"

Pointing at Omar, she shook her head emphatically. "Isn't it a federal crime to transport someone like him?"

"Donna, he's just been given a pardon for all his crimes from the president. I saw it myself. He's the one who made the Miami raid possible. He helped to stop the killing."

Standing stock-still, she shifted her gaze from one man to the other and back again. Clearly she had no reason to trust her ex-husband, let alone this wild scenario of his. On the other hand, he'd once been in Special Forces, and no matter what she thought of him, he did know what he was talking about.

Finally she sighed, slowly nodded. "I'll do it. But, Greg, if you make me regret this, it'll be the last time you see Robby for the rest of your days."

Fort Huachuca—minutes later

Concealed by the falling curtains of snow, Delia snuck back to her car, hurried inside and started it with a terrifyingly slow chugging of the over-chilled engine. When it turned over at last, she slammed it awkwardly into gear and sped away, heedless of the wintry streets.

She was ten miles from Huachuca before she allowed herself the luxury of slowing down to posted speeds, grasping the cell phone even more tightly against her lap. Within its invisible circuitry lay not only the key to her survival but her chance at vindication against all the injustice piled up against her.

Part of her felt like a naive ingénue, assuming the best from some very dark and serious men commanding her. Somewhere she could just imagine that officials with impressively decorated uniforms were laughing at her, she just knew it. Sitting around and slapping their knees, guffawing at the thought of a military officer believing an American president would let the leader of al-Qaeda live free among his constituents.

She shook her head bitterly and growled under her breath. How could she have been so gullible?

What came next would wipe those smirks from their faces, she assured herself.

White House cabinet room, West Wing—4 hours later

The table usually reserved for cabinet secretaries was now surrounded by a half-dozen generals from every branch of the armed forces, as well as crisply suited civilians from affiliated agencies.

Each face seemed glazed over by the satisfaction of sitting in such an august place on such a gratifying errand—to receive the profuse congratulations of the president of the United States. Only a few knew the full truth's unsavory details; that they were being honored for treachery and murder, carried out in the solemn interest of the security of the American homeland.

A rear door opened, and as a single body the men stood from their seats, rigid and proud. Their commander in chief sauntered in, acknowledging them with a curt nod.

He had a visitor with him.

"Men, you've been gathered here to receive the thanks and congratulations of a grateful nation for the elimination of two grave threats, all within a three-hour period."

The unknowing generals nodded with grins of ill-concealed pride.

"However, the agenda has changed."

At that moment a large monitor screen flickered to life behind him.

On it glowed the face of a young woman in an army uniform. A captain.

"Gentlemen, meet Captain Delia Kilgore."

The generals who didn't know snickered inwardly.

Those who did know felt a chill of shock and fear race down their spines.

"Unfortunately, Captain Kilgore is joining us from a satellite linkup down in the southwest, and only at the last moment, which is a shame. You see, she deserves to receive thanks and recognition as well. It's Captain Kilgore who unearthed and championed the old Tabula Rasa protocol that became Project Forgiven. In fact, I would say she's the only one here who deserves any kind of favorable recognition."

The ponderous faces around the table now jerked abruptly toward the president's.

The image on the screen shifted to the poorly lit faces of two wide-eyed men, huddled together in some kind of cavern.

"Gentlemen," continued the president, "meet Omar Nirubi, very much alive as of a few hours ago. On the run for his life, by the way, from elements of our very own United States Armed Forces. And also—Captain England, did I forget something important about these two men?"

She smiled at him meekly, then faced the cordon of reddening faces.

"Only, Mr. President, that these fugitives are risking their freedom to prevent the New Year's Day plot from being carried out during the next few hours. It seems treachery and murder did not produce the desired result."

Delia nodded, trying to restrain the thrill coursing through her body, and thanking God for the vicarious pleasure of this two-way video feed, which now allowed her to see the self-importance and arrogance drain from every downcast face around that table.

National Counterterrorism Center, McLean, Virginia

Once the data from a certain Captain Delia Kilgore had cleared the proper channels and been authenticated, it took the NCC's computer staff only minutes to cross-check the Caltech grad students involved in chemical warfare research against the FBI and Homeland Security suspect files.

Immediately a strong candidate popped up.

His name was Jack Woodward, a recent convert to Islam, and to top it off the lead student on Caltech's nerve gas project.

Minutes later, word arrived at the Pasadena office of the FBI. Within fifteen minutes a dozen cars screeched wildly from the office's parking garage.

Teams converged on both Jack Woodward's laboratory and apartment. At the residence they found plenty of incriminating evidence, including a refrigerator full of vials. But no sign of Jack. He was gone, on his way to join in the holiday's festivities.

The attack was in progress.

CHAPTER 48

The Rose Bowl, Pasadena, California

It was still a few hours before kickoff, and the stadium hosting the Rose Bowl game—granddaddy of all college football match-ups—was already a madhouse of milling crowds and frantic preparations. Its vast parking lot was overflowing with early birds and tailgaters alike. Television trucks and college transport buses lined the stadium's ivy-covered flanks.

And all this came prior to the arrival of Homeland Security.

The first sign of their invasion was the thumping sound of helicopters—eight Black Hawks, all in a row, followed by a Bell Ranger and an aging Huey. Without regard for the snarled traffic or flow of pedestrians, the choppers landed in every available space within a quarter mile of the stadium fence.

The reaction was immediate as the sky filled with careening dust devils of food wrappers, paper programs, and stray bits of clothing. Eventually the rotor blades slowed and the aircraft began unloading passengers by the dozens.

They failed to greet anyone, apologize for the inconvenience of such a disruptive arrival, or even make eye contact. Many struggled with the weight of oversized metal cases in their fists, while others led German shepherds on leashes, all of them rushing toward the stadium.

Captain Kilgore exited the third helicopter, for it was her own tip, and her adamant assertion of its validity, that had caused this whole ruckus in the first place. She'd already been warned that if her information proved false, she'd be spending the remainder of her career as an Aleutian crossing guard. But now was not the time to dwell on that; now was the time for action. Following the long column of operatives into the perimeter, she stopped and looked around for Greg and Omar.

Within a couple of minutes the game's preparations had fallen into chaos. A two-star general nearly canceled the game outright, citing presidential authority as his justification, when a Rose Bowl official attempted to deny the invaders entry. Even the locker rooms and private suites were intruded on by shouting officers and bomb-sniffing dogs.

On the field itself, last-minute chalking came to an abrupt halt as large explosives scanners were wheeled out to the fifty-yard line. The stadium's gates were replaced by metal detectors, hastily erected from the bulky metal cases.

Next, a minivan made its way through the crush of cars and people, and Greg and Omar stepped out.

Leaning in to make apologies to his wife and son, he quickly turned and the pair began running with the same urgency as the chopper teams.

Delia, scanning the crowd with a pair of binoculars, had just spotted the two men when she was interrupted by a tapping finger on her shoulder.

"Captain Kilgore, I've been instructed to tell you that the

preliminary sweep has resulted in a negative finding. No sign of any chemical agent or suspicious activity."

She scowled at the messenger. "You realize he could hide the entire dose in a soda can," she said. "A sweep that fast can't be the final verdict."

"Captain, the metal detectors and roving dogs will be the only ongoing presence."

"Great," she snapped as she raised her arm and began waving over the crowd. Just then her satellite phone rang.

"Delia, we see you!" shouted Greg over all the noise. "But the officers won't let us through without tickets or some official document!"

"Maybe it's for the best," she said. "The teams aren't finding anything. They're starting to turn skeptical. Hold on. Something's happening."

She glanced around as one by one the other officers' cell phones began ringing. One dark-suited official snatched a radio from a waiting police officer and jerked it to his ear.

"What's going on?" she muttered to herself. She raised her phone again. "Greg, something weird is happening. People are being called away, all at once. I just saw an agency executive almost clobber a cop for his radio."

On the other side of the security perimeter, Greg was wracking his brain. He still believed the Pasadena clues were correct, as well as Omar's strong reaction to the rose allusion. But if not the game . . .

Greg's face turned white and he literally struck himself upside the head.

"The Rose Parade!" he shouted.

Indeed, something strange and unusual was happening along the parade route. In the past several minutes, hundreds of people had fallen unconscious at the float staging area, requiring a convoy of ambulances to come to the rescue. It was first assumed that some exotic species of flower petal had inflamed rare forms of allergies, at least until later, when rounds of allergy medicine administered to the sick had failed to help them.

By now, the parade's legendary floats had drifted out onto Colorado Avenue.

Within a few short minutes, nearly forty people had died in the viewing stands. Panic swept through the crowds as nobody could guess the contagion's source.

CHAPTER 49

Miles away at the Rose Bowl Stadium, Greg heard the news through his satellite link with Delia.

"That's it!" she exclaimed. "The parade! Greg, can you get there? Because I'm stuck!"

Looking around frantically, Greg spotted a news helicopter parked among army vehicles. He and Omar began sprinting toward the craft.

"Can you fly this thing?" Omar yelled as they climbed aboard.

Greg nodded. He'd once flown choppers for the army.

Instantly Greg began flipping switches and firing up the rotors. Before it was even considered safe to lift off, he jerked back on the stick and took the bird airborne. Below them, spectators ran for cover, terrified by the hasty departure.

Rising into a blue sky, they both craned their necks in search of the parade.

"I don't know where it is any more than you do," Greg panted. "Look for some kind of sign."

"There!" Omar shouted. He pointed southward, where the sky was cluttered with a chaotic array of helicopters, hovering up or down in rapid landings and takeoffs. "That has to be it."

Greg aimed the chopper's nose in that direction and began racing toward the scene.

"When we get there, what do we look for?" Omar asked.

"I have no idea. We've gotten this far, though. I just pray we'll know it when we see it."

"And then be in a position to do something about it."

"Right," agreed Greg.

"Look!" This time Omar was pointing out in front of the helicopter.

Below them stretched the most colorful streets either of them had ever seen, filled with the Rose Parade's famous flower-petal floats.

"How beautiful. But is it one of them killing the people, or something else?"

"Just look at the mayhem going on down there!" Greg said.

The crowds below were spreading apart in a series of waves sweeping through the streets. The vacated areas revealed bodies, lying motionless, as onlookers ran for cover.

"It looks like the carnage is traveling down Colorado Avenue," said Greg. "I'll bet it's a float."

"Most likely a float that involves some use of smoke or steam," Omar added. "It would be a perfect way to diffuse an airborne gas."

Then they saw it. Moving down the avenue at the head of the progression was a magnificent rose-covered re-creation of a Mississippi steamboat, complete with working smokestacks. All the people who had lined its decks now lay dead. The vapors rising from the two stacks appeared thicker and darker than they should be.

"That's the one," both men stated at once.

"Can you lower the helicopter onto the float's deck?" asked Omar.

Dipping sideways and dropping as low as he could for a better view, Greg peered down, hovering there for a moment, then shook his head.

"I can't. Too many wires and structures in the way."

"Then how are we going to stop this thing? I must get down there and stop him!" Omar gave Greg a panicked look, turned and opened his door while unbuckling his seat belt.

"Oh, no you don't!" screamed Greg.

"It's the only way!" Omar shouted back, and then without hesitating leaped from the helicopter.

Even for a crowd in the throes of a terrorist attack, the sight was shocking. A man, plummeting through the air, landing on the float, and instantly collapsing its flimsy outer layer. Above the chaos, a gasp rose up from all those who had witnessed the stunt.

Omar had struck the roof of the float's pilothouse, then crashed all the way through the successive layers of cheap construction to the bottom deck of the float—the flatbed of a truck chassis. Breaking a leg and several of his ribs in the process, he was sure.

Still ambulatory from the overdose of adrenaline surging through his veins, Omar slowly stood, putting all his weight on his good leg. Within his first few breaths he reeled backward, his left arm shaking uncontrollably.

Feeling his body and limbs leave his control, he knew at once this was not a symptom of the fall but of the poison itself. Omar realized that he'd chosen the right target.

In a corner of the float stood a man who looked more like

a surfer than a soldier of jihad. Yet the chemical mask gave him away, along with the ampule he held up with two fingers.

"I thought you'd been killed, my master!" the man cried out, his voice garbled by the mask.

"Stop this right now!" shouted Omar. Swaying from the float's erratic course, as well as from his injuries and inhaling the poisoned air, he could hardly stay on his feet.

"But I'm serving jihad!" the man insisted. "I'm killing the infidels! What I hold in my hand is the final, ultimate dose. The first ones were but tests, while this will kill a million of the American dogs!"

"I am telling you," Omar said, grimacing, "this murder will stop now!"

Omar stumbled forward and grasped the man's arm. The two men struggled, lurching forward, then back again, desperate for control of the dose. As their grips tightened, Woodward, or Azzam, dropped the ampule. For a split second, the glass vial flashed in the air, tumbling freely.

Omar released his hold on Woodward, threw himself to one knee, his fractured leg screaming in pain, and lowered a cupped hand. Just above the deck, the vial fell into his palm and remained intact.

Mad with rage, Woodward raised a small handgun and fired straight into Omar's chest.

"I won't be stopped!" he screamed.

Clutching his chest, Omar collapsed, brought down by the bullet's force.

As Woodward was about to bend down to take back the ampule, determined to finish the mission, another shot rang out and he was thrown back onto the float, near the deck's edge.

Greg, hovering only feet above the float, had delivered the

shot, firing through the open helicopter door. It was Greg's shot of a lifetime, in so many ways.

Somehow Woodward got himself back up, staggered, then went down again, this time crashing through the thin side wall of the float and tumbling onto the street. A double bump and lurching smokestacks announced the float's passage over the terrorist's body.

Flaring the chopper ahead of the now-stalled float, Greg set the runners down on the pavement and hopped out. By the time the chopper's blades had stilled, the remaining gas had been swept away in the rotor wash.

Running through the debris, Greg jumped up onto the float and rushed over to the body of his friend. When he saw the extent of the wounds, Greg inwardly groaned.

He drew near to Omar's bloodied face. "Why did you do that?" he implored.

"It was my job to do," Omar said, his speech slurred. "Here . . ." With a shaky hand Omar handed the ampule to Greg. "Take this . . . and have it destroyed."

"You did good, brother," Greg whispered, receiving the lethal dose from him. "Remember—"

"I know," said Omar as he clasped Greg's hand. "I'm for-given."

Then his grip grew weak, his fingers relaxed, and his features took on a peaceful expression. He smiled and breathed, "I see Him, Greg. Coming for me. I feel His love. . . ."

Another face appeared behind them. Delia Kilgore, who had commandeered a chopper and followed them nearly step for step. Her face now tear-stained, she stepped forward, knelt, and took both men by the hand.

"I'm so sorry for my part in this," she managed to say.

Greg looked up at her. "This is not a defeat," he said softly.

"Today's victims, they're the casualties. But this is not one of them."

Delia rested her chin on Greg's shoulder, and they wept together for the man they had alternately despised and loved, rejected and embraced, then watched become transformed in the crucible of a few pressure-packed days.

Riding in silence, Delia escorted Greg in a military vehicle through the chaotic streets of downtown Pasadena and back to the stadium.

"What are you going to do now?" Greg asked as he took hold of the door handle.

She shook her head. "I have no idea. I know one thing, though. There's a wonderful man back in Arizona who I hurt pretty badly, and who I'd like to mend fences with."

"Is that what you call it in Arizona? Mending fences? If that's true, I hope the two of you mend a lot of those fences."

She reached over and cradled his cheek with her hand.

"You've got a bit of fence mending of your own to do, Greg. I hope for your sake that the darkest days are behind you."

He nodded. "I think they are. Omar Nirubi, probably the unlikeliest of men on this earth, taught me to forgive myself."

She smiled, said a final good-bye, and Greg stepped from the vehicle and waved as she pulled away.

Searching through the crowd, it was a full twenty minutes before Greg spotted Donna's van. In front of its mosquito-spotted grill stood mother and son.

It was clear to him that Donna and Robby, on seeing him approach, had been worried for his life. The anxiety and concern in their eyes moved him to tears.

"Daddy!" This time there was no obstruction—no hedge branches, no police officer's arm, no legal document saying that a father could not hold his son in his arms. This time Robby leaped up and made contact with his father's bloodstained chest, not caring what stain he received in return.

"Robby, I'm so glad you're okay," said Greg, holding his boy tightly. Over his son's shoulder he saw Donna and met her softened gaze. "I'm glad to see you're safe too."

"I saw what you did," she said. "People were watching it all as it happened—on cell phones, laptops, portable televisions. The whole world was tuned in. And, Greg, you came through. You did something here," she said, her eyes rimmed with tears. "You made a difference. You saved people."

Still holding Robby in his arms, Greg walked up to her and stood close. He leaned in and whispered so only she could hear him. "Is it too late to save this family? Because I'm through being angry. I'm through holding grudges. We've both hurt each other. Can we forgive and start over, do you think?"

She looked deep into his eyes, saying nothing.

Then, finally, she gently nodded her head. "I can try," she whispered back.

Together the threesome wove their way through the crowd and mayhem, a family on the mend at last.

ABOUT THE AUTHOR

MARK ANDREW OLSEN, acclaimed author of the novels *The Warriors* and *The Watchers*, also collaborated on bestsellers *Hadassah*, *The Hadassah Covenant*, *The Road Home*, and *Rescued*. Mark grew up in France, the son of missionaries, and is a graduate of Baylor University. He and his family live in Colorado Springs.